I wasn't sure how I felt about him, but I was sure I didn't want to lose him...

Garrett sat with his head in his hands. He looked up at me with those sad eyes. "Do you know what this means? A cop, maybe someone in my own precinct, may be a killer. I look at everyone with suspicion now, my own colleagues, the guys I trust with my life every time we go out on a call. It's driving me crazy. I feel like I can't trust anyone. I hate myself for it."

I realized that was the reason he had hustled me away from the campsite before I ran into the cops on their way up. He was trying to protect me.

"Well, how do you know the kid wasn't killed by another druggie?"

"It was too professional. Too methodical. The way he was killed, the way he was buried. It has all the marks of someone who knows what he's doing."

"Like a cop."

He nodded and ran his hands through his hair again. "Another thing. The kid was buried up there by the police shooting range. Very few people outside the force even know that range is up there. Or how to get to it."

"But how do you know it was a cop from your precinct? There are more than one in Pineland Park, aren't there?"

"There are two precincts in town, and also the county sheriff's office who oversee the outlying areas. I might not even know the guy. But that doesn't make it any easier to swallow."

If there was one thing I knew about Garrett, it was his fierce loyalty. I knew he was anguished at suspecting one of his fellow officers of such dreadful things. Also, for the first time, I felt genuinely fearful for his life.

Travel columnist, Ryn Lowell, has been away from Trout Fork, Colorado, for barely a month when a frantic call from Alma sends her hurrying back. One of the Trout Forkers is in jail for the murder of another of the locals. With Jack, her "traveling cat," secured on her motorcycle, Ryn heads back to her home away from home and the people she has come to care for.

Will Ryn be able to help solve the murder? Can she get her friend out of jail? And what about Detective Garrett Easterbrook? Why isn't he on the case? Everyone knows something has been bothering him lately, but what can it be? Is there still a spark between him and Ryn? Will it become a flame or peter out?

The Mountaintop Murders is the exciting sequel to *Death in Trout Fork.*

KUDOS for *The Mountaintop Murders*

In *The Mountaintop Murders* by D M O'Byrne, travel writer Ryn Lowell is back in Trout Fork, Colorado, trying to solve another murder. This time it's Sarge who has been killed. A local, Hank, has been arrested for the murder. But Ryn is convinced he is innocent, and she is determined to prove it. However, her editor is not pleased with her for being back in Trout Fork and she could end up without a job. Then there's the relationship between her and Detective Garrett Easterbrook. He wants a commitment, but she just isn't sure. And why isn't he on the murder case, working to free Hank? Ryn knows something is bothering him, but he isn't willing to talk about it. Like all of O'Byrne's books, the character development is excellent. It's like being with old friends. Combine that with suspense, intrigue, and fast-paced action, and you have a first-class whodunit. ~ *Taylor Jones, The Review Team of Taylor Jones & Regan Murphy*

The Mountaintop Murders by D. M. O'Byrne is the second book in her Ryn Lowell Colorado Mysteries Series. This time Ryn, our intrepid travel writer, is called back to Trout Fork, Colorado, because Sarge has been murdered while he and Hank were camping. Hank admits to being drunk and passed out, and he has been arrested for the murder. But Ryn doesn't believe Hank is capable of killing anyone and she wants to clear his name, even though she knows her editor will be most unhappy with her and her mother will freak if they find out she is back in Trout Fork on the scene of another murder. The first thing she notices when she gets to Trout Fork is that Garrett Easterbrook, the detective she fell for the last time she was there, is not on the case. And something is troubling him—something he doesn't seem to want to talk about.

Can Ryn solve the crime, keep her job, and finally decide how she feels about Garrett, or will she end up being another victim? *The Mountaintop Murders* is well written and fast paced, with plenty of twists and turns that will keep you guessing until the very end. ~ *Regan Murphy, The Review Team of Taylor Jones & Regan Murphy*

ACKNOWLEDGMENTS

Thanks to my hubby, Tom, who proofread every word and provided a gauge as to how the mystery was shaping up.

I appreciate the residents of Deckers, Colorado, the tiny village on which Trout Fork is based. Even though I know none of them and didn't base my characters on anyone who lives in Deckers, the general atmosphere I describe in the books is accurate and could only be created by those who live in such a delightful little place.

OTHER BOOKS BY

DM O'BYRNE

AND

BLACK OPAL BOOKS

Dangerous Turf

Three to One Odds

Death in Trout Fork

THE MOUNTAINTOP MURDERS

Ryn Lowell Colorado Mysteries

DM O'BYRNE

A Black Opal Books Publication

GENRE: MYSTERY-DETECTIVE/WOMEN SLEUTHS/SUSPENSE

THE MOUNTAINTOP MURDERS
Copyright © 2019 by DM O'Byrne
Cover Design by Jackson Cover Designs
All cover art copyright © 2019
All Rights Reserved
Print ISBN: 9781644371374

First Publication: MAY 2019

Published by Black Opal Books **http://www.blackopalbooks.com**

DEDICATION

This book is dedicated to all the readers who offered glowing reviews of Death in Trout Fork and who let me know they are dying for the series to continue.

CHAPTER 1

Ryn! Oh, thank God I caught you." Alma's voice on the phone trembled, her breath coming fast.

I pushed Jack Kerouac, my orange tabby cat, off my lap onto the bed and sat up. "Alma. What's wrong?"

"Oh, my God. It's Sarge. He's *dead*. Somebody killed him. Up at his campsite. It's so *awful*."

I pictured the old fisherman they called Sarge eating breakfast at the café, and I remembered Ashley saying she hated waiting on him. "He smells funny," she'd said, wrinkling her nose.

"That's terrible. Who would do such a thing to that harmless old man?"

Her breath caught as she choked back a sob. "That's bad enough," she wailed, "but what's worse is that Hank's been arrested. They think he did it. He's *in jail*."

"No! Hank?" I remembered the night Hank, the proprietor of Trout Fork Liquors, arrived at Alma's cabin earlier that summer with a bottle of wine and a single red rose. But his hopeful beginning of a romance with Alma was halted by her ex-husband's reappearance.

I tried to sound calm. "There must be some mistake. Does Garrett know?"

"Yes. We called him as soon as Hank came down

from the campsite and told us he woke up and found Sarge dead. Then the cops came up to investigate. That was two days ago, and they came back today and arrested Hank! We're all just sick about it." Her voice broke again.

"What was Hank doing at Sarge's campsite?"

"Oh, they were drinking and playing cards up there. They do that a lot. I mean…they did."

"Well, what does Hank say happened?"

"He doesn't remember. Anything. Anything at all! You know how he drinks. He says he woke up and there was Sarge…dead. Oh, my God! Poor Hank. In jail!" She began to weep loudly into the phone.

"Take it easy, Alma. There has to be a reasonable explanation." Then I thought about the murder of the waitress in Trout Fork earlier that summer. The explanation for that was anything but reasonable.

"Where are you, Ryn? Will you be coming this way again?"

I looked at the Colorado road maps strewn all over the bed in my motel room. "I'm at a dude ranch near Fairplay. I just finished my column, and I'm not sure where I'm going next."

"Why, that's not more than an hour from here. Oh, please come back to Trout Fork. At least for a while. To help find out what happened. Garrett says he can't do much because—"

"It's not his jurisdiction," I interrupted with a sigh. "I know the drill." Although Trout Fork was fifty miles from Denver, crimes committed there were still in Denver's jurisdiction, and Garrett, the local detective, was prevented from getting involved in Denver's cases. Officially, at least.

"No. That's not it," Alma said. "Sarge's campsite is just over the county line, so it's Pineland Park's jurisdiction. But Garrett says he's involved with something else right now and can't look into it. They've assigned another detective to the case."

It seemed odd that Garrett wouldn't fight to be involved in the investigation of the murder of a Trout Fork resident, and I wondered what he could be doing that he considered more important. "Tell you what. I'll come back to Trout Fork until I figure out where I'm going next. Maybe I can snoop around a little. Would that help?"

Alma exhaled heavily. "Oh, thank you, dear. Just having you here would be such a blessing. And I know Ashley misses you."

I didn't know if there was anything I could really do, but my journalist's instincts had served me well in the past. At least I could ask a few questions. I felt sure that Hank Edwards was no murderer, and if I could help prove that, it was worth a trip back to Trout Fork. "Okay. As soon as I check out and pack up my stuff, I'll be on my way. I should be there this afternoon."

Alma brightened. "I'll make sure Ashley's room is ready. Oh, she'll be delighted. And Sasha! She'll be so excited to see Jack."

I smiled at the vision of Jack being groomed by Sasha, Ashley's black and white tuxedo cat, like a sultan enjoying the ministrations of his favorite concubine. "What about your new waitress? Isn't she bunking with Ashley?"

Alma giggled. "Zoe? No. Turns out she's terribly allergic to cats. Her face blew up like a balloon the first night she was here. I'm letting her use one of the cabins in the back. I can't rent it out anyway. Too close to the burned out area. See you soon, dear. Oh, I'm so relieved."

I hung up and pulled Jack onto my lap. I stroked his

silky fur while he closed his amber eyes and purred. "Well, Jackie, it looks like you'll be seeing your girl-friend today. Remember Sasha?"

He opened his eyes slightly at the name. *Do cats have memories of one another?* I was sure they did.

Sitting there in that lonely room, memories of my time in Trout Fork flooded my mind. Foremost among them was Garrett, with his steel blue eyes, unruly black hair, athletic physique, and his love of opera and the Romantic poets, so incongruous for a detective. The days I had spent with him after the fire, living innocently together in his cabin, sitting together in the evenings with Jack purring between us on the sofa, came back to me in sweet, melancholy remembrance. I shook my head. *Stop that*, I chided myself. *Don't idealize him. You know where that will lead.*

I got off the bed and began stuffing my belongings into the battered suitcase, flicking a few dead bugs from its surface with my finger. Riding strapped on the back of my Honda motorcycle these past few weeks had given the suitcase a somewhat shabby appearance, which seemed to fit perfectly with my lifestyle.

I picked up Jack's basket, and he began pacing back and forth across the bed and meowing. He liked nothing better than flying down the road, strapped in his basket in front of me on the bike. He was a traveling cat, relishing the nomadic lifestyle of his namesake, Jack Kerouac, the poet and travel writer.

Jack looked up at me with a question in his eyes and gave me his usual chirp that sounded like *"Brrrt?"*

"I should have named you Burt instead of Jack." I stuffed my laptop into the suitcase and took it out to the Honda and secured it to the back of the bike. Then I went to the office to check out.

Buck, the manager, stood at the desk and greeted me

with a huge smile. He knew I was writing about the dude ranch for my travel magazine column, "Out of My Way," and he had been more than accommodating this week.

He tipped his cowboy hat with old-world courtesy. "Checking out, Miss Lowell? I hope you enjoyed your week with us." He tapped on the keyboard of the iMac computer on the counter that seemed out of place in the ranch-themed office with its pot-bellied stove and pine log walls covered with horseshoes and a huge bearskin.

"It's been wonderful. Thanks for everything."

"Our pleasure."

I gave him the magazine credit card, wondering briefly how my editor, old Cranky Crenshaw as I called him, would feel about me going back to Trout Fork. I had already done a column from there, and he had made it clear it was time to move on. Since then, I had written columns about a golf resort, a winery, and now the dude ranch. He wanted several columns from the Colorado ski resorts, but it was still too early in the season. The snow wouldn't begin falling for at least two more months.

Buck gave me his most ingratiating grin. "When will we see the column? I hope you said some nice things about us."

"Very nice. It will be in the October issue. The magazine will send you several complimentary copies."

I took the receipt and headed for the door.

"Ya'll come back now, hear?" Buck called after me.

I smiled at his folksy comment and waved. *His name is probably Lester, and he's really an insurance salesman from Chicago,* I thought as I closed the door behind me. I shook my head. *When did I become so cynical?*

I went back to the room, put Jack's harness on him, and carried him and his basket out to the bike. Strapped into the basket in front of my seat, he sat up eagerly, gazing out the windshield, his tail swishing back and forth. I buckled on my helmet, straddled the bike, and turned the key. The engine purred to life, and I felt the familiar thrill of the open road before me. We pulled slowly out of the parking lot and turned onto the main road that would wind through the mountain pass and take me back to Trout Fork. The rugged peaks of the Rocky Mountains loomed in the distance, the tops of some still covered in snow, even now in mid-August.

In less than an hour, I breezed through the town of Pineland Park and turned north onto the county road that led to Trout Fork. As I passed the police station on the outskirts of town, I noticed Garrett's gray pickup wasn't parked in its usual spot. Hopefully, he was at Alma's Café trying to get to the bottom of Sarge's murder. I was sure he knew as well as I did that Hank couldn't have done it, although Garrett could be maddeningly slow to reach his conclusions.

As I sped down the winding road, leaning into the curves and watching Jack adjust to the bike's movement, the joyful sensation of freedom was tempered a bit by feelings of loneliness inherent in doing the kind of work I had chosen. I pushed the feeling away. *Travel writers travel*, I reminded myself. *That's all there is to it. So suck it up.*

Flying along the mountain road, I had the feeling of returning home, even though I had only spent a few weeks in Trout Fork that summer. I smiled at the thought of the quirky Trout Fork residents and how much I looked forward to seeing them again. Not just Alma and Ashley, but Gil Acevedo, the bait shop owner, whose all-American, pro-military, law-and-order stance belied his tender heart. Of course there was zany Madam Gauzie, the elderly owner of the antiques store, whose knowledge of the history of Trout Fork and its residents, combined with her uncanny intuition, made her a valuable resource.

I shook my head at thoughts of Zach, the one they had called Rev, whose bizarre religiosity had led him to murder that waitress and then to take his own life. And poor Hank, tortured by memories of the wife who had deserted him and caused him to lose himself in alcohol. They were an eccentric bunch, but I had come to feel a warmth toward them I had always found lacking in my feelings toward my own family. That one of them was in jail and the rest in turmoil was disturbing, and I hoped there was something I could do.

We sailed into Trout Fork, pulled into the parking lot, and stopped in front of Alma's Café alongside several cars and motorcycles. I shut off the engine and gazed around at the area, one of those places that seem to be stuck in a time warp. The four stores—the café, Gil's bait shop, Hank's liquor store, and Madam Gauzie's antique store—hadn't changed a bit. They huddled together under one shingled roof, tourists ambling along the wooden walkway that connected them.

One of the many motorcycle clubs that rode through the area had just pulled into the lot. Several gray-haired men in leather motorcycle pants and jackets were peering through the darkened window into Trout Fork Liquors, closed now that its proprietor sat in a jail cell.

Jack sat up in his basket, his whiskers quivering as he gazed at the familiar surroundings. I dismounted and set my helmet on the seat. Jack was struggling against the straps tying him to the basket, so I unbuckled him and set him on the ground. I connected the leash to his harness, and we strolled toward the café.

I took a deep breath. The scent of pine from the trees on the hillsides surrounding the little hamlet filled the air. The crystal blue Colorado sky with its puffy clouds sailing above the Rocky Mountains never failed to take my breath away. From across the street came the familiar murmur of the Trout Creek as it flowed gently down-stream.

Jack and I entered the café to find Ashley and Zoe hurrying with plates of food between the rustic dining room and the patio. The lunch rush was in full swing, and the blond oak tables were crowded with the tourists, hik-ers, bikers, and fishermen who frequented the area.

Ashley, on her way in from the patio, spotted me and cried, "Ryn!" and rushed to give me a huge hug. Although it had only been a month since I'd last seen her, I could have sworn she grew another two inches. Her glossy chestnut hair was pulled into a pony tail and secured with a flowered band. Her chocolate brown eyes shone with delight. "And here's Jack!" She bent down to stroke Jack while he rubbed his head on her hand in greeting. She stood and held onto my arm. "Oh, I'm so glad you're here," she gushed. "I guess you heard about Hank. Isn't it the worst? Mom's been freaking out. That poor old Sarge. I feel bad now for not wanting to wait on him. Did you see Garrett? He's out on the patio talking to one of the renters."

I smiled at her breathless teenage effusiveness. "Yes, I heard about Hank. No, I haven't seen Garrett yet. I just got here."

She led me toward the patio. "Come sit outside, and I'll get you some lunch. Have you seen Mom?"

"No. I'm sure she has her hands full in the kitchen. I'll see her in a while."

Just then, Alma's voice boomed from the kitchen. "Orders up, girls!"

A wave of nostalgia washed over me. A month ago, that would have sent me scurrying to the kitchen window to pick up my orders and deliver them to the tables. I picked out a metal mesh table in the shade on the patio. Jack sat up on one of the chairs and began washing his paws. Jack always knew when a meal was coming.

The scent of the purple and fuchsia flowers cascading from planters along the railing mingled with the pine smell from the trees surrounding the stores. The faint murmur of the creek flowing nearby was the only sound until another group of motorcycles pulled into the parking lot. The winding mountain road between Pineland Park and Trout Fork was a favorite destination of bikers from all over, and Trout Fork was often inundated with motorcycle clubs during the summer.

Garrett sat across the patio with his back to me, deep in conversation with a man in a fishing cap and waders. They got up and shook hands, and the fisherman picked up his gear and left the patio. Garrett started to sit down again, but he looked around and his eye caught mine. I felt that familiar rush.

He came to my table, sat next to me, and grasped my hand. "The prodigal returns," he said with a smile. "Both of them." He stroked Jack's head with his other hand.

"Well, you know what they say about the bad penny." I noticed he made no attempt to release my hand, not that I wanted him to.

His disconcertingly blue eyes gazed into mine. "You've heard about Sarge?"

"Yes. Alma asked me to come back for a while, and I'm between assignments, so I thought I might be able to help. Garrett, why aren't you investigating? I know Alma would feel better with you on the case."

He ignored my question, still grasping my hand as though afraid I would disappear again. "How have you been, Ryn? The last time we spoke, you were going to visit some wineries on the Western Slope."

"I've been here and there. This past week I've been at a dude ranch. I'm not sure where I'm going next." My constant traveling was a bit of a sore point between us, so

I switched subjects. "Is it true they've arrested Hank? How can that be? You don't think he could have done it, do you?"

He sat back, released my hand, and ran his fingers through his thick black hair. "We don't really know anything much. Only what Hank told us. He said the two of them went to the campsite and got drunk and passed out. He doesn't remember anything else until he woke up in the morning to find Sarge with his skull crushed. He came down to the café, and Alma called me. The captain assigned another detective to the case."

"But why?"

He shrugged. "I've got something else on my plate. And maybe the captain thinks I'm too close to the people here, ever since that business this summer. Anyway, Detective Sloan is a good man. He and his team looked at the campsite and took Sarge's body to the coroner's office in Denver. Then they came back today and arrested Hank. That's really all I know."

"That's terrible. Who would want to kill a harmless old guy like Sarge? Especially Hank?"

"I don't know, but they must have some evidence, or they wouldn't have arrested him."

"Well, I'd like to know what they think they have on him."

Just then, Alma burst onto the patio, her round red face wreathed in smiles, her bright blue eyes shining. "Ryn dear, Ashley said you were out here."

I stood and allowed her to wrap me in the motherly hug I had grown to love, the kind I had never received from my own mother. Alma was short and pudgy and full of life.

I kissed the top of her head that barely came to my shoulder.

"Hello, Garrett. Sorry to interrupt."

Garrett stood. "No problem, Alma. I have to get back anyway. I'll call you, Ryn." He smiled at us and walked away. I watched him go, admiring his well-muscled back and shoulders and his slim waist.

Alma gazed after him. "I think he's been pretty lonely since you left. Maybe that's what's been bothering him."

"How do you know something is bothering him?"

"Just a feeling I get." She smiled at me. "Anyway, you're here now. Have some lunch, and then we'll get you settled in with Ashley again. Oh, I can't wait to see Sasha's reaction. She's been missing Jack since you left."

"Okay. Just a hamburger and—"

"And an extra plate for Jack. I remember." She hugged me again. "Welcome home."

CHAPTER 2

When Zoe delivered my hamburger, her arched eyebrows over her curious hazel eyes told me she recognized me from the day she came to Trout Fork to take the waitress job I was giving up. "Oh, you're back," she said, backing away slightly from Jack who was sitting up at the table, his amber eyes regarding her placidly.

"Just for a little while. How do you like the job?"

"It's okay. Alma is nice to work for. And there's some interesting people here." Her eyes flickered momentarily toward a handsome young man slouching casually at a nearby table with several young teens, all wearing matching T-shirts with the YMCA logo. I remembered there was a YMCA camp across the road from the Trout Fork stores. He looked up and flashed a captivating smile at Zoe, who flushed and raised her eyebrows at him. She cleared her throat and said, "Anything else I can get you?"

"I'm good. Thanks." I cut some of the hamburger into small pieces and put it on the extra plate for Jack. As I ate, I watched Zoe clear the tables nearby. She was about eighteen, short and stocky, with strawberry-blonde hair in a long braid down her back. She glanced up now and then at the handsome young guy who followed her with his eyes. I didn't need to be a crack investigative journalist to know there was something going on between them.

The warm summer breeze wafted through the patio, ruffling the umbrellas slightly. I leaned back and sighed, enjoying the sensation of coming home again. Memories of my real home and family in New York City moved fleetingly through my mind. I would have to call Mother soon, which I dreaded, knowing her reaction to the news I was back in Trout Fork would be, "Really, Kathryn, can't you find somewhere more suitable to spend your time?" To Mother, everything in life was deemed either suitable or unsuitable, depending on how closely it conformed to her New York society standards.

The pleasant quiet was shattered by a woman's grating voice coming from inside the café demanding service. I peered through the door to the dining room to see a heavy-set woman with tightly curled, iron gray hair, her glacial blue eyes flashing at Ashley who was hurrying toward her table. The woman wore ostentatious clothes and jewelry, completely incongruous for an outing to Trout Fork. Her bony, thin-haired husband sat quietly perusing the menu. His body language spoke of a desire to be invisible.

The woman surveyed the café and wrinkled her nose disdainfully. "I don't know what would bring Richard to this depressing dump. No wonder he drank."

The husband didn't respond.

"Young woman," she said to Ashley, "who might be able to give me some information about my brother?"

Ashley looked confused. "Your brother?"

"Yes, my brother. Richard Horner. I received a call from the police saying he was found dead here two days ago. He lived here for years. Surely someone here must have known him."

Richard Horner must be Sarge's real name, I thought. Somehow putting a name and family members with him made his death seem more real to me.

"Oh, you mean Sarge," Ashley said. "Gil knew him better than anyone. You should talk to him. He owns the bait shop next door."

"Humph. I'll have the grilled cheese. Howard, stop staring at that menu and order something. We don't have all day."

The mousy husband kept his eyes averted from Ashley as he quietly ordered something I couldn't hear. *Why do bossy, controlling women always marry men like that? And both end up miserable. Another reason not to get married.*

"Oh, there's Gil now," Ashley said, motioning to Gil who had just come into the café. Gil looked the same as I remembered him, tall and thin with dark graying hair, a hook nose, and intense brown eyes under dark bushy brows. His profile always reminded me of a bald eagle. He strolled over to the table in his usual unhurried style.

"Gil, this is Sarge's sister. She wants to talk to you about him." Ashley took the menus and scurried away, apparently glad to leave the obnoxious woman to Gil.

Gil pulled out a chair and sat with the couple. "You must be Estelle. Sarge mentioned you."

"Yes. I'm Estelle Milner, Richard's only living relative. This is Howard, my husband."

Gil nodded to the man. "How did you find out about—"

"The police called the VA and they contacted me. I'm here because I want to know what happened to my brother, why this Hank person killed him. And what was he doing here anyway? The last I heard from him, he was working in Pineland Park. What brought him to this…place?"

Gil shifted in his chair. "Sarge hadn't actually worked in years. He had a bit of a substance abuse problem."

Estelle sniffed. "That doesn't surprise me. But why was he living in a tent like a homeless person?"

"He lived with me during the winter. I have a cabin behind my store. But he preferred his tent when the weather permitted. I think he enjoyed the solitude."

She peered at Gil. "How did you know my brother? I don't remember him mentioning you."

"I've known him for years. We met in a bar in Pineland Park and got to talking about the military."

"Were you in the Marine Corps too?"

"Army."

The woman's eyes bored into Gil's. "Who is this Hank who killed him? And why?"

Gil leaned forward and returned her gaze in a way that said he was unfazed by her intimidating presence. "I don't believe Hank killed him. Hank wouldn't hurt a fly."

"Humph. Well, the police have different ideas. Or do they arrest people for no reason around here?"

"I don't know what evidence they have, but I know Hank couldn't have done it."

"Well, someone did. And we're not leaving here until we get some answers."

"We all want answers, ma'am. Sarge had his problems, but he didn't deserve to die like that."

"Indeed." She looked around scornfully. "I don't suppose there's a hotel nearby."

Gil got up from the table. "There's some motels in Pineland Park. Or you can rent one of the cabins. Talk to Alma. She owns the rentals."

The husband looked up at Gil hopefully. "How's the fishing around here?"

"Great. Come to the bait shop, and I'll fix you up with whatever you need. I'll give you a map of the area, too."

"Thanks. I will."

The woman scoffed at the two men. "This isn't a vacation, Howard. Once we're finished with the formalities, we'll be on our way back to Albuquerque."

Howard seemed somewhat crestfallen, but he said quietly to Gil, "I'll stop in when we get settled." His wife gave him a withering look. Gil gave the man an understanding nod and moved to the ordering counter.

Ashley delivered their lunch then came to my table and began clearing the dishes. She glanced several times at the Milners with a quizzical expression.

"Anything wrong, Ash?"

"Did you ever have the feeling you've seen someone before, but you can't remember where?"

"Sure. Who have you seen before?"

"That brother-in-law of Sarge's. I could swear he's been here before." She gathered up the dishes and took them back to the kitchen.

Gil still stood at the counter where Zoe was ringing up his lunch. He paid her and took his to-go order toward the door. Then he caught sight of me through the door to the patio and came out. "Ryn. I heard you were coming back. Alma was telling everyone this morning."

"Hi, Gil. Nice to see you again. Sorry to hear about Sarge. And Hank, too. What a shame. Can you sit down for a while?"

"I better not. Have to get back to the store. I just came in to get some lunch to go."

"Okay. Maybe I'll see you later.

"Why don't you join us for the poker game tomorrow night? We're one player short."

I saw the sadness in his eyes. I had no doubt he missed Hank and wondered if he felt somewhat responsible for Sarge.

Gil had always had a soft spot for anyone involved with the military or law enforcement. I believed that was why he took both Hank and Sarge under his wing and tried to help them deal with their substance abuse. I was sure he felt that he had failed them both.

"Maybe I will. Thanks."

c∽e∽ɔ

Later that afternoon, Ashley and I sat on her bed in the room we shared in Alma's cabin behind the café. The room hadn't changed in the weeks I'd been gone, except for the pile of books on Ashley's desk. The pine log walls, the painted dresser, the tiny closet, the lace curtain over the one window, and the small bathroom were just the same.

Jack and Sasha, Ashley's black and white tuxedo cat, lay quietly on Ashley's bed together, purring and watching us through half-closed eyes. The two cats had greeted each other joyfully, touching noses and sniffing each other. Then Sasha pounced on Jack and the two rolled over on the bed, swatting each other playfully in mock combat.

Ashley was writing in a notebook on her lap, her long, slim legs tucked under her. She looked up at the cats. "Sasha missed Jack like crazy. The first few days after you left, she prowled around meowing and looking under the bed for him. How does Jack like riding in his basket?"

"He loves it. He's a born traveler."

"That's awesome." She looked at me hopefully. "Are you going to stay for a while this time?"

"I'm not sure. Your mom wants me to try to help find out what happened to Sarge."

Her impish grin lit up her face. "I bet Garrett is glad. He's been moping around since you left."

"Moping?"

"Yeah. He's like distracted or something."

I changed the subject. "I guess you met Sarge's sister today."

"That's one scary lady. Mom rented them Zach's old cabin. I think the sister's going to snoop around, and he's gonna fish."

I gave a slight shudder. "Zach's cabin? Wow." The last time I was in that cabin, I was tied up with Ashley while an insane Zach sharpened a hunting knife to kill us both. It was only by sheer luck, or the providence of God, that we escaped with our lives.

"Yeah. Weird, huh?"

"Definitely. So what's been going on since I left? How are things between your mom and dad? Still reconciling?" Ashley's parents had been divorced since Ashley was little and had been brought together by Ashley's abduction.

She shrugged. "Who knows? Sometimes I think they are. But then I hear them arguing and…I don't know. I can't figure them out. Dad gets on my nerves. He's been playing papa bear lately, all protective and stuff."

"You have to expect that after what happened."

"I get that, but it's not like every guy I meet is going to try to kill me. But that's the way he acts. There's this guy…" She looked at me shyly.

"Oh? Tell."

"He works over at the YMCA camp. His name is Derek and he's cool. But Dad's like 'you don't know anything about him.' How can I find out about him if Dad gives us the stink eye every time he sees us together?"

"Was that Derek I saw today at the café? He was on the patio with some kids from the YMCA camp."

"That's him. He's a counselor for the summer. Cute, isn't he?"

"Yeah." I thought about the way he had flirted with Zoe and hoped Ashley wasn't heading for heartbreak. "So when does school start?"

"Two weeks." She gestured to the pile of books on her desk. "I've already got a ton of stuff to do, prep for my AP classes."

"How's that going?"

"Okay. All except French Three. It's killing me. I'm afraid I'll be behind before the class even starts."

"I wish I could help, but I took Spanish. Maybe you should get a tutor."

"That's what Mom says. She says I should ask Philippe."

"Who's Philippe?"

"One of the tourists here for the fishing. He's renting a cabin from Mom for a few weeks. Nice old guy. He spends all his time fishing. Mom says he's fluent in French."

I knew "old guy" could mean anyone over thirty to Ashley. "With a name like Philippe, I don't doubt it. Maybe you should ask him."

"I don't know. He's here on vacation, and I don't want to bother him. Maybe he'd think it was weird."

I stood and began to unpack my suitcase. "You'll never know if you don't ask. The worst he can do is say no."

She went to the dresser and picked up her hairbrush. "I guess." She brushed her long chestnut hair and tied it up in a ponytail. "I better get back. Zoe gets testy if I don't help set up for dinner. I'll be glad when school starts and I only have to work weekends." She gave

Sasha one final pat and headed for the door. "See you later."

"Bye." I finished unpacking and sat on the bed. Jack came to me and stretched out on my side, sighing as I scratched behind his ears. I leaned back against the pillow and pulled aside the lace curtain covering the window. The area behind the stores and cabins was still blackened from the fire, the stumps of the trees standing stark and skeletal against the sapphire sky.

Memories of the terrible forest fire that nearly wiped out Trout Fork came back to me—the acrid smoke that jarred us from sleep, the eerie red glow from the hillside behind the cabin, the swirling embers, the sound of the trees exploding as the sap within them boiled, the terrified residents in night clothes fleeing in their cars, the wailing of the sirens.

I let the curtain fall back in place, stared at the ceiling, and thought about Garrett. What was it Ashley said? That he was distracted? What could be distracting him? His job with the Pineland Park Police couldn't be all that stressful. After all, that's why he'd left the Denver PD and moved to a smaller department. Mostly what he investigated here was car break-ins and thefts. Was it really my being gone that he was moping about? I doubted it. Garrett wasn't the moping type. We had spoken on the phone about once a week since I'd left Trout Fork, and each time he seemed his usual self. If he really was distracted about something, it must have happened recently.

A woman's voice brought me out of my reverie. "Yoo-hoo. Ryn, dear. Are you there?"

I hopped off the bed and hurried into the cabin's living room. I would have recognized that voice anywhere.

Madam Gauzie stood at the door. She dashed to me and enfolded me in her arms before I could say a word, her numerous beaded necklaces making indentations in my chest as she held me close. She wore her usual multi-colored skirt and top with a flowing gossamer shawl. Her smoky gray hair was swept up in a bright magenta scarf.

"Oh, my dear," she said, holding me at arms' length. "Let me look at you." She squinted at me analytically. "A little pale, I think, but now that you're back, we'll take care of that."

"Hello, Madam G. How have you been?"

"Just fine, dear. Of course there's this terrible business with Sarge and Hank. We're all in an uproar about it." She took my arm and led me to the door. "Come to my cabin and I'll make us a nice hot cup of tea."

Before I could answer, she linked her arm through mine and guided me along the path behind the stores, still chattering away. We passed Gil's cabin and the one Hank rented, now dark and forlorn-looking.

"Have you seen Garrett yet? Of course you have. He must be delighted you're back." She peered at me. "You *are* back, aren't you? No more gallivanting around?"

"Only for a while. I'll have to be moving on eventually."

She shook her head disapprovingly. "Tsk, tsk. You young girls. Always looking over the rainbow. You know, my dear, very often what we're looking for is right under our noses, if only we can get our heads out of the clouds long enough to see it." She unlocked the door to her cabin. "Well, here we are. Make yourself at home while I brew the tea." She scurried to the kitchen while I sat on the flowered sofa and smiled at the quaint, old-fashioned décor. Crocheted pieces covered the tables and mantelpiece. I always felt I had stepped into a Victorian novel when I visited this cabin.

I leaned back and listened to the old woman humming in the kitchen. I noticed a faded wedding photo on the end table and picked it up. The young bride wore a

'70s style, floor-length dress, and her dark hair was inter-twined with tendrils of flowers. The smiling groom was in a blue uniform with a white cap. "Is this you and your husband?" I asked when she brought the tea tray to the coffee table.

"Yes, that's me and my Edgar. Weren't we a hand-some couple?"

"Very handsome. I guess Edgar was a soldier?"

She handed me a steaming cup. "Sailor. That was during the Vietnam War. He was afraid they would draft him into the army, so he enlisted in the navy right out of high school. We got married just before he shipped out."

"That must have been hard for you, being newlyweds and all."

"It was, but at least I knew he wouldn't be fighting in some God-forsaken jungle. It was bad enough being on a ship in the South China Sea." She opened the photo al-bum on the table and thumbed through it. "Here's a pic-ture of Edgar and some of his shipmates."

A group of tanned young men grinned from the pho-to, their arms draped nonchalantly over each other's shoulders, standing in front of a sign that said "USS Kirk."

"That was taken in 1971, right after the Kirk was commissioned. He was so proud of that ship. He talked about it like it was his baby."

"How long was he there?"

"Until 1975, when the US finally left Vietnam." She shook her head. "He had some awful memories of those last days."

"Was he involved in the fighting?"

"No, thank God. But when Saigon was evacuated, there was absolute chaos. He told me about the last days when his ship took on hundreds of refugees fleeing from Saigon as the North Vietnamese were bombing the city.

The South Vietnamese who had worked with the Americans were terrified they would be killed by the Communists when they took over. Those poor desperate people tried to come out to the US ships in leaky rowboats, rafts, anything that would float. Some of them even tried to swim. Many of them drowned."

I sipped the sweet, hot tea. "Seeing that must have been traumatic for him."

"It was. The Americans tried to get many of them out and they did, thousands of them, but many more had to be left behind. It got so bad the helicopters evacuating civilians started landing on Edgar's ship, which really wasn't equipped for it. They allowed them to land anyway. But the deck was too small to store the helicopters, so he and his crewmates were ordered to push them overboard to make room for the next one landing. Can you imagine? Millions of dollars' worth of aircraft pushed into the sea."

She poured more tea into my cup. "He had a soft heart, my Edgar. He had nightmares about those days for years. It's a wonder he never took to drink after those experiences."

I thought for a moment. "Wasn't Hank in the military about the same time? During that war, I mean?"

"No. He was too young for service in Vietnam. Why?"

"I wondered if he had similar memories, the kind that haunt soldiers and drive them to drink or turn to drugs. We know more about PTSD than they did then, and the servicemen get better treatment now. But back then, they pretty much had to tough it out on their own. What if Hank's drinking has its roots in his military experiences?"

She placed her cup and saucer back on the tray. "I really don't think so, dear. It wasn't until his wife left him that Hank started drinking heavily. Hank's only real problem was his temper."

I thought about the day I first met Hank. An innocent remark caused him to snap at me, what Ashley referred to as being "Hanked." His quick temper was well known.

"Let me ask you something. Do you think Hank could have lost his temper with Sarge over something and killed him? I mean, nobody wants to believe it of him, but how do we really know what goes on in someone's mind?"

She looked at me thoughtfully. "I wouldn't want to speak ill of anyone, especially a sad case like Hank, but…"

"But?"

"Well, I do know that Gil heard Hank and Sarge arguing about something as they were on their way up to Sarge's campsite that night."

"Arguing about what?"

"Gil didn't say. But whatever it was, it got pretty heated."

We chatted for a while longer. Then she got up and began clearing the tea things. As I watched her, I began to wonder if I was on a fool's errand, coming back to Trout Fork to try to help clear someone who might actually be a murderer. I didn't want to believe that, but how many people in Trout Fork, besides Gil and Hank, even knew Sarge? Could this have been a random killing? If so, was there a murderer lurking somewhere, waiting for another victim?

CHAPTER 3

I woke late the next morning, forgetting momentarily where I was. Jack was in his usual spot, stretched out along my side under the covers. One glance around the room told me this wasn't another dreary motel room. It was home, or as much of a home as I had had in the past year. I raised myself on one elbow and checked the other bed, which was empty except for Sasha, who was sitting up watching me. Ashley was up and, no doubt, already at work serving breakfast in the café.

I stroked Jack and wondered why he and Sasha weren't prowling by the bedroom door, meowing for their breakfast. *Of course, Alma has already fed them. No creature, whether two- or four-legged, ever goes hungry in Alma's cabin.*

I sat up and looked at the clock. Almost eight. My first thought was whether Garrett would be breakfasting in the café, and that possibility propelled me into the shower. I dressed quickly in jeans, tank top, and my Birkenstocks, taking just a bit more time with my short hair than I usually did. *Stop fussing,* I chided myself. *He's probably not even there.*

I left the cabin and stood on the step for a moment, breathing in the clean mountain air. Drops of dew glistened on the grass, reflecting the golden morning sunlight. The trees were filled with the chirping and singing of birds. A squirrel scampered past with a pine cone in his mouth.

I crossed the lawn between the stores and the cabins and entered the café kitchen through the back door. I found Alma at the grill, turning eggs, bacon, sausages, and pancakes with the spatula she wielded with an expertise born of many years' experience. Her face was even redder than normal with the heat from the grill. I went to her and hugged her tightly. "Thanks for feeding Jack."

"Of course, dear. I'm surprised he didn't wake you scratching at the door. Did you sleep well?"

"Dead to the world." I sniffed at the goodies on the grill.

"Have a seat in the dining room. I'll send out a stack of pancakes for you."

I hugged her again. "You're the best."

"I think Garrett is still out there," she said with a mischievous grin. "I'm sure he'd like some company."

I pushed through the familiar swinging door to the dining room and found Garrett at his usual table near the fireplace. I had the overwhelming sense of *déjà vu*. That table had been the scene of several crucial events, including our first serious argument. It was also at that table where we sat waiting for news from the search parties scouring the area for Ashley after Zach had abducted her.

Garrett was finishing his coffee and reading the paper. He glanced up and smiled as I approached. Then he stood and pulled out a chair for me. "Good morning," he said.

I was struck once again by the depth of his blue eyes and that shock of black hair that fell over his eyes in the most endearing way. I was more pleased to see him than I wanted to admit. "What are you doing here so late?"

"I'm going up to Sarge's campsite this morning to look around, so I stopped for breakfast first."

"Are the cops finished up there? I mean, is it accessible to the public?"

"No. The area is still cordoned off. I just want to see if there's anything they might have missed."

Ashley approached with my pancakes. "You're up," she said with a grin. "I was beginning to wonder."

"I know, I know. I'm a slug. Bring me some coffee, will you?"

I poured syrup onto the steaming pancakes and dug in, suddenly ravenous, while Ashley brought the coffee pot. Then she went back to the kitchen window to pick up more orders. I could see Zoe working the tables on the patio.

"So are you still riding that death machine?" Garrett had once referred to motorcycles as "donor cycles," a name supposedly given to them by emergency room physicians.

"Yep. Still riding. Still alive."

Garrett watched me eat, making me a bit self-conscious. There was a look on his face that I could only describe as parental. It was the one thing I disliked about him, the way he could make me feel like a child who needed protecting from herself. I guess I couldn't blame him, though. The last time I was in Trout Fork, I nearly managed to get myself killed.

His staring at me made me uncomfortable, so I tried to make conversation as I ate. "So what are you looking for up at the campsite?"

"Anything that might help figure out what happened up there."

I set my coffee cup down and gazed at him. "Mind if I go with you?"

He squirmed a little in his chair as though undecided. "I guess it wouldn't hurt to have two pairs of eyes looking around."

We finished breakfast and left the café, crossing the road to the trail that led to Sarge's campsite. Once on the trail that followed the creek winding through the pine-covered hills, Garrett took my hand. We walked along quietly, enjoying the sounds of the forest—magpies calling to one another from the treetops, squirrels chattering, the rippling water cascading over the rocks, and the splash of the occasional trout leaping from the water for sheer joy. The sunlight filtered through the trees and cast waving shadows on the trail. The layers of pine needles dampened the sound of our footsteps.

At one point, we passed the rock I had sat on the day Jack dug in the dirt and uncovered the fingers of the waitress buried there. I pushed that memory out of my mind, not wanting to spoil this beautiful morning.

The trail climbed steadily upward, leaving the creek far below, and I found myself slowing down and panting slightly. I wondered how long it would take me to completely adapt to Colorado's thin air and altitude.

Garrett tucked my hand into the crook of his arm. "Here. Hang onto me. It's not far now."

"This is quite a climb." How had Sarge, who was in his sixties and not exactly athletic, managed to climb that hill every day?

The trail turned to the right, and there was the yellow police tape surrounding the campsite. It was eerily silent. Sarge's olive green canvas tent was still erected, although it sagged and showed signs of having been searched by the police. In front of the tent were the remains of the campfire. Beer bottles and other trash lay scattered around the site.

Garrett held up the tape and we ducked under it. "Don't touch anything."

I watched him walk around the tent, stopping several times to stoop down and look more closely at the ground. Each time, he straightened up and slowly moved on. I searched the area in front of the tent, not exactly sure what I was looking for. I knelt down next to the fire pit, picked up a stick, and started poking through the ashes. Expired campfires usually contained mostly ashes and the remains of whatever fuel was used such as the branches of trees and bushes. But as I dug through the ashes, I uncovered several things that seemed out of place.

"Garrett, look at this."

He came and squatted down beside me. "What is it?"

"Does this look like cloth to you?"

He took my stick and used it to carefully prod the ashes where I pointed. Then he put on a pair of rubber gloves, pulled up a piece of material about two inches square, shook the ashes off it, and placed it on a nearby rock. He found several more pieces of khaki fabric like the army surplus clothes Sarge usually wore.

"It looks like he, or someone, burned some of his clothes. I'm going to have to call the detective on the case and see what they recovered from his tent."

"Why would anyone want to burn his clothes?"

"Beats me." He swept the stick through the ashes again. He reached in and brought up what looked like the corner of a piece of paper. He shook the ashes from it and peered closely at it. "There's writing on it."

We stared at the paper, our heads close together. I could make out several words. One was "Gil," and another the name "Greer." The rest of the writing was blurred.

I searched Garrett's face. "He was writing something to Gil?"

"Maybe. Or it could be part of a journal or diary."

"Sarge didn't strike me as the type to keep a diary. I think it's more likely a letter or note to Gil. But about what? And why would he bother writing to Gil when he saw him nearly every day?"

Garrett sat back on his haunches and looked at the tent. "Maybe whoever killed him burned his personal possessions to destroy evidence of something. Maybe Sarge knew something about someone, and that's what got him killed." He took a plastic bag from his pocket, picked up the pieces of cloth and the fragment of paper, put them in the bag, and sealed it.

The sound of footsteps coming down the trail startled us, and we looked up the hill to see a middle-aged man with a camera coming toward the campsite. His wrinkled long-sleeve shirt was open at the collar, with a dark tie hanging lopsided. He was medium height, with salt-and-pepper hair, watery blue eyes, a thick mustache, and a three-day-old beard.

He stopped suddenly when he saw us, a wary look crossing his face. Then it disappeared, and he grinned. "Well, if it isn't Detective Easterbrook."

Garrett stood and helped me up. He took off the rubber gloves and put them in his pocket with the plastic bag. "Hello, Bodmin. What are you doing up here?"

The man sauntered to us. "What I'm always doing, following the story. Find anything interesting?" When Garrett didn't answer, the man gazed at me curiously. "I didn't know you worked with a partner."

"This is Kathryn Lowell. She's a journalist, not a cop. Ryn, this is Vince Bodmin, editor of the local paper."

He shook my hand. "Managing Editor, *Pineland Park Star*. What kind of writing do you do?"

"I'm a travel writer." I told him the name of the magazine I wrote for.

He whistled. "New York, eh? Impressive." He studied my face closely. "Wait a minute. I remember now. You're the one who caught that religious nut, the one who killed that waitress a couple of months back."

"I didn't exactly catch him, but yes, that was me."

"And now you're working with the police on this case?"

"Ryn is just a friend," Garrett said. "She's not working the case. What were you doing up the trail, Bodmin? Nothing much up there."

The man shifted uncomfortably. "To tell the truth, I was looking for a place to relieve myself. That's all."

Garrett narrowed his eyes at the man, and I could tell his detective's radar was on full alert. "Well, don't let us keep you."

He leaned in closer to Garrett. "You'll let me know if there are any new angles on this case, right?"

"You'll be the first to know."

"That's my boy. Goodbye, Miss Lowell. Nice meeting you. Drop by the *Star* one of these days, and I'll show you around the newsroom. It's not exactly the *Times*, but we call it home. Adios, Easterbrook." He started down the trail, whistling.

Garrett watched him thoughtfully. "I wonder why he didn't send a reporter up here to look around."

I shrugged. It did seem an odd thing for a managing editor to do, but small town newspapers weren't usually well-staffed.

Garrett looked back up the trail Bodmin had come down. "Are you up for a little more hiking?"

I looked skeptically at the steep hill. "Uh…"

He smiled. "Okay, city girl. You stay here and look around some more. I won't be long."

I watched him head up the trail, admiring his athletic stride. Then I poked around the campsite again. Finding nothing, I sat on a fallen tree trunk to take in the scenery. I understood why Sarge would find the site appealing. The campsite was nearly at the top of a steep hill over-looking the valley, and the view was spectacular. The creek ran so far below that the sound of the water couldn't be heard up there. The silence was almost op-pressive, and I glanced up the trail, hoping to see Garrett. As I listened for his footsteps, I thought I heard popping noises, very faint and very far away, coming from over the hill. They came in rapid succession, followed by si-lence, then more popping.

Garrett appeared at the top of the hill, coming quick-ly down the trail while talking on his phone. He discon-nected the call as he reached me, the expression on his face grim.

"What's wrong?"

He took me by the arm and pulled me away from the campsite. "There's a body buried up there, about a hun-dred yards from here. I just called the precinct. They're sending a detail up. They should be here in twenty minutes." He took the plastic bag out of his pocket. "Here, take this. I want you to show it to Gil. Ask him what he thinks it means. Wait for me in the café."

I took the bag reluctantly. "But don't you have to turn this in to the detective on the case?"

He avoided my eyes. "I'm going to hold onto it for a while."

We heard the same popping noises again. "What is that? Do you know?"

Garrett looked vaguely up the hill. "Our police shooting range is just over that hill. Now hurry. I don't want you to run into the cops on their way up. And, Ryn. Keep this to yourself."

I could see the uneasiness in his eyes and wondered why all the secrecy. But I knew Garrett well enough to realize asking him would be pointless. I nodded and started down the trail with the plastic bag. About halfway to Trout Fork, I could hear the faint sound of sirens wailing in the distance. I broke into a jog and covered the rest of the distance in minutes. My morning runs along this trail earlier in the summer were always so pleasant. This one had a sense of foreboding about it.

I crossed the road in front of the stores, entering Gil's Bait Shop just as two police cars careened down the road, screeching to a stop at the trailhead across the street. Several uniformed officers and a rather paunchy plainclothes detective got out and started up the trail. I didn't envy them the hike up that hill.

"What's going on over there, Ryn? Any idea?" Gil was standing at the counter behind the register. The store was empty of customers. I wasn't sure how to begin, remembering that Garrett warned me to keep the discovery of the body to myself.

I smiled at him. "Hi, Gil. Garrett and I were just up at Sarge's campsite, and we found something. He was wondering if you can help with it."

"I'll do what I can. Anything to help the police."

I showed him the little scrap of paper. "We found this in Sarge's campfire. It looks like he was writing something to you. Do these words mean anything to you?"

Gil pulled his reading glasses from under the counter and put them on. He peered closely at the scrap of paper. "Greer. Well, I'll be damned."

"Is Greer someone you and Sarge know?"

He handed the scrap back to me. "I knew him. Sarge only knew him from what I told him."

"Who is he?"

Gil took off his glasses and put them slowly under the counter. His expression was pained. "One of the few rotten apples in the military barrel. When I was stationed at Fort Riley, there was an officer named Greer there who was involved in some shady deals."

"Like what?"

He seemed reluctant at first to share anything detrimental to the reputation of the service. "It was rumored that he was dealing coke to some of the men in his command. I didn't believe it at first, but the truth came out eventually. There was a young soldier who was one of Greer's customers. But the kid got religion or something. Anyway, he told some of his buddies that he was going to the base commander and rat out Greer. But before he could do that, he disappeared. They assumed he had gone AWOL and put out a search for him. His body was found buried in a remote location on the base."

"How awful."

"It was Greer, of course. He killed the kid and buried him. He thought he'd get away with it, but the soldier's buddies came clean, and Greer was arrested and court-martialed. He's serving life at Leavenworth."

I looked down at the paper. "But why was Sarge writing to you about Greer?"

"Beats me. We haven't talked about that whole thing for years. I'm surprised he even remembered it."

The door opened and several fishermen came in. Gil greeted them and answered their questions about bait and lures.

I left the shop and sat on the bench outside. I stared again at the paper, trying to put myself in Sarge's place. He saw Gil nearly every day, but for some reason he had decided to write a note to him about a long-ago event they hadn't talked about for years. Then, for some reason, he burned the note in the fire before he could deliver it. Or maybe someone else burned it before or after Sarge was killed. Was it the killer who burned it? And what about this new body Garrett had just found? Did that person have anything to do with Sarge's death? And where did Hank fit in with all this? I had no clue. But one thing was certain. Trout Fork had its secrets, and those who try to uncover long-buried secrets often wish they hadn't.

CHAPTER 4

As I sat on the bench waiting for Garrett, a silver Mercedes pulled into the parking lot and stopped in front of the café. Ashley's father, Robert, stepped out of the car and headed for the café. I followed him, noting the expensive suit that covered his tall, lanky frame. With brown hair just graying at the temples and piercing brown eyes, he looked like he had stepped out of the pages of GQ, making him seem out of place in Trout Fork. Then I remembered Alma saying he was an attorney in a Denver law firm.

The lunch rush was just ramping up, so Ashley and Zoe were already busy taking orders. I waited at the ordering counter under the sign that said "Order here or be seated for table service" and watched Robert take a chair at one of the dining room tables. He sat tapping his fingers and eyeing Ashley, who was waiting on Derek and some of the young teens from the YMCA camp. Ashley flashed her most engaging smile at Derek, tossing her long auburn hair back from her face in a manner that told me she had her sights set on him. Robert sat glaring at them, tapping his fingers on the table. I couldn't help smiling as I remembered Ashley saying he was in his "papa bear mode" lately.

Ashley glanced over at her father, and the smile faded from her face. Leaving Derek's table, she went to her father. "Hi, Dad. Here for lunch?"

Robert gave her a stony look. "I'm here for the weekend."

"Oh, great," Ashley said, but her cautious brown eyes indicated she was anything but thrilled at the prospect of being watched all weekend.

Alma came out from the kitchen and joined me at the ordering counter. "What can I get you, Ryn?"

"Just a coffee, I think. I'm waiting for Garrett."

She glanced nervously at Robert and Ashley, who flounced away from her father's table to rejoin Derek. "Oh, dear," she said quietly. "I hope they're not going at it again."

"Robert said he's here for the weekend. Alma, if the cabin is too crowded, I'm sure I can bunk with Madam Gauzie for a few days. It's no problem."

"I won't hear of it. There's more than enough room. Now have a seat, and I'll have Zoe bring your coffee."

Alma hurried back to the kitchen, and I chose a table by the window so I could watch for Garrett. Zoe brought the coffee and set the cup down with a little more force than necessary. I saw her eyes flash as she glared at Ashley and Derek. Derek was apparently teasing Ashley about something, making her giggle. The room was positively awash in emotional drama. The pheromones were flying between Ashley and Derek, Zoe was firing darts of jealousy in their direction, and Robert sat nearby fuming in parental disapproval.

I was relieved when Garrett finally came in. He was accompanied by a paunchy, balding man in his fifties wearing an ancient, disheveled suit jacket and shabby trousers that bagged at the knees. He was sweating profusely. Garrett led him to the cooler next to the back wall and leaned in for a bottle of cold water. "Here you go, Sloan. It's on me."

The man guzzled the entire bottle of water at one time. "Ahh," he said producing a huge burp to emphasize his satisfaction.

Garrett put his hand on the man's shoulder. "Better?"

"Yeah. Thanks." He wiped his forehead with his sleeve. "That's quite a climb. I wonder that old buzzard didn't croak from it before somebody whacked him."

"But then look at all the fun we'd be missing."

Sloan snorted. "Right. I better get back to the station. The uniforms can wait up there for the coroner."

Garrett stood watching him meditatively as the man shuffled out the door of the café. Then he noticed me and gestured to me to join him outside. We stood next to his pickup watching the hefty policeman amble toward his car across the street.

"Is he the one investigating Sarge's murder?"

"That's him. Detective Marvin Sloan. I knew him when we both worked in the Denver PD. He had a good rep up there."

"What's he doing in Pineland Park?"

He shrugged. I wondered if I had touched a sore spot with Garrett who I knew had left the city police for a lower-key job here. He told me once that the crime rate in Denver was beginning to get to him, and that he preferred the small town atmosphere.

He turned to me. "What did Gil have to say about the note?"

I related what Gil had told me about the army officer named Greer who had been running a drug ring and killed one of his men and buried him on the base.

Garrett just nodded.

"So what do you think that means?" I prompted.

He shrugged and gazed off into the distance. Then he

turned to me. "Don't forget about our dinner tomorrow night. I'll pick you up at seven."

"Of course I won't forget. But what about the note? Does it mean anything to you?"

"Maybe. Look, I can't talk now. I need to get back to the station. See you tomorrow night."

He took the plastic bag with the note and pieces of cloth in it from me then opened the door of his truck and got in, his face stony and his manner determined. I stepped back onto the wooden walkway and watched him drive off. Alma was right. Something was bothering him. But what?

☙❧☙

It was after nine o'clock that evening before the café was closed and cleaned up. On my way over from the cabin, I met Ashley coming back from the café. She was staring down as she walked and looked frazzled.

"Hey," I said. "Busy dinner shift?"

She looked up suddenly. "Oh, hi. Yeah, I'm fried. I was hoping to study tonight, but I don't know. Are you going over for the poker game?"

"Yep. It won't be the same without Hank, though. He always livened up the game."

She rolled her eyes. "I'm sure Mom and Dad will provide plenty of excitement, no doubt gossiping about their annoying teenage daughter."

She looked so sad, and I reached for her arm in sympathy. "What's wrong, Ash? Anything I can do to help?"

She shrugged me off. "No. It is what it is."

I watched her open the door of the cabin, remembering my own teen years and that awful feeling of conflict with the two most important people in my life. I longed to tell her how lucky she was to have parents who were

concerned about her. My father, the Wall Street investment banker, and my mother, the society matron, had
given me all the material privileges of our class. But their
time, attention, and affection were carefully parceled out
in small doses, all the while conveying the impression
that I didn't quite measure up to their expectations.

My little brother's death in the swimming pool was
the final blow, splintering my family and leaving just the
shell of pretense we showed to the world. It was no wonder I fled as soon as the chance presented itself. I made
very little money as a travel writer, and my trust fund
wasn't accessible for another two years, but living hand-
to-mouth with just Jack for company seemed like bliss
compared to the stifling, austere atmosphere of our luxu-
ry New York apartment.

I could only hope that Ashley and her parents could
recapture the joy and relief they felt just a month ago
when she was found safe in Zach's cabin. The memory of
their tearful embrace that terrible night had filled me with
envy for that kind of closeness.

I shook off the disturbing memories and went
through the back door of the café, determined to glean as
much information about Sarge and Hank as possible. I
also planned to pump Alma about Garrett. Something had
gotten under his skin, and it wasn't just my journalist's
natural nosiness that was prompting me to dig deeper. As
reluctant as I might be to admit it, Garrett was incredibly
important to me. Thoughts of him intruded into my daily
routines and filled my dreams at night.

The poker table was already set up in the dining
room. Madame Gauzie, who always attended the games
but never played, was flitting around filling cups and
glasses while offering an assortment of homemade goodies to the players. Alma, Robert, and Gil greeted me as I
pulled out a chair at the table.

"Sorry I'm late. You should have started without me."

Alma patted my arm. "Did you have a nice nap, dear?"

"Very nice. I don't know what it is about your cabin that always makes me sleep so well."

Gil dealt the first hand. "Jacks or better to open."

We all looked at our cards and made our opening bids. Robert had changed into casual, although still expensive-looking, clothes. He glanced at me and asked casually, "Did you see Ashley on her way back to the cabin?"

"Yes. She's going to try to study."

Robert scoffed. "About time she thought about something worthwhile instead of mooning around over boys."

Alma frowned at him. "That's hardly fair. She's just turned sixteen. You have to expect her to be interested in boys."

Gil apparently decided it was time to change the subject. "So, Ryn, did Garrett find anything else at Sarge's campsite?"

"Not that he told me, but you never know with Garrett. Sometimes he clams up. I told him what you said about the note, and he just said, 'hmm.'"

Alma's eyes met mine. "What note?"

I wondered if I had said more than Garrett wanted me to say. "Oh, just something Sarge had scribbled. Apparently he burned it, so it probably didn't mean anything."

Alma shook her head. "Poor old Sarge. Who would do such an awful thing? And why? That's what I can't figure out. How could anyone hate him enough to kill him? He always seemed so sad, or hunted, or something."

"We all have our secrets," Robert said. "People should be left to keep them as they wish."

"Sarge didn't have secrets as much as he had bad memories of his time in the Marine Corps," Gil said. "He enjoyed the service, but Vietnam haunted him. He never could get past the memories. It's why he drank and smoked weed."

Madam Gauzie, who had been sitting quietly in the corner waiting for an opportunity to feed us, piped up. "My Edgar was the same way. He never could forget the awful things he saw."

Gil turned to her. "I didn't know your husband was in Vietnam. Where was he stationed?"

"On the USS Kirk."

Gil nodded. "Oh, a navy man. Sarge was assigned to the US Embassy in Saigon. He was helping evacuate the American personnel and the South Vietnamese who worked there. Pretty chaotic, from what he told me. Although he didn't talk about it much. But I know he did have flashbacks. Whether it was PTSD or what they used to call 'shell shock' in previous wars, he just couldn't get past it. Some men never do."

The hand finished with Alma winning with her full house. Robert took the deck from Gil and began to deal another hand. "We never should have been in that stupid war to begin with. It was entirely illegal. What danger were the Vietnamese to us?"

Gil's eyes flashed at Robert. "It's easy to see that now, but in those days, they thought the threat of communism needed to be stopped before it spread. The generals knew what they were doing and could have won that war. It was the idiot politicians in Washington who couldn't make up their minds. Typical."

I decided to try a different tack before the argument became political. "But why did the cops arrest Hank?

Garrett doesn't know, but he says they must have evidence or they wouldn't have taken him in."

Robert offered a lawyer's perspective. "Well, think about it. He was alone with Sarge at the campsite, he has no alibi, and he was seen arguing with Sarge on their way up there. Isn't that what you said, Gil?"

Gil scoffed. "They were always arguing about something. Like an old married couple. There was never anything to it."

"But the police don't know that. All they know is there was some kind of conflict between them. The fact that Hank says he can't remember anything doesn't help his cause."

"What I don't understand is Garrett," Alma put in. "Why didn't he insist on being assigned to the case? I would feel so much better if he was the lead detective. But he says he's involved with something else right now. I don't know what could be more important than getting Hank out of jail and finding the real killer."

I thought about my date with Garrett the next night. Maybe he would open up about whatever it was he was doing that prevented him from investigating Sarge's murder.

We played on until about eleven. Then I went back to the cabin and tiptoed into the room I shared with Ashley. She was asleep with her phone next to her on the pillow.

I could guess who she'd been talking to late into the evening. I moved the phone to the dresser and stroked Sasha who got up from Ashley's side to head-butt my hand.

Jack was sitting quietly on my bed, gazing out the window. He turned to me, his usual affectionate expression in his eyes.

I sat next to him and scratched his ears as he purred.

"Are you up for an early morning jog, Jack?" I whispered to him.

Jack's penchant for jogging with me in his harness and leash were well known in Trout Fork and didn't raise eyebrows here like it did in other places we had visited lately. I undressed quietly and got into bed. Jack curled up by my pillow, and soon we were both sound asleep.

I woke early the next morning. Ashley was still asleep, so I dressed quietly in shorts and running shoes. When Jack saw me pick up his harness and leash, he dashed to the bedroom door and paced back and forth. We tiptoed into the living room where I saw Robert's briefcase and jacket on the sofa. I glanced at Alma's bedroom door. I knew she would be up soon to prepare the café for breakfast, but it was still early, and there was no sound from her room.

We left the cabin and stood on the front step, breathing in the cool mountain air. I did a few stretches before we started down the hill toward the trail. The sunlight was just hitting the tops of the pines, but the trail was still heavily shaded. I jogged along, Jack trotting easily at the end of his leash, with none of the foreboding I had felt earlier in the summer after the body of the waitress had been found. This was just a beautiful, peaceful morning. A hawk flew from the treetops and skimmed over the water, while two squirrels played tag on a nearby tree, chasing one another around the trunk like stripes on an old-fashioned barber pole.

Normally at this hour, the creek was a popular place for trout fishermen, but today only one lone angler was standing midstream in his waders. He didn't notice us as we passed by. We continued on for about a half mile before Jack begin to fade, so I picked him up and put him on my shoulder as I walked along.

I finally turned back and began to retrace my steps.

Just before reaching the trailhead again, the fisherman I had seen in the creek approached from the opposite direction.

When we met, he smiled and tipped his baseball cap. "Lovely morning, isn't it?"

I set Jack down on the trail. "Just perfect."

The man was small with graying black hair and slightly slanted brown eyes that crinkled in the corners when he smiled. His manners were genteel and old world, reminiscent of someone from another century. "I see your cat is in a harness. Does he like that?"

"He loves to jog with me and ride on my motorcycle strapped in his basket, so he knows whenever I pick up his harness that adventure is on its way."

He bent down and ran his hand along Jack's back. "How charming."

I didn't remember seeing him in Trout Fork before, so I asked, "Do you live around here?"

He straightened up and said, "No. I live in Denver. I'm here for a fishing vacation. I'm renting one of the cabins behind the stores."

"Oh, then you must have met Alma."

His smile broadened. "Yes. A most delightful person and very helpful. She and her lovely daughter have been most accommodating." He wiped his hand on his vest and extended it to me. "I am Philippe Tran."

I shook his hand. "Oh, you must be the Frenchman. I'm Kathryn Lowell. Ryn to my friends."

"Pleased to meet you, Ryn. I'm only half French actually. On my mother's side."

"But I understand you speak the language fluently."

He seemed flattered and just a little embarrassed. "Yes, I'm afraid our mother insisted we all learn it."

"Forgive me for asking, Mr. Tran, but Ashley is struggling with her French Three Advanced Placement class preparation. Do you think you would be able to give her some pointers? I think it's the verbs that are confusing her."

He smiled ruefully. "Ah, yes. *Les verbes.* They can be most troublesome."

"I'm sure any hints you could give her would be appreciated."

"I would be delighted. I will talk to her and her mother this afternoon."

"Wonderful. Thank you so much."

"*Un plaisir,* I assure you." He tipped his cap again. "Good day, Miss Lowell."

"Ryn, please."

"Good day, Ryn." He bent down to pat Jack on the head. "And good day to you, too, *mon petit chat.*" He strolled away humming to himself.

I continued down the trail with Jack strolling by my side. I felt a glow of satisfaction for helping to solve one of Ashley's problems. She had had enough drama for one summer, and I hoped working with Philippe would lighten some of her burden. I was beginning to think of her as more of a little sister than my own sister back in New York. If there was any way I could be a supportive big sister to her, I was going to do it. I was also determined to try to help her navigate the rough waters of the teen/parent experience.

Now if only I could figure out how to solve Sarge's murder and get Hank out of jail. Then there was Garrett. Something was on his mind, and, although he was going to hate my poking into his psyche, I was determined to get to the bottom of it.

CHAPTER 5

I took Jack back to the cabin and fed him. Watching him eat reminded me that I was ravenous, as I always was after an early morning jog. I took a quick shower and dressed.

Robert was sitting on the living room sofa with his morning paper and coffee when I left the bedroom. He seemed right at home in an old sweatshirt and pants. He looked up as I came in. "Good morning, Ryn. Have a nice run?"

"Lovely. Such a beautiful morning. I guess Alma and Ashley are over at the café?"

"Yes. My two girls are slaving away. I almost feel guilty." He stretched his long legs and plopped his stocking feet on the coffee table. "But not quite." He gave me that little boy grin that I knew Alma found so disarming.

"They do work hard, don't they? I'm amazed at Ashley sometimes. She seems so mature for sixteen. Oh, I have good news for her. I think I've found her a French tutor. I don't know if you've met Philippe. He's an older man here for a couple of weeks for the fishing. I ran into him on the trail, and he said he'd be happy to help her out. His mother is French."

He laid his paper in his lap. "Well, that is good news. I know she's been worried about that class. She knows she needs a high GPA to get into a good school. Where did you attend college?"

"Columbia. Journalism major."

He nodded. "That makes sense. Tell me something, was it worth the money? Sometimes I wonder if Ashley shouldn't just go to a Colorado university. There's nothing wrong with a state school. But she seems to have her heart set on Stanford."

I wondered if Ashley really had her heart set on anything right now besides Derek, but I didn't suppose her father wanted to hear that. "I can't really say if Columbia was worth the money. My father paid for it. I don't even know how much it cost." I was surprised at how much admitting that embarrassed me. I cleared my throat. "I'm going over to get some breakfast. See you later."

Alma was at the grill when I came in the back door of the café. She smiled at me and waved her spatula. "I'm so glad you're here, Ryn. It's like old times again."

I hugged her. "I'm glad, too. And guess what? I met Philippe on the trail this morning. I asked him about tutoring Ashley. He said he'd be happy to help her with her French."

"Wonderful. He's a nice man, isn't he?"

"Very nice. He says he takes fishing vacations every August."

"Well, what luck that he came here this year."

"I'll go tell Ashley." I headed for the dining room. "How about a stack of your delicious, award-winning pancakes?"

She rolled her eyes in a good-natured way. "You don't have to flatter me, dear. I'll feed you regardless."

The dining room was about half full, and I looked around for Ashley. She was waiting on Sarge's sister and her husband and not looking particularly happy about it. I wondered if Estelle was giving her a hard time.

As I approached the table, I heard the woman complaining in a loud voice.

"This coffee is cold, young lady. I want some fresh. *If* it's not too much trouble."

"Yes, ma'am," Ashley said, picking up the cup and saucer. She passed me on the way to the coffee pot, and whispered, "I can't believe that old witch is Sarge's sister. Sheesh."

I sat at a table nearby so I could eavesdrop. Anything I could learn about Sarge might help find out who had a motive to kill him. But there was no conversation between them. They seemed to be one of those old married couples who had long ago lost interest in one another.

Ashley returned with a fresh cup of coffee that she put down in front of Estelle. Ashley gazed at the husband for a moment, then the light of recognition came into her eyes. "Now I know where I've seen you," she said.

Howard looked up warily. "Me?"

"Yes. You were here earlier this summer, around the end of May, wasn't it? You were talking to Sarge."

Estelle looked at her husband and thunderclouds immediately gathered in her blue-green eyes, while lines of suspicion dug sharply between her eyebrows. "What's this?"

"She's mistaken," he said, dismissing Ashley with a wave. "This is the first time I've been here."

Estelle narrowed her eyes at him then at Ashley who had come to my table. She poured a cup of coffee for me, bent down, and whispered, "I know he was here. He and Sarge sat right over there by the fireplace. I'm sure of it. He had a piece of paper he kept pushing under Sarge's nose like he wanted him to sign something. Sarge kept shaking his head and saying 'no.'"

We looked back at the couple and saw Estelle staring at us.

"He can deny it all he wants," Ashley whispered. "But I know it was him."

Just then Zoe came from behind the counter with a tray loaded with breakfast plates. She glared at Ashley. "Hey, Ash, are you working today or what? The orders are piling up in the kitchen and I'm slammed."

Ashley rolled her eyes. "The prima donna calls."

She hurried to the window where Alma was banging on the bell with her spatula and calling, "Orders up, Ashley!"

I drank my coffee while watching Estelle and Howard. What had brought him here earlier this summer, and why was he keeping it from his wife? And what was he trying to get Sarge to sign? Did it have anything to do with Sarge's death? I had a hard time believing that mousy little man could be involved in anything violent. But I had felt the same way about Zach when I first met him. *You just never know about people.*

Zoe delivered my pancakes which I wolfed down in minutes. Then I leaned back, drank my coffee, and continued to watch the people come and go in the café. My mind wandered to Garrett and our date that evening. I wondered if Ashley would let me borrow something to wear. I could always go into town to do some shopping, but I didn't think my finances could take the hit.

Thoughts of my uncertain future began to disturb the peace of the morning. So many decisions, both wise and unwise, had led me to this time and place. My job writing a travel column had certainly freed me from the stifling confines of the office, but it had left me perpetually broke. Selling my car and buying the motorcycle had saved a lot of money, but winter was coming and the thought of being snowed in somewhere, unable to get out and about, scared me. I had come back to Trout Fork at Alma's request to help exonerate Hank, but that had put me right back into a relationship with Garrett that was heading where? Leaving here a month ago hadn't solved anything, only postponed it. How long could I expect Garrett to wait for me to make up my mind about our future? That I had strong feelings for him was undeniable. But the thought of "as long as you both shall live" terrified me. I had seen firsthand too many marriages that seemed to serve no other purpose than to make two people miserable.

As though verifying my thoughts, I heard Estelle rip into her husband again about his having been to Trout Fork without telling her. He continued to deny it, and their voices rose in anger at one another. I shook my head. *If that's what marriage turns into, I'll pass.*

The café door opened and Derek came in, this time without his young charges from the camp. Both Ashley and Zoe looked up at him, each with a different response. Ashley beamed at him, her face flushed, while Zoe's lip turned up as she studiously ignored him. She flounced past him on her way to the kitchen without so much as a nod.

Hmm, I thought. *Apparently the bloom is off the rose of that romance.* Ashley followed Derek to a table on the patio and handed him a menu. Their demeanor was one of mutual attraction and shared affection, that first pulse-pounding blush of romance that can either lead to joy or disappointment. Zoe appeared to have found the latter.

Just then Robert came into the café, looked around, and spotted Ashley and Derek on the patio. His eyes smoldered as he strode toward them in a way that said this wasn't going to end well. Robert took Ashley by the arm, marched her through the dining room, and banged open the swinging door to the kitchen. Soon I could hear them arguing loudly enough to cause the customers in the dining room to look toward the kitchen with concern.

I decided to see if I could help keep the peace in this family I had come to love. In the kitchen, Robert was bearing down on Ashley with an intensity that must have served him well in the courtroom. But badgering her like a hostile witness clearly wasn't working. She stood with her feet apart and her arms folded, staring at the floor. Alma tried to intervene, holding Robert by the arm and begging him to calm down.

But he wasn't about to let up. "Have you been seeing him outside of work? Is that where you were the other night when I called?"

"Dad, it's not a big deal. He took me over to show me the camp and introduce me to some of the kids over there. A lot of them are my age. It was cool meeting them."

Robert was fuming. "I don't want you out at night with him. I don't care where he wants to take you."

"But why? What do you have against him?"

"I don't trust him. We know nothing about him."

"What do you want to know? He just graduated at the top of his class. He volunteered to counsel the kids at the YMCA camp this summer. He was class president and captain of the debate team. He wants to be a lawyer. Like his father. Like you."

Alma let out a sigh of relief. "See there, Robert? He's going to be an attorney. He can't be all bad." She forced a smile.

Robert's eyes narrowed. "What's his last name?"

"Adamson."

"Is his father Frank Adamson? With Adamson, Henley, and Schultz?"

"I think so. Why?"

Robert ran his hands through his hair in frustration.

"Because Adamson is known for shady practices, that's why. He was nearly disbarred a couple of years ago. And he represents the dregs of the criminal world. If Derek's anything like his father…"

Ashley's eyes flashed. "Like father, like son, is that it?"

Alma continued to try to placate the two of them. "Now, Ashley, your father isn't saying that. He's just concerned for you. You can't blame him after what happened this summer."

Ashley had had enough. She straightened her shoulders and spoke in a stilted voice. "I have tables to wait on. Can I go now?"

Robert just glared at her, but Alma said, "Yes, go. I can't afford to lose customers."

Ashley walked stiffly through the swinging door, her head held high.

Robert stared after her. "I'm going to look into that Adamson kid," he said quietly.

Alma patted his arm. "You do that. You might just find out he's the kind of boy you want for your daughter."

He scoffed. "Frank Adamson's boy? I doubt it."

"He seems like a very nice boy. Ashley said he's been accepted to Stanford."

I cringed inwardly. *Oh, no. That's the last thing Robert needs to hear.*

His face turned red. "I should have known," he said through clenched teeth. "No wonder she wants to go to Stanford. Well, over my dead body." He stormed out the back door.

Alma and I regarded each other like two onlookers at a prize fight. "Whew," she said, wiping her face with her apron. "You know what their problem is? They're too much alike."

"I can see that."

"I've been the referee in too many of these fights, and to tell the truth, I'm getting tired of it. We were better off when it was just me and Ashley. I thought having the family back together again would be great, but..." She shook her head sadly, and my heart went out to her.

"No family is without its problems," I said, hugging her. "You'll work it out. You love each other and care about each other's lives. That's worth more than anything."

☙❧☙

Late that afternoon, I sat on my bed with Jack, pondering what I was going to wear for my date with Garrett. Ashley came in and stared woefully at the pile of books and notebooks scattered on her bed. Sasha followed her and looked hesitantly at the bed then trotted over and hopped up on my bed. She settled down next to Jack with her paws tucked under her chest.

Ashley laughed. "Poor Sasha. She can't even find a place to sleep on my bed anymore. Look at this mess."

"Aren't you going over for the dinner shift?"

She moved some books and papers over and sat on her bed. "Nope. Mom gave me the night off. Zoe can handle it. Hey, thanks for talking to Philippe. He came in this afternoon and offered to tutor me."

"You're welcome. When will you start?"

She opened her French textbook and took out several pages of notes. "Tomorrow. He gave me some things to brush up on before we start."

I felt a glow of satisfaction at being able to help her. "That's great, Ash." I went to the closet and stared at my meager wardrobe. I saw Ashley's burgundy top hanging there and wondered if I should ask to borrow it again. But

Garrett had already seen me in that. I poked through some of the other things hanging there.

Ashley must have read my mind. "Help yourself to anything you find. I'm going to get a bunch of new stuff for school anyway."

I pulled down a pale blue top with lace trim and held it up in front of me. "What do you think?"

"Awesome. It brings out your eyes. Where's he taking you?"

I turned to the mirror to admire the effect. "He didn't say. Wherever it is, I hope it perks him up."

"Yeah, he hasn't been himself lately. What's going on with him?"

"I don't know. What I don't understand is why he wasn't assigned to Sarge's case."

"But didn't he take you up to the campsite? Why would he do that if he wasn't on the case?"

I sat next to her. "Listen. He told me not to mention this to anyone, but..."

She looked at me eagerly, her eyes twinkling. "I'm not anyone. Spill."

"Up there, at the campsite, we found some things in the ashes of the campfire—some pieces of cloth, like someone had burned his clothes and personal belongings. And there was a piece of a note or letter that he was writing to Gil. He mentioned this guy named Greer that Gil told him about."

"Who's he?"

"An officer Gil knew in the army. He was involved in drugs, and it turned out he killed one of his men and buried him on the base."

"Whoa. Why would Sarge be writing to Gil about that?"

"Good question. The funny thing about it is that when I asked him if he was going to give the note to the detective on the case, he said he was going to hang onto it for a while."

She furrowed her brow. "So?"

"If it's not his case, he'd be obligated to turn it in, wouldn't he? That's not like him. He's usually so anal about procedure."

"Huh. That does seem odd."

"He started acting all secretive after he found the body buried up off the trail. He hustled me out of there like he didn't want the cops to see me at the campsite."

"Do you know who it was he found buried?"

"No, but I'm going to ask him tonight."

She sighed and chewed on her pencil. "Men. Do you realize how much of our lives we waste trying to figure them out?"

"They'd probably say the same thing about us." I picked Jack up and held him close to me, stroking him. "Why can't men be more like cats?"

"What, furry and cuddly? Works for me."

"Speaking of men, what's up with you and Derek? Anything serious?"

"I like him. I like spending time with him. He's smart and funny."

"And gorgeous."

She gave me that impish grin of hers. "That too."

"So what happens when school starts?"

She shrugged. "He goes off to Stanford, and I go back to Pineland Park High. And that will be that."

"That doesn't seem to bother you all that much."

She looked at me steadily. "I'm a realist. That's why Dad getting his boxers in a twist about him is so annoying. I know nothing will come of it. Why can't Dad see that?"

"You can't blame him after—"

"After what happened with Zach. I get it. It's still

annoying." She went back to her notes.

I watched her as she studied, thinking how mature she was and how sensibly she regarded her relationship with Derek. I tried to remember how it felt to be sixteen having my first crush, but it seemed too long ago. All I could recall about my teen years was the enduring sorrow over little Davey's death and the silence that enveloped the family like a thick fog. It was more than ten years ago, but since then my parents' relationship had become one of silent tolerance, while my brother's marriage had disintegrated. I had no idea what path my little sister's life had taken, other than she was spending next semester in Florence studying art. Mother kept me apprised of her activities, but what did I really know about her? *Why do some families drift so far apart while others remain closely connected? Do fractured families produce more fractured families?* If so, was there any chance for me to have a successful long-term relationship with someone?

I leaned back to watch a magpie strut along the window sill outside and thought about Garrett. He had left me in no doubt that he was hoping for a future with me, and the thought of that was certainly appealing. Yet I couldn't bring myself to commit to him. Was it because I was afraid of my family's history repeating itself? Or was there something else? Did I really know Garrett? Did I really trust him?

CHAPTER 6

Garrett arrived promptly for our date, wearing a smart gray blazer and ice blue shirt that brought out the blue in his eyes. I heard him talking with Robert at the front door. As I came into the living room, they stopped talking, but not before I heard Garrett say, "I'm sure they screen their counselors very carefully."

Garrett's eyes lit up as he assessed my outfit which, I had to admit looked pretty fabulous. I only wished my own clothes looked half as attractive on me as Ashley's did. I was grateful we were about the same size.

"Where are you two off to?" Robert asked.

"Dinner at Borelli's," Garrett said. "Ever been there?"

"No. Alma only gets one night a week off from the café. But we'll have to try it."

"I'm sure she'd love it," I said, hoping he would take both Alma and Ashley for a night out.

Garrett opened the door and held it for me. "Ready?"

Outside, the late afternoon sun was just dipping behind the mountain tops to the west, casting lengthening shadows on the lawn. The August air was still and warm, with just a hint of autumn we were beginning to sense in the evenings. Garrett took my hand as we followed the path next to the café on our way to the parking lot. Passing the patio, I noticed Zoe serving some customers there. Seeing her reminded me of Derek.

Garrett opened the door of his pickup for me. "Garrett, what was Robert asking you about when I came in?"

"Hmm? Oh, he was wondering about the YMCA camp up the hill. He wanted to know how the counselors are chosen. Whether they do background checks on them."

I knew what that was about. Robert had said he was going to check up on Derek. "Well? Do they?"

"I don't have any specific knowledge about that camp, but these days anyone who works with kids is very carefully checked. It's standard procedure. And the YMCA is a good organization."

He got in, started the engine, and exited the parking lot onto the road toward Pineland Park. He was quieter than usual. The low hum of the police scanner on the dashboard was the only sound in the cab.

"So," I said. "We're going to Borelli's?"

He glanced over at me almost as though he had forgotten I was there. "You don't mind, do you? I know we've been there before."

"Of course I don't mind. The food is great."

"I have to make a quick stop at the station first to pick up some work."

"Garrett. It's Saturday night. Do you really have to work this weekend?"

He sighed. "Williams gave me a pile of paperwork yesterday. It'll take me days to get through it."

Any hope I had of a romantic, after-dinner interlude began to fade like last week's flowers. We drove the rest of the twenty-mile trip in silence. I sensed he was lost in his own thoughts, and I didn't want to intrude.

He pulled into the parking lot at the police station. "I won't be long. Want to come in?"

The lobby of the small police station was deserted except for the young, fresh-faced officer behind the desk who looked up as we opened the door. "Hey, Garrett," he said with a smile.

"Address him as Detective," a stern voice said. Captain Williams, who I had met before, stepped out of his office behind the desk and cast a disapproving look at the officer.

"Detective," the young man mumbled, his face turning red.

Williams was just as I remembered him, a tall, well-dressed black man with a pencil thin mustache. His manners were courtly, almost aristocratic. He held the gate open for us, bowing slightly from the waist like the maître d' of a posh restaurant. "Miss Lowell, isn't it?" he said with a smile that showed his perfect white teeth. "Nice to see you again. Garrett said you had left the area."

"I was on assignment at some of the resorts."

"Oh, that's right. A travel writer, correct? That must be fascinating."

Garrett started down the hall toward his office. "I'll be right out."

Left alone with the police captain, it seemed a good time to ask about Hank. "Can you tell me how Hank Edwards is doing?"

He looked perplexed. "Edwards?"

"Yes. He's in your jail. He was arrested for the murder of Sarge…Richard Horner…at the campsite near Trout Fork."

"Oh, yes…yes. Mr. Edwards is our guest, isn't he?"

I couldn't tell whether he was being sarcastic. "I was just wondering how he's doing."

"I can assure you that our prisoners receive the best of care." He hesitated for a moment, a cloud crossing his face. "Although Mr. Edwards is in a certain amount of discomfort."

"Oh? What kind of discomfort?"

"The kind experienced by all alcoholics when they are deprived of alcohol."

Before I could inquire further, Garrett reappeared from his office, staggering under a mound of paperwork vast enough to make a Washington bureaucrat green with envy. The pile began to wobble, and Williams reached out to steady it. "Need some help, Detective?"

"No, sir. I can manage. Get the door, will you, Ryn?"

"Good night, Miss Lowell," Williams said with a slight bow. "Enjoy your dinner."

Once we and the mound were squeezed into the cab of the pickup, I said, "Your boss said Hank isn't doing too well in jail. Have you seen him at all?"

"No. He's not my prisoner. I'm not on that case, remember?"

"Why is that anyway? I would have thought anything that happened in Trout Fork would be of interest to you."

He laid his hand on the pile of papers between us. "I have more than enough to do."

"What about the evidence we found in the campfire? The note and the pieces of cloth. Have you given them to Detective Sloan?"

"Not yet. I'm hanging onto them for a while."

He offered no further explanation, so I decided to let the matter drop temporarily.

We pulled into Borelli's crowded parking lot. I got out of the pickup, and the smell of pasta and other Italian delights washed over me. My stomach reacted with a loud growl, reminding me that I hadn't eaten since Alma's pancakes early that morning.

Garrett came to my side of the pickup. He was certainly handsome, even if he was being annoyingly mysterious lately, and I was proud to be seen with him.

Although the restaurant was crowded, the atmosphere was tastefully subdued. The soft lighting was enhanced by candles glowing in red globes on each table. Italian arias playing softly in the background added to the ambiance. White-coated waiters glided unobtrusively from table to table, some pouring wine from bottles wrapped in white linen, others depositing delicious-looking entrees in front of diners with a flair bordering on the theatrical.

We ordered the Italian sampler plate for two, and Garrett chose a bottle of expensive merlot which the waiter brought quickly. He poured a small amount into Garrett's glass, waiting deferentially while Garrett tasted it and nodded.

We sipped our wine and talked about innocuous things like the weather and current events. I was relieved that he hadn't asked about my plans for the future or how long I would be in the area. The longer we sat there, the more relaxed he became, and soon we had reestablished the warm familiarity we had nearly lost. In no time, it was as though there hadn't been a one-month break in our relationship. He reached across the table and held my hand as he talked.

The waiter brought the sampler plate, and we devoured the different pastas, sauces and meats, along with the garlic bread. I ate until I thought I would burst.

After the waiter had cleared our plates, Garrett glanced toward the hostess stand where a heavy-set, mustached man wearing a tuxedo was greeting customers. Garrett got up from the table. "Excuse me a minute, Ryn. I'll be right back."

I watched him walk up to the man and tap him on the

shoulder. They had a somewhat heated conversation, the other man gesturing wildly at one point. I could see the anger in his eyes as he shook his head vehemently in response to Garrett's questions. His raised voice was beginning to attract attention until the hostess intervened with a calming look and a hand on his arm.

When Garrett came back to the table, I asked, "What was that all about? Who's that man?"

"That's Mario Borelli, the owner."

"What was he shouting about?"

"Nothing. Police business."

"I think I'm going to have to talk to your boss about overworking you," I teased. "First, that pile of paperwork, now interrupting a lovely dinner with—"

His eyes flashed at me. "Stay out of my professional life, Ryn. It has nothing to do with you."

Garrett's harsh response to my teasing shocked me. It was so unlike him.

"I...I'm sorry. I shouldn't have snapped at you. I didn't mean anything by it." He looked around warily and then at me again. He ran his fingers through his hair. "Do you want dessert?"

"No...no, I'm fine." I leaned forward and took his hand again. "Garrett, what is it? Can't you tell me?"

He looked away and gestured to the waiter for the check. The waiter placed it on the table, and Garrett laid some twenty dollar bills on the check. He put his wallet away. "Ready?"

I was disappointed that the evening was being cut short. He must have seen that in my eyes because he said quietly, "We can talk at my place."

He took my arm and propelled me toward the door. We passed the hostess stand where the owner still stood. He avoided making eye contact with us.

As we drove toward Garrett's cabin, the atmosphere in the truck was heavy with the silence of conflict. Garrett was exhibiting the annoying combination of a troubled spirit with a silent tongue, and I was beginning to be more than a little irritated with him.

"Are you sure you don't want to just take me home?" I asked stiffly. *Two can play that game.*

"Yes, quite sure."

We pulled into his driveway and parked in front of his cabin that sat back from the road in a tranquil setting. He turned off the engine and handed me his keys. "Open the door. I'll bring in this load." He followed me to his door, struggling with the paperwork pile.

The cabin was a bit messy, which was unusual for Garrett. He was normally so tidy and put together. Papers were scattered on the sofa and coffee table, along with empty coffee cups and fast food wrappers. This, too, surprised me. Garrett usually ate only healthy food.

I picked up the cups and took them to the kitchen. The sink was full of dirty dishes and the stove had some burned food on the surface.

Garrett dumped the load of paper on the small kitchen table and plopped into a chair with a sigh.

"Why don't I make us some coffee?" I asked.

He looked up at me gratefully, fatigue and stress radiating from his eyes. "That would be wonderful. Remember where it is?"

"Yes. Should I make it decaf?"

"Not for me. I'll be up for a while."

I joined him at the table after I set up the coffee pot. "You're tired, Garrett. You really look like you've been working too hard."

He gazed at me, and I noticed the dark circles under his eyes. "That's not it."

"Is it me? Our relationship? Look, I know it's frustrating that I can't make up my mind about the future. I'm a bit up in the air right now and—"

"That's not it either." He smiled for the first time since we left the restaurant. "You're not all that hard to put up with."

"Then what? There's something going on with you. Everyone's noticed it, and they're concerned about you. I'm concerned." My eyes searched his, and I could see the sadness around his eyes beginning to soften, along with his resolve.

"Okay. But what I'm going to say can't leave this room. Promise? Not even to Alma or Ashley."

"I promise. Not even to Jack," I quipped, hoping to ease the tension a little.

He leaned forward and spoke softly. "A couple of weeks ago, I picked up a guy on drug charges. Nothing serious. He wasn't dealing or anything like that. As I was questioning him, he told me he had some information that he would exchange for a lesser charge. He said he knew about a dirty cop who is supposedly involved in dealing drugs and running a protection racket."

"Protection racket?"

"Yeah, you know. A bad guy shakes down local business owners. Either the owner pays a certain amount for protection or his place gets robbed, or his business burns down, or he's turned in for code violations. That kind of thing."

"Did he tell you who the cop is?"

"No. All he would say was it's somebody on the Pineland Park force, and he would name him in exchange for a charge of disorderly conduct or public intoxication. I thought he was just trying to weasel out of the charges, so I ignored him. He got out on bail, partly because he had no record and has family in the area. Also, he had a stable job. He worked as a busboy at Borelli's."

"Is that what you were talking to Mr. Borelli about tonight?"

"Yeah. The kid told me he saw Borelli giving the cop money one night. Tonight I asked Borelli if he was paying someone for protection. He got pretty hot. Denied he knew anything about it. But I'm sure he was lying."

"Okay, but why does that have you so upset? It seems pretty minor."

He took a deep breath. "Remember that body we found buried up the hill from Sarge's campsite?"

"Yeah?"

"It was the busboy."

The coffee pot timer went off, causing us both to jump. I got up to pour the coffee and brought the cups to the table.

Garrett sat with his head in his hands. He looked up at me with those sad eyes. "Do you know what this means? A cop, maybe someone in my own precinct, may be a killer. I look at everyone with suspicion now, my own colleagues, the guys I trust with my life every time we go out on a call. It's driving me crazy. I feel like I can't trust anyone. I hate myself for it."

I realized that was the reason he had hustled me away from the campsite before I ran into the cops on their way up. He was trying to protect me.

"Well, how do you know the kid wasn't killed by another druggie?"

"It was too professional. Too methodical. The way he was killed, the way he was buried. It has all the marks of someone who knows what he's doing."

"Like a cop."

He nodded and ran his hands through his hair again. "Another thing. The kid was buried up there by the police shooting range. Very few people outside the force even know that range is up there. Or how to get to it."

"But how do you know it was a cop from your precinct? There are more than one in Pineland Park, aren't there?"

"There are two precincts in town, and also the county sheriff's office who oversee the outlying areas. I might not even know the guy. But that doesn't make it any easier to swallow."

If there was one thing I knew about Garrett, it was his fierce loyalty. I knew he was anguished at suspecting one of his fellow officers of such dreadful things. Also, for the first time, I felt genuinely fearful for his life.

CHAPTER 7

We sat at the table and drank our coffee in silence. The sadness in Garrett's eyes reminded me that here was a man who was loyal, faithful, and principled. Having to be suspicious of other policemen must have been tearing him apart. I also remembered Alma saying once that men like Garrett don't come along every day, and if I lost him, I would regret it. I felt a rush of affection for him and reached over to take his hand.

He looked mournfully at the massive mound of paperwork on the table. He took several folders from the top of the pile and opened the first one. "Here's the incident report from the crime scene where they found Sarge's body." He tossed the folder on the table and picked up another one. "And here's the autopsy report from the Denver coroner." He laid it on top of the first one and opened another folder. "These are background checks on the principals." He laid it down on the others and must have seen the eagerness in my face. "I shouldn't be showing these to you, but what the hell."

That was music to my ears, just what I had been waiting for. Maybe these files would help us find out who killed Sarge so we could get Hank out of jail. I grabbed the first folder—the crime scene report—and began reading hungrily.

The report was very detailed, even down to the GPS coordinates of the campsite. The area had been thoroughly searched by Detective Sloan and his team. They had noted the campfire where someone had burned Sarge's clothes and other possessions, meager though they were. The murder weapon, a rock that had Sarge's blood and hair on it, was found near the body. There was a notation stating the nature of the scene seemed to indicate a crime of passion, possibly with anger or revenge as the motive. When I read that sentence, I said, "Hmm."

Garrett sipped his coffee. "Anything interesting?"

"They seem to think whoever did it was mad about something. There was considerable violence evident throughout the scene." I didn't want to think about Hank's well-known volatile temper or the fact that he had been seen arguing with Sarge. No wonder he was suspected.

Garrett was silent, so I handed him the folder and took the next one. The tab at the top said, "Autopsy: Richard Horner."

After reading a bit, I said, "Listen to this, Garrett. Cause of death was a single blow to the head with the rock found by the body."

"We knew that."

"But there was something else. The fingers of both his hands were broken."

Garrett perked up a little and peered at the report. "Pre- or post-mortem?"

"Post."

He gazed out the window and said, almost to himself, "Why would someone who had just killed him with a rock bother to break his fingers?"

One of the things that made Garrett a good detective was his instinct for finding a killer's motivation. Solving the psychological puzzle was what he found most fascinating about police work.

I read more of the report. "Here's something else. They found a piece of paper in the pocket of his jacket. It had the letters w-i-n-d handwritten on it."

He looked at me and wrinkled his brow. "Wind? Like the West wind?"

"Or maybe it's wind with a long i, as in 'wind up and throw.'"

"That's all it said?"

I skimmed through the rest of the report. "That's about it."

He drummed his fingers on the table and gazed off into space. Then he stared at me intently. "We need to find out whether Sarge wrote it."

"How?"

"We'll compare it to the note he was writing to Gil. If the handwriting doesn't match, then that word may give us a clue to the motive."

"Wind?" I laughed and couldn't resist saying, "So we may be looking for some kind of crazed meteorologist?"

He grinned at me. "Or maybe someone had it in for Sarge because he had a problem with offensive flatulence."

I was so glad to see Garrett's mood change that I continued to offer silly motives until we were both holding our sides from laughing.

Finally, he wiped his eyes and said, "There's only one person who can shed some light on any of this, and that's Hank. I think our next move is to question him."

"But didn't the other detective already do that?"

"Yes, but Sloan didn't get much out of him. Now that he's had a few days to dry out and sober up, he may remember something we can use. Nothing like some time in a jail cell to jog the memory."

I was delighted that Garrett used the word "we." He was usually such a stickler for procedure and kept his professional and personal lives separate. But maybe he was suspicious enough of his colleagues to trust me. Whatever it was, he finally said. "Let's visit Hank tomorrow. I'm sure he'd like to see you."

We spent hours going through the reports and folders on the table until Garrett began yawning. I looked at the clock. It was past midnight. "I guess you'd better take me home. While you can still drive."

He lifted one eyebrow. "You can always stay here."

As tempting as it was, I didn't want to rush into something that wouldn't be so easy to get out of. "They'll be wondering where I am, and I'd rather not give Ashley any ideas."

Garrett got up reluctantly and stretched his back. "Okay. Why don't you meet me at the station at eleven tomorrow to visit Hank? I'll go in early. It's always quiet on Sunday, and I want to look up a few things."

⟡⟡⟡

The next morning, I took a short jog with Jack. Then I fed him, showered and changed, and went over to the café for breakfast. Gil and Madam Gauzie were sitting together at a table near the patio. Madam Gauzie waved to me. "Yoo-hoo, Ryn dear. Come join us."

I sat with them and ordered from Zoe, who was looking a bit ragged. Her normally bright green eyes were somewhat bloodshot, possibly indicating a late night.

Gil and Madam Gauzie had eaten and were just finishing their coffee. Gil was reading a Denver newspaper,
grumbling about the coverage, which, according to him,
had a definite liberal slant.

Not wanting to risk having him launch into a political diatribe, I said, "I'm going to visit Hank today. Anything you want me to tell him?"

Gil looked up from his paper. "Tell him his buddy
Gil misses him. It's just not the same around here without
him."

"Oh, maybe we should go see him, Gil," Madam
Gauzie put in.

"I don't know if he can receive visitors. I'm going
with Garrett. I can find out, though."

"Do that, dear," she said, shaking her head. "The
poor man. Such a dreadful thing to happen to him."

"Does Garrett have any leads?" Gil asked.

"Well, he's not officially on the case. A Detective
Sloan is in charge. But…" I hesitated, not knowing how
much to reveal. "Gil, is W-I-N-D a military acronym?"

He thought a moment. "Not that I know of, but
there's so many of them it's hard to keep track. What's
this all about?"

"I saw the autopsy report on Sarge last night. He had
a piece of paper in his pocket with that word on it. We're
wondering what it means."

"What else did the report say?" he asked.

"That he was killed by a single blow to the head with
a rock."

Madam Gauzie gasped and her hand went to her
heart. "Oh, dear. The poor man."

"The cops also know they were arguing that evening.
That, and his fingerprints on the rock, was enough to arrest him."

Gil shook his head and said, "Damn. I'm the one that

told the cops that. But those two argued all the time. Everything from sports to politics to the best fishing spots."

Madam Gauzie leaned in toward me. "Hank had his problems, God knows. But he couldn't kill anyone. He has a heart of gold. Gil, do you remember that time with the rats?"

Gil grinned. "Yeah."

I looked back and forth at them. "Rats?"

Gil said, "We had a problem with rats chewing the telephone wires in the back of our stores. Oh, this was years ago when we all had land lines. They were becoming a real nuisance. I suggested putting some rat poison out to stop them, but Hank wouldn't hear of it. If he couldn't bring himself to kill a rat, how could he kill a man? And not just any man, his friend." He shook his head. "No, I'll never believe it."

Madam Gauzie nodded in agreement. "Anything else in the report, dear?"

"One odd thing. The fingers on both his hands were broken."

"All of them? How strange. How did that happen?"

"The police don't know, but it appears they were broken after he died."

Gil furrowed his brow. "This gets weirder and weirder."

Zoe brought my breakfast, and I dug in. I talked as I chewed. "The scene also seemed to indicate anger or revenge. I guess it was the way things were destroyed and burned."

Gil and Madam Gauzie gave each other uncomfortable looks.

"What?" I said between mouthfuls.

The old woman sat back and sighed. "Well, we all know about Hank's temper. Especially when he's drinking, he becomes another person."

I nodded, remembering the first day I met Hank and said something innocent, only to have him demonstrate his Jekyll and Hyde personality. It was amusing at the time, but it always made me tread softly around him after that, careful not to say anything to set him off.

Gil stood. "Give him my best. I hope he's out soon. If he doesn't get back to his store pretty quick, he could lose his liquor license. Then how will he make a living?"

Madam Gauzie got up and pushed her chair in. "I'll walk out with you, Gil." She laid her hand on my shoulder. "Give him my love, too. Tell him I'm sending good thoughts his way."

I watched them leave the café and smiled at the odd pair. Even in all my years in New York, I had never met two such unique individuals.

∽∾∽

Garrett's gray pickup was parked in front of the police station when I pulled my bike into the lot and switched off the engine. I removed my helmet and sat for a minute reveling in the Sunday morning quiet.

I opened the front door to find the lobby empty, so I went through the small gate toward Garrett's office. He wasn't there, so I sat in the chair facing his desk to wait for him. The other office doors were closed. I assumed most of the force had Sunday off. Either that or they were all out on patrol.

Garrett came in carrying a folder and sat at his desk, but not before closing his office door. His appearance was a bit disheveled, his eyes indicating a lack of sleep.

"Good morning," I said.

He looked up and smiled. "Hi."

"What's up?"

He lowered his voice furtively and showed me the

note we had found in Sarge's pocket. "I've been in the evidence room. I looked at Hank's statement and compared it to the handwriting on the note with the word 'wind' on it. The handwriting's not the same."

"So maybe Sarge wrote it?"

"Look." He took Sarge's note to Gil and laid it next to the note that said "wind." The two writings were also completely different.

"If Hank didn't write it and neither did Sarge, it must have been the killer."

Garrett put both notes in his drawer and stood. "We don't know that for sure, but we do know it wasn't either of them. Let's go see Hank."

We left the office and descended the stairs to the basement. It smelled of mold, dampness, sweat, and urine. Two small cells sat across from each other with a narrow aisle between them. A square of sunlight from the only window cast a barred shadow on the floor. One cell was empty. In the other, sitting on a narrow bunk with his head in his hands, was Hank.

He looked up at us, and my heart went out to him. He had lost weight and looked ten years older. His bushy red beard and hair were lank and ragged-looking. His pale face made a stark contrast against the bright orange jumpsuit. His bloodshot eyes seemed to have difficulty focusing on us as he blinked and squinted.

We stood in front of his cell. "Hello, Hank," I said. "Remember me?"

He hesitated a moment, then got up and walked unsteadily toward the bars. "Ryn? What are you doing here?"

I tried to smile cheerfully, hoping my face wouldn't show how appalled I was at what was before me, a mere shadow of the strong character I had once compared to a mountain man I had seen in a movie. "I came to see you.

And to tell you Madam Gauzie sends her love. And Gil said to tell you he misses his buddy."

He reached out, his hands trembling, and grasped the bars to steady himself. "Tell them I miss them too."

Garrett held out a Snickers bar to him. "Here, Hank. I brought you something."

Hank's hands shook violently as he grabbed the candy bar and tried to remove the wrapper. Garrett took it gently from him, ripped it open, and handed it back to him. Hank managed to get it into his mouth, chewing slowly while his hands continued to shake.

Garrett spoke to him quietly. "We were hoping you might be able to remember something about the morning you found Sarge."

Hank looked at Garrett vacantly. Then huge tears welled up in his eyes. "Sarge is dead, isn't he?"

"Yes. He's dead. Do you remember what happened to him?"

Hank stared into space then he looked fearfully back and forth at me and Garrett. "Did I kill him?"

I stared at this wreck of a man, wondering if it was possible he killed his friend.

"Can you tell me what happened when you woke up that morning?" Garrett said gently.

Hank's bleary eyes fixed blankly on the wall behind us. He appeared to be trying to remember. "There was blood. Lots of blood," he mumbled.

"That's right," Garrett said. "Do you know how the blood got there?"

"Did I do something to him? Was it my fault?" Lines of strain and remorse dug into his forehead.

"That's what we're trying to find out," Garrett said, placing his hand on Hank's arm. "Do you remember anything at all about the night before?"

Hank's jaws worked vigorously. "We played cards."

"What else? Were you arguing about something? Gil said he saw you arguing after you left your store."

He looked up at us, a bit of recognition in his eyes. "The Broncos."

"What about them?"

He straightened his shoulders indignantly. "He said they stink. And they'll never win another Super Bowl. That really pissed me off."

"That was the argument? The Broncos?" I could tell Garrett was getting frustrated. "Can you remember anything else about that night? Besides playing cards?"

"We had a few drinks, and he smoked a couple of joints."

"Did you see anyone near the camp?"

Hank's forehead wrinkled. "I didn't. But Sarge said he saw someone the night before."

Now we're getting somewhere, I thought. I moved in closer to him. "Who was it, Hank? What did he say?"

His hands rubbed his temples and tears began to form in his eyes again. "I don't know. I don't know. I can't remember."

Garrett patted his arm. "It's okay."

His eyes pleaded with me in desperation. "I need a drink. Can you get me a drink?

"I'm sorry. I wish I could."

Garrett took my arm. "We'll come see you again soon. Get some rest."

Hank mumbled something incoherent and weaved back to his bunk.

Garrett guided me toward the stairs. "We weren't going to get anything out of him. He's in withdrawal. Did you see the way his hands shook?"

"So sad. How long will that last?"

"Could be as long as a week. After that, we can visit him again, and maybe he'll make more sense. I'm convinced he knows more about what happened than he can recall right now. We'll just have to go slow and hope it starts to come back to him. In the meantime, I'm going to concentrate on that note. I'm convinced the word 'wind' means something. It has to."

He walked me out to my bike and stood gazing at the mountains while I strapped on my helmet.

"I forgot to tell you what Ashley told me," I said. "You know Sarge's sister and her husband?"

Garrett nodded. "Alma told me they were in Trout Fork. What about them?"

"Well, Ashley swears the husband, Howard, was here earlier in the summer talking to Sarge. She said he kept pushing a piece of paper at him, trying to get him to sign it."

"Did he sign it?"

"Not according to Ashley. She said Sarge kept refusing and Howard got mad. When Ashley brought it up, Howard denied ever having been in Trout Fork."

"Huh," he said in his annoyingly noncommittal way.

"Don't you think that's interesting?" I prompted. "Maybe you should tell Detective Sloan so he can look into it."

His face clouded. "Maybe." He leaned over and kissed me on the cheek. "Be careful on that thing."

CHAPTER 8

Several days later, I sat in the bedroom Ashley and I shared. She was with her parents in the living room.

Robert had made a rare mid-week visit, and I had decided to give them some space. Jack and Sasha were curled up together on my bed, Sasha having given up trying to find a few clear inches on Ashley's bed among the books.

I hadn't seen Garrett since we visited Hank on Sunday. I knew he was busy, but when I didn't hear from him, I started to worry about the possibility that someone in his precinct might be a danger to him. I finally told myself that he was a capable detective and could take care of himself. He didn't need me to protect him.

I had given Alma, Gil, and Madam Gauzie an update on Hank, leaving out the more disturbing details of his condition. Alma said she would make some of Hank's favorite chili and send it with Garrett the next time he came in.

After putting off calling my mother for weeks, I sighed and pulled out my phone, hoping this might be one of those times Trout Fork's spotty phone service would be unavailable.

Damn, I thought as the New York number began to ring.

My mother's cool voice breathed into the phone. "Hello. Lowell residence."

"Hello, Mother. How are you?"

"Ryn. I was just thinking about you. Where are you, dear? Still in Colorado?"

"Yes. I'm back in Trout Fork for a visit."

"Trout Fork? Isn't that where that dreadful man—"

I sighed. "Yes, Mother. The very same Trout Fork."

"But I thought you were doing columns in other parts of the state. Why are you back in that place?"

I could picture her nose wrinkling as though a foul order had wafted in as she spoke of *that place.*

"I came back for a visit, to see some friends and take a break before my next assignment." I didn't dare mention another murder in Trout Fork for fear she would send the Pinkertons to drag me home by force.

There was silence on the other end of the phone. Then she said hesitantly, "Is there any chance you might be going to Vail next?"

"As a matter of fact, Mr. Crenshaw wants me to do several columns from there and the other ski resorts, but it's too early in the year. Why?"

"You remember the Blanchards, don't you?"

"Of course I remember them." Dexter Blanchard had some connection with my father's investment firm. His Armani suits declared it was quite a lucrative connection. Marilyn Blanchard was an uptight, snooty society matron involved in numerous charities. Their son, Dansby, a year older than me, grew up in stuffy New York society which he hated as much as I did. Whenever we were forced to endure some boring function, Dan and I inevitably found a corner where we could sit and poke fun at the crowd.

We had drifted apart after high school and I'd lost touch with him.

"Well, we saw them at a charity do last week. Marilyn tells me Dansby lives in Vail now. He has become some sort of...oh what's the word...someone who works very little and skis a lot."

"Ski bum?"

"That's it. A ski bum. His father is quite put out about it. All that education gone to waste. He graduated from Yale, you know. He worked in the City for a year then decided to throw away a perfectly good career. He just packed up and left. Then he called his parents to say he was working in a ski shop in Vail and wouldn't be coming back. His father was livid."

I tried not to laugh out loud. I was tempted to gloat and say I was glad to hear I wasn't the only refugee from that hideous lifestyle, but decided there was no point in pouring salt on her wounds.

"Ryn? Are you still there?"

"Yes, Mother, I'm here."

"I was thinking..."

Uh-oh. Here it comes.

"...why don't you get in touch with Dansby? I'm sure he'd love to hear from you, and since you're so close to Vail, maybe you two could get together."

The thought of reconnecting with someone from that scene held no appeal whatsoever, although seeing Dan again might be very amusing. "I'll have to do that."

She exhaled into the phone. "Oh, I hoped you'd say that. As a matter of fact, I gave Marilyn your number, and she said she'd pass it on to Dansby. You can expect a call one of these days."

"That will be nice. How's Dad? And Jarrod?" I knew from our last phone conversation that my brother's marriage was on the rocks.

Mother sighed. "Your father is the same, working long hours. Jarrod is still trying to work out a settlement with Meredith."

"So I guess the marriage is over?"

"Yes, I'm sorry to say. But Jarrod seems resigned to it. At least they have no children. What about you, dear? Did you go back to Trout Fork because of that detective you were seeing? Easterbrook, wasn't that his name?"

"Yes. Garrett Easterbrook. He's not the reason I came back, but I am still seeing him." My cell phone beeped, reminding me I had forgotten to charge it. "Look, Mother, my phone is about to die. Give my love to Dad. I'll call again soon."

"All right, dear. I hope you hear from Dansby. Perhaps you two can—" Her voice cut off.

I plugged the phone into the charger and sat on the bed stroking Jack. I wondered why talking to my mother always produced a profound depression in me. My childhood was hardly one of abuse or deprivation, if you didn't count emotional deprivation. Hearing her voice always triggered images of the looks of disapproval she perpetually wore. She disapproved of everything and everyone. Even her own husband and children couldn't live up to her standards, no matter how much they achieved or how successful they became.

I thought about Garrett and where our relationship was heading. I knew from his not-so-subtle hints where he hoped it was heading, and I had no doubt he would make someone a wonderful husband—caring, considerate, intellectually stimulating. But was it enough? *Don't all couples believe their marriage will beat the odds and be the one that survives fifty years?* I shook my head. My feelings for him, although strong and growing stronger, were tempered by reality. I had seen too many bad marriages and precious few good ones.

As though to verify my thoughts, the sound of raised voices came from the living room. Then the bedroom door burst open, and Ashley stormed in, her face like thunder. She stomped into the small bathroom we shared, slamming the door behind her. Jack and Sasha both looked after her, their eyes wide.

Through the door to the living room that Ashley had left ajar, I heard Alma and Robert arguing. For once, Alma wasn't being the conciliator, and her tone was just as strident as her husband's.

"You're overreacting, Robert. At best, this is nothing more than a summer fling."

"Fling? Fling?" he shouted. "You want your daughter flinging with a criminal? Is that it? What kind of mother are you?"

"Don't overdramatize everything. You're jumping to conclusions. It could be something as minor as a speeding ticket. The boy is hardly a criminal."

"Hardly a criminal? What do you call someone ordered by the court to do community service? A Boy Scout?"

"There's no need to be sarcastic."

"Alma, did you hear what I told you? The reason he's over at that YMCA camp is he was ordered there by the court. And this is the guy you want your daughter going out with? Well, over my dead body. If I have to camp on your doorstep to keep her away from him, I will."

Alma's voice rose to match his volume. "This is exactly what happened to break us up in the first place, Robert. You've always been so controlling. You, the bigshot lawyer, and me, barely graduating from high school. And you never let me forget it. Well, in case you haven't noticed, I'm not that girl you married. I have my own business, I own all these cabins and the surrounding land,

and I raised our daughter with little help from you. So get off your high horse."

I felt guilty eavesdropping on their conversation, so I got up and closed the door. Ashley came out of the bathroom, her eyes red from crying, and flopped on the bed. Sasha got off my bed and went to join Ashley, who grabbed the little cat and held her close.

My heart went out to both Ashley and her parents. "Ash? Are you okay?"

She nodded mutely. "My life sucks," she wailed. "He's going to ruin what's left of my summer."

I smiled to myself, remembering how huge and emotionally-charged teenage relationships could be. I had no words of comfort for her. I knew in a few weeks school would start, and she would forget the drama of the summer and probably forget Derek as well. But the last thing she needed was to hear me blow off her concerns. "I'm sorry. I know it's hard."

"Sometimes I wish Dad would just stay in Denver. Why does he have to come down here and get involved with us after all this time?"

"Maybe he's trying to make up for lost time."

"Lost time is just that—lost. We'll never be the Brady Bunch."

"You have to give him credit for trying, though. Even at this late date."

"All they ever do is argue. That's not my idea of a family."

How little she knows about families, I thought.

ᒍᕬᒍᕬ

The next morning, I sat in the café eating breakfast and ruminating about my phone call to Mother. The depression those calls usually produced had subsided for the most part, but as I watched Estelle Milner sitting alone, I thought again about the number of miserable married couples I had seen in just the last few years.

The woman glared at the café's front door, tapping her fingers on the table in apparent impatient irritation. As though in response to her unspoken call to him, her husband entered the café dressed in waders and an old fishing cap covered with hooks, lures, and miniature beer cans. It was so out of character for him that I nearly laughed out loud. Ashley was just passing with a tray full of breakfast plates and rolled her eyes at me, nodding toward the man.

Howard sat with his wife, cringing as she lit into him about his lateness. His demeanor was that of a puppy being scolded for peeing on the carpet. His previously cheerful expression faded, and he sighed and quietly ordered a coffee from Zoe.

Garrett came into the café carrying his morning newspaper. He smiled when he saw me and came to join me at our usual table. He signaled to Ashley, who came over to take his order. He noticed the Milners sitting nearby. "Oh good. They're here," he said quietly. "I'm going to talk to him about Sarge. I'll have to get him alone, though."

I snickered. "Good luck on that. She rarely lets him out of her sight." I watched him scan the front page of the paper. "So tell me, any news about the busboy? Are you any closer to knowing what happened to him?"

"Nope. I haven't heard anyone at the station talking about it either. It's like it never happened. I asked the captain about it, but he just said Detective Sloan is on it. But Sloan hasn't asked me about my interview with the kid."

"Is that unusual?"

"I put in my report when I arrested the kid that he had some information about a Pineland Park cop, information he was willing to trade for lesser charges. If Sloan was doing his job, he should have asked me about it."

"Isn't Sloan also the one investigating Sarge's death?"

Garrett nodded. Ashley brought his breakfast, and we both ate quietly. We had just finished when we saw Estelle leave her husband alone and head down the hallway toward the ladies' room.

"Excuse me," Garrett said as he got up. He went to Howard's table, which was just barely close enough for me to hear their conversation.

Garrett slid into an empty chair at the table and pulled out his ID. "Mr. Milner, I'm Detective Easterbrook. I'd like to ask you a couple of questions about your brother-in-law, if you don't mind."

Howard looked at him, his brow furrowed suspiciously. "I guess."

"You were here earlier this summer talking to your brother-in-law."

"Was I?"

"You know you were. The police are investigating a murder, so don't play coy with me. A witness saw you arguing with Sarge...Richard Horner...about signing some kind of document. What was that all about?"

Howard squirmed in his seat, casting glances toward the ladies' room. He leaned in toward Garrett. "Look. My wife doesn't know anything about this." He hesitated for a moment. "I was trying to get him to sign over his half of our house in Albuquerque. His father...his and Estelle's...left the house to the two of them. Sarge was never there. It was of no use to him. But we couldn't sell it or refinance it as long as he owned half of it. If I could get him to sign the paper, we would own the house outright. But he refused."

"Well, you own it now, don't you?"

Howard bristled. "Now look. Don't go trying to pin that on me. I had nothing to do with it."

"You benefitted from his death though, didn't you? Now the house belongs to you and your wife, doesn't it?"

Howard was sweating and pulling at his collar as Garrett bored in on him.

"Did you kill your brother-in-law, Mr. Milner?"

Listening to Garrett grill the man gave me a different perspective on him. He may love opera and the Romantic poets, but when it came to doing his job, he could be a pit bull.

"No. I didn't. I didn't," Howard said, his voice rising.

Garrett sat back when he saw Estelle emerge from the hallway. "How long will you be in Trout Fork, Mr. Milner?"

"I don't know. It's up to my wife."

Garrett stood and nodded genially to the two of them. "Well, enjoy the fishing."

Estelle regarded the two men through narrowed eyes.

Garrett came back to our table and threw a couple of dollars down. Then he took my arm and said, "Come on."

As we headed toward the door, I could feel Estelle's eyes boring into my back. Outside the café, I squinted at the bright sun. "Where are we going?"

"Didn't you say Gil was close to Sarge?"

"Sarge lived with Gil during the winter months. They've known each other a long time."

He propelled me toward the bait shop. "Good. Maybe he can shed some light on that family."

We found Gil deep in conversation with a customer about the difference between brown trout and rainbow trout. He nodded to us when we came in. The fisherman left and Gil came to us. "Going to take up fishing, Garrett?" he said with a smile.

Garrett fingered some of the paraphernalia on the counter. "Maybe someday. But right now I need some information."

Gil folded his arms, revealing the US Army tattoo on his upper bicep. "Whatever I can do to help."

"You were close to Sarge, weren't you?"

Gil shrugged. "As close as anyone could get to him. What do you want to know?"

"Did he ever talk about his sister and her husband? About the deed to their house in Albuquerque?"

Gil grimaced slightly. "I thought that would come up. I guess you know about Howard coming here a few months ago."

Garrett nodded. "I'm wondering about that. Did Sarge ever talk about it?"

"Never before, but he sure talked that day. He was pretty steamed. He told me Howard pressured him to sign the property over to him. Sarge detested him because he's such a weenie and because he allows Estelle to dominate him. I guess their father was pretty brutal and controlling, and Sarge hated him. That's one reason he joined the Marine Corps right out of high school. He wanted to get out from under their father's thumb."

"Did Sarge say why Howard was trying to get him to sign?"

"He said he suspected Howard wants to sell the house because he needs the money to pay his gambling debts. Hank said he mentioned something about owing somebody in Las Vegas. He came here alone because he didn't want his wife to find out about it." Gil glanced sideways at Garrett. "Do you think Howard killed Sarge?"

"I don't know. But it would solve his money problems, wouldn't it?"

Gil shook his head. "Hard to believe that wimp could kill anyone."

"Maybe. But if those Vegas loan sharks are after you, you can get pretty desperate. Those boys don't mess around."

Garrett thanked Gil and asked him to get in touch if he remembered anything else.

We left the bait shop and stood next to Garrett's pickup. I could almost see his mind whirling as he gazed at the trailhead across the street. "Ryn, can you meet me at the station around dinner time?"

"Sure. Why?"

"I need to talk to Hank again. It's been four days since we last visited him. Hopefully he's regained some of his memories of that night."

"Okay. I'll bring him some of Alma's chili."

"About six o'clock. Most of the day shift will be gone by then."

I watched him drive off then went to the café kitchen where I found Alma thumbing through some recipes. She smiled at me, her bright blue eyes twinkling in her round pink face. "There you are. What have you and Garrett been up to?"

"We're going to see Hank again tonight. I can bring him the chili you made for him."

"Wonderful. It's all packed up in a container in the fridge. There's some of that cornbread, too. He loves that."

I left the kitchen and took a seat on the patio. Zoe came by and asked if I wanted anything. Her normally outgoing manner seemed subdued. I asked her for coffee, and said, "So how's it going, Zoe? How do you like the job? And living in Trout Fork?"

She shrugged noncommittally. "It's okay, I guess."

"What are you planning to do for the winter?"

She looked at me somewhat suspiciously. "Why? What's it to you?"

Her abrupt manner took me back. "I'm just interested. Some would call it nosy. Occupational hazard for a journalist, I guess."

She took out a tissue to wipe her runny nose. "I don't know what I'll be doing after the summer. It depends on...lots of things. I'll get your coffee."

I watched her walk away and wondered how closely she had been involved with Derek and whether the downturn in that relationship was causing her to lose her sparkle. She brought my coffee and the check and turned away without another word.

I sat on the patio for about an hour, just enjoying the sun and the clear Colorado sky. The scent from the purple and fuchsia flowers in the planters on the railing mixed with the pine smell from the trees. I breathed deeply and thought about the strange inconsistency of this tiny, peaceful community and the two murders that had occurred here in one summer.

After midmorning, I decided to take a hike on the trail to work off my breakfast. As I passed through the dining room, I saw Ashley at a corner table with Philippe. Her French book and notebook were open before them, and they were poring over her notes. They looked up and waved as I passed. Philippe's smile crinkled his eyes, while Ashley looked resigned and somewhat less than thrilled.

I silently breathed a prayer of thanksgiving that I was finished with formal education forever. *I may be broke,* I thought, *but at least I'm free—not stuck in a stifling classroom or chained to a pile of huge, boring textbooks.*

As I strolled along the trail enjoying the feeling of freedom that was so incredibly important to me, I couldn't help shuddering at the thought of Hank stuck in that tiny cell for a crime he didn't commit. I was more determined than ever to do whatever I could to free him.

CHAPTER 9

Late that afternoon, I struggled into an old pair of jeans which seemed just a bit tighter than I had remembered. I turned sideways to gaze at my profile in the mirror. Was it Alma's pancakes that had caused me to put on a couple of pounds? Or was it that I would be twenty-nine in October and my girlish figure was beginning to rearrange itself?

Jack was watching me from his usual perch on my bed. "Oh, don't look at me like that," I told him. "You're not getting any younger either."

He stood and stretched. Then he sat with his tail wrapped around his front paws and regarded me with his inscrutable amber eyes.

I turned back to the closet and sighed. My sparse wardrobe was beginning to depress me. I had a fleeting memory of those shopping trips along Fifth Avenue with my father's credit card burning a hole in my pocket. But those New York days were long gone. Now I was lucky to afford gas for my motorcycle.

Pulling a top and light jacket off their hangars, I wondered if Garrett would suggest we have dinner together after our visit to Hank. If he did, I wouldn't be dressed for anything more exotic than Burger King. I patted Jack on the head and told him to be a good boy while I was gone.

He said, "*Brrrt?*"

I found Alma's chili and cornbread in Tupperware containers and wrapped in a plastic bag in her refrigerator. I took them out to the bike and strapped them onto the seat behind me.

Zoe and Ashley were waiting on customers on the patio. I waved to Ashley who looked up as I started the engine. I noticed Zoe looked more frazzled and unkempt than she even had that morning. What was going on with her?

Maneuvering along the winding road to the police station, I felt a slight chill that reminded me autumn was rapidly approaching. In the mountains of Colorado, winter came early, and even now in mid-August, the feeling of cooler weather was already in the air. How would I ever afford the heavier clothes I would need to get around on my bike in the winter?

I hadn't received a check for the last three columns I'd written, but I dreaded calling the office for fear my editor, old cranky Crenshaw, would demand to know where I was and what I was writing about now. I had no doubt he would reach for his Rolaids when I told him I was back in Trout Fork.

The poor man's blood pressure was a victim to the quirks of his travel column writer. I often wondered why he put up with me.

I pulled into the parking lot in front of the police station and parked the bike next to Garrett's gray pickup. I was just dismounting when the door opened and Detective Sloan waddled out the door and headed for a dilapidated Ford, one of the few cars in the lot beside Garrett's. He nodded to me as he passed by, got into his car, and drove off in the cloud of black smoke belching from the

Ford's exhaust. Whatever brought him down here from the Denver PD, clearly it wasn't the pay.

The door opened again, and Captain Williams came out. "Good evening, Miss Lowell," he said with a slight bow when he saw me. "The detective is waiting for you, I believe."

"Thank you." Normally, I would say "Thanks," but there was something about the captain's courtly courtesy that always put me on my best behavior.

"Have a good evening."

I watched him go, then took the plastic bag of food off the bike, and entered the station. The desk sergeant barely looked up as I opened the gate and started down the hall. Either Garrett told him he was expecting me, or he had seen me often enough to know me.

I found Garrett in his office, his eyes glued to his computer screen. I slid into the chair facing his desk and waited for him to notice me. One thing I had learned about Garrett—his powers of concentration were formidable. I took the opportunity to examine his face more closely than I usually did because I never wanted him to catch me staring at him. His steel blue eyes were framed by dark intense eyebrows and long, almost feminine, lashes. His forehead was broad, but his hairline was low, the reason his thick black hair tended to fall forward, causing him to push it back absent-mindedly. An aquiline nose and sensuous lips completed the picture. I smiled to myself. All in all, he was quite a looker. That great physique didn't hurt the image either.

After a minute or two, I cleared my throat. He started and then grinned at me. "You're here. Sorry. I didn't see you."

"I'll try not to take that personally. I have Hank's chili. Has he eaten yet?"

"I doubt it. I haven't seen the caterer tonight."

"Your prisoners get catered food?"

"Well, maybe 'outsourced' is a more accurate description." He looked back at the screen. He saw me watching him and said, "I'm searching databases for crimes involving notes left at the crime scenes."

"Any luck?"

"Nada." He got up and switched off his computer. "Let's go down and see Hank. Maybe Alma's chili will jog his memory."

We stopped in the tiny break room where I heated the chili in the microwave and added a plastic spoon I found in a drawer. Then we descended the narrow staircase to the cells in the basement. As soon as Garrett opened the door, the unpleasant odors accosted me, causing me to wrinkle my nose. "Ugh."

"Sorry about the smell," Garrett said. "We really need to air this place out."

We found Hank lying on his bunk with his arms crossed behind his head. He got up when he heard us and came to the bars. He looked much better than when I'd seen him several days before. His eyes were clearer and his hands had stopped their awful trembling. He seemed surprised to see me. "Ryn. When did you get back in town?"

Garrett's eyes met mine, and he shook his head slightly. I guessed he was trying to tell me that Hank's alcoholic withdrawal symptoms were playing tricks with his memory.

"Just a few days ago. I'm staying with Alma for a while." I held up the container. "She sent some of her chili and cornbread. She knows how you love her chili."

His eyes glowed with delight, and he smiled through his bushy red beard. He reached through the bars to take the container from me. Then he sat on his bed and dug into it. "This is great. Tell Alma I said thanks a lot," he said, spewing crumbs everywhere as he shoved huge pieces of cornbread into his mouth.

We waited for him to finish and watched him wipe his beard with the napkin Alma had included. He sighed and looked around as though wanting more.

"Hank," Garrett said, "I was hoping you might remember more about the night Sarge...died."

He came to us and placed his hands on the bars between us. "I been thinking about that."

I held my breath.

"I been thinking that I couldn't have hurt Sarge. He was my buddy. But I drank too much. Like always. If I hadn't passed out, I mighta been able to protect him from whoever..." He shook his head and pulled at his beard. "Why didn't they kill me? Why Sarge? He never hurt anyone."

"That's what we're trying to find out. Can you help us?"

"How?"

"Try to remember what you and Sarge talked about that night. Did he say anything about a note he was writing to Gil?"

"Gil? No."

"Did he ever mention an army officer named Greer?"

Hank rubbed his hands across his eyes. "I don't know. Maybe. I just don't remember. It's all so fuzzy."

"All right. Forget about that for now. What about Sarge's sister? Did he mention her at all?"

His brow furrowed in concentration. "Yeah. Well, not the sister. Her husband. He called him a weasel."

"What did he say about him?"

"That he was trying to steal their house, the one he grew up in. Somewhere in New Mexico."

"Albuquerque."

"Yeah, that's it."

Garrett moved closer to the bars. "Now this is really important, Hank. Did he say anything about seeing someone near the campsite? Or maybe farther up the hill?"

I knew Garrett was fishing for information about the busboy he'd found buried up there.

A look of recognition flashed over Hank's face, and he broke into a sly smile. "Yeah, he did. He saw something."

"What did he see?" Garrett asked quickly. "Did he see a body being buried up there?"

"A body? Geez, no. One night he saw two kids in the woods farther down the trail. Doing the deed." He grinned again.

"Two kids having sex? Did he know who they were?"

"He didn't say. He just said he watched them for a while." He snickered. "The old goat."

I felt a little sick. Could it have been Derek and Ashley the night they went up to the camp together? Was Ashley foolish enough to get involved with Derek and risk her future? I didn't want to believe it.

Garrett spoke softly. "Can you remember anything else about that night, Hank?"

Hank shook his head sadly and tears formed in his eyes. "I drink too much. That's how I lost my wife. Did you know that?" His eyes searched ours. "She left me because of the booze. I'm such a jerk." He pounded his hands on the bars. "When I get outta here, I'm not touching another drop. I'm gonna sell the store and—How is the store, Ryn? Do you know?"

I didn't want to tell him he was in danger of losing his liquor license and his livelihood. "I think Gil is keeping an eye on it for you. Don't worry."

"Gil," he mumbled. "He's a good man—good man."

We could see that he was growing tired and losing his focus, so we said our goodbyes, and I promised I would bring him some more chili. We left him sitting on his bed with his head in his hands.

As we ascended the rickety stairs, I said, "Can Gil come to visit him? I think it would do him a world of good."

"I'll see what I can do. Poor guy. He could use a friend."

♥❧❧

After our visit to Hank, Garrett walked me out of the station to my bike. "I've got a ton of stuff to do before I can leave tonight. Do you mind?"

"Of course not," I said, trying not to show my disappointment. I straddled the bike and pulled on my helmet.

"Tell you what. Saturday night I'll have you over for dinner."

"Lasagna and opera again?"

"No. I'll woo you with my chicken cacciatore this time."

I started the bike. "Works for me. But I'm easy."

He leaned over and kissed my cheek. "That'll be the day."

The sun had gone behind the mountain tops to the West, and the early evening shadows were shrouding the road. I drove slowly, thinking about Hank and the wife he was still pining over. Maybe he really would kick the booze when he got out of jail. But if he didn't get out soon, there would be nothing for him to go back to, and like most alcoholics, it was likely he would find solace in the bottle again. It was imperative we find something to exonerate him, and that meant finding the real killer.

I went over the people I thought might have a reason to kill poor old Sarge, but none of them seemed to have a strong enough motive. I decided to lay it all out for Ashley when I got back. Maybe a fresh perspective would help clarify things. For a sixteen-year old, she was remarkably logical and perceptive.

Jack was waiting patiently for me when I opened the bedroom door. He meowed to me and rubbed against my legs as I changed into my old sweat pants and T-shirt. I sat on the bed and played with him, throwing his favorite mouse for him to chase until he wore himself out. Then I opened the window and sat in the darkness watching night fall over the forest. The moon, silver-white and crystal clear, peeked over the treetops and flooded the area with light. I remembered how difficult it was to see the moon in New York because of the skyscrapers. I felt no longing at all for New York and was even beginning to think I belonged in Trout Fork. It wasn't only the beauty of the area. It was home to the people I had come to love.

Ashley came in and switched on the light. "Hey. How come you're sitting in the dark?"

"Just enjoying the peace. Are you finished for the night?"

She tossed her purse on the bed. "Yep. Zoe is helping Mom close up so I can get some studying done. I don't know how much help Zoe will be, though. She's a real zombie these days."

"She does look a little out of it lately. What's that all about?"

Ashley shrugged and sat on the bed with her books.

"How's the French going? Is Philippe helping at all?"

"Yeah. It really makes a difference speaking the language and not just doing grammar exercises. Only sometimes he talks so fast he loses me. So I say *Je ne comprends pas* a lot. It's my favorite expression. So what have you been up to?"

"Garrett and I went to see Hank. I brought him some of your mom's chili."

"Poor Hank. How's he coping?"

"Better, I think. But that jail is a stinking hole."

"Is Garrett any closer to finding out who did it?"

"I know there are a couple of suspects, but nothing concrete."

"Like who?"

I hesitated, not sure whether I should mention Garrett's suspicion about one of his fellow officers. Although I had my suspicions about Derek, I didn't want to implicate him for fear she would lump me in with her father and other nosy adults. "Well, there's Sarge's brother-in-law, for one. You know he was pressuring Sarge to sign over his share in the family home."

She pulled Sasha close to her. The little cat cuddled up with her and purred. "So that's what he was trying to get him to sign."

"Yeah. Now that Sarge is dead, the house belongs to him and his wife. So he had motive."

"But they weren't here when Sarge died."

"Their story is that they came after the VA called his sister, but who really knows?"

"Okay. Who else?"

"Well, I probably shouldn't tell you this, but—"

She grinned at me. "You always say that, and you always end up telling me."

"I know, I know. It's just that I trust your instincts. And it's good to say these things out loud. It helps me think."

"Go on."

"Remember when I told you about the note Sarge

was writing to Gil about a dirty army officer?"

"Yeah. You said Garrett didn't want to turn the note in to the detective on the case."

"Right. Well, Garrett has been freaking out about that note. He's afraid Sarge was trying to tell Gil about a corrupt cop. Now Garrett suspects every one of the cops in his precinct, and it's killing him. He hates himself for it."

"Bummer. Is there anyone in particular he suspects?"

"Not that he's told me. And I hate to keep at him about it. I figure when he knows something, he'll tell me." I watched her for a moment, then said, "Ash, let me ask you something. That night you were with Derek, the night your dad couldn't get you on the phone, where did you and Derek go?"

"Just up to the YMCA camp. He showed me around and introduced me to some of the kids up there. There's a bunch of log cabins and a big hall with a huge stone fireplace. It was nice."

"What else did you do?"

She looked at me sideways. "Nothing else. We walked around, hung out with the kids, and came home. Why?"

I stroked Jack and watched her eyes. "You didn't take a walk up the trail? Toward Sarge's camp?"

"No. What's this all about? Why are you asking?"

I hated her to think I suspected her of getting physically involved with Derek, but if I didn't ask, I wouldn't know. And I felt strongly that I could be a big sister to her and counsel her in a way her parents couldn't. I knew she looked up to me, and having shared a horrible experience earlier in the summer had cemented the bond between us.

I took a deep breath. "Sarge saw two kids having sex in the woods one night. Up the trail from the camp."

Her eyes smoldered. "And you assumed it was me and Derek, is that it?"

"I didn't assume anything. And I'm not here to judge you. But if you're having sex, I just want you to know you can talk to me."

She pulled her books toward her on the bed. "Well, I'm not. I'm not stupid."

"I know you're not," I assured her. "You're one of the smartest kids I've ever known. Way smarter than I was at your age. I just don't want you to do anything to mess up your future. So if there's anything you ever want to talk about…"

Her expression softened. "Thanks." She got that impish grin on her face. "As long as we're doing the whole true confessions thing, what's up with you and Garrett? I mean, if you want me to be honest with you…"

"We're not having sex, if that's what you're asking. I admit I've thought about it. But I don't want to rush into anything until I'm sure."

"Sure of what? You'd have to be blind not to see he's crazy about you. What are you waiting for?"

I grimaced. I knew that question was on Garrett's mind as well. "I don't know, Ash. All I know is I don't want to make a mistake."

"Well, you know what Mom says—letting him get away would be the mistake." She got up and went into the bathroom.

In a moment I heard the shower running. I sat back and stared at the ceiling. How long would I be able to put Garrett off before I made the commitment he was always hinting about? I suspected that once Sarge's murder was solved and Garrett found out whether there was a dirty cop in his precinct, he would no longer be distracted by his job. Sooner or later, I would have to make a decision, not only regarding our relationship, but my future with the magazine. How long would I be able to sustain this nomadic lifestyle before it all fell apart?

I turned over and hugged Jack, enjoying his furry warmth and feeling just a little sad that his presence and affection were about the only things I was sure of.

CHAPTER 10

I woke the next morning to the sensation of Jack's whiskers tickling my face, which was his way of telling me it was time to get up. I pulled him next to me under the covers in hopes of getting a few minutes more of sleep, but he wasn't about to be discouraged. First he kneaded my side with his paws then with his claws. I pushed him away, but he grabbed my hand with his front paws and began chewing on my fingers. Realizing it was hopeless, I threw back the covers and sat up. Bright sunlight streamed in the window. I looked at my phone, shocked to see it was nearly ten o'clock.

I had a fleeting thought about Crenshaw, who was no doubt wondering where I was and why I hadn't sent him a column in over a week. I checked my account on my bank's website and saw that the magazine had deposited a check for my last three columns. Now I had no excuse. I would have to make a decision soon, or I would find myself without a job. Would old cranky Crenshaw really fire me? I'd always been able to appease him in the past by putting on my perky personality act, but that might be wearing thin. I'd have to call him soon.

I showered and dressed and strolled over to the café. I avoided the back door to the kitchen, where Alma would no doubt razz me about sleeping late, to take a table on the patio. A large crowd filled the dining room.

Ashley came to wait on me, looking harried.

"Hey. What's with all the people?"

"Some kind of tour group. It would have been nice if they had warned us they were coming. And Zoe would pick today to be sick." She put air quotes around "sick."

"Oh, sorry. Do you want me to jump in and give you a hand?"

Relief was written all over her face. "Would you? That would be so awesome."

"No problem. It's the least I can do." I went to the kitchen where Alma was trying to keep up with all the orders. Her face showed the stress of trying to organize the tickets on the wheel and work the grill at the same time. I told her I would replace Zoe for the day.

She seemed incredibly relieved. "Oh, thank you, dear. I don't know what's happened to Zoe lately. She's been so moody. Take a pad of tickets from the drawer." She turned back to the grill.

I left the kitchen and scanned the menu on the blackboard. Nothing unusual. Ashley hurried by and asked me to take care of the patio while she dealt with the crowd in the dining room. I went back to the patio, passing the coffee pots along the way and wishing I had had time for a cup.

The patio was full, and many of the customers looked at me expectantly. I guessed some of them had been waiting for some time. I had no idea where to start, so I called out, "Sorry for the delay, folks. We're a little shorthanded. So who's been here the longest?"

They all looked at each other, then an elderly couple tentatively raised their hands. I went to their table and took their order. I took several more orders before I noticed Derek sitting alone at a table at the back of the patio. He smiled at me in a way I could only describe as predatory. I started to ignore him, but then I decided it might be useful to pick his brain a little. Whatever he knew and whatever he was up to, I knew it probably wasn't good. And maybe he was even connected to Sarge's death.

I approached his table. "Sorry for the wait," I said. "It's really busy."

"No problem. I didn't know you worked here."

"I'm just helping out for the day."

"Nice of you. Ryn, isn't it? Short for Kathryn?"

I gave him my most ingratiating smile. "You've done your homework."

"Always—where a pretty girl is concerned."

I tried not to gag. "And you're Derek. Ashley's mentioned you."

"She had nice things to say, I hope."

I nodded. "Of course. What can I get for you?"

"A ham sandwich and a coke."

"Okay." I started to walk away.

"You forgot to ask about dessert," he called after me.

I turned back to him. "Did you want dessert?"

"Yeah. For dessert, I want you to join me. I'd like to get to know you." There was that smarmy smile again, accompanied by an appreciative glance up and down my torso that made me feel like I needed a shower.

I looked around at the crowded patio. "It could be a while. But I'll try." I fluttered my eyelashes at him, nauseating myself in the process. But anything for information.

It was nearly an hour before the patio emptied out, and I was surprised to see that Derek had waited that long. As I approached his table, he pushed out a chair for me with his foot, but didn't get up. His curly blond hair, blue eyes, athletic build, and charismatic smile made quite a picture. I could easily see the attraction for Ashley. But it wasn't his appearance that worried me.

"Thanks for joining me. Now tell me all about yourself. What brings you to this backwater burg?"

I told him about my job as a travel writer, my relationship with Alma and Ashley, my background in New York, and anything else I could think of. If I told him all about my life, he could hardly object to my probing into his background. Finally, I said, "Enough about me. What brings you to Trout Fork?" One thing I had learned as a journalist is how to question people in a way that made them want to offer information.

He told me about his home in Denver, his family, and the high school he was about to graduate from. His achievements and honors were proudly enumerated, and I could almost see him puffing up as he described himself, like a rooster in a barnyard trying to impress the hens. It nearly made me laugh.

"So what brought you to the YMCA camp? Some kind of community service, isn't it?"

His arrogance faded. "Who told you that?"

I smiled to put him off his guard. "I'm a journalist, remember?"

He ran his hand through his hair and rolled his eyes. "Okay, you got me. I'm here on a com-serve assignment. It was what they call a 'youthful indiscretion.' It won't happen again."

"What kind of indiscretion, if you don't mind my asking?"

"Nothing serious," he said evasively then began talking about himself again. At one point, he hinted, with little subtlety, at his female conquests, which gave me the opening I was waiting for. I leaned in toward him. "So you're quite the ladies' man. Was that you having sex with someone in the woods one night last week?"

To say he looked shocked would be an understatement. He had that same expression I had seen when interviewing small town officials in upstate New York. While working on a story, I had uncovered a corruption and graft scheme. When I confronted the mayor with what I knew, he had that same guilty look that Derek wore now.

Before he had a chance to lie, I bluffed, "I know it was you. What I want to know is who the girl was. Do I have to remind you that Ashley is a minor and you could be charged with statutory rape? And that will get you way more than community service. Like a prison term."

He bristled and leaned in closer to me. "It wasn't Ashley."

"The kids in the camp are minors, too."

He looked around nervously. "It wasn't one of them either. It was…"

"Zoe."

He nodded. "She's eighteen. Believe me, she was more than willing."

"Bowled over by your charm, no doubt," I said with a sarcasm I couldn't repress.

"That and what I can do for her," he said smugly.

"Like what?"

He sat back, clearly sorry he had said so much. He stood quickly and laid a ten-dollar bill on the table. "Keep the change," he said, and strode quickly off the patio to the parking lot. I watched him cross the lot and head up the trail toward the YMCA camp. At least now I knew there was something unpleasant going on between him and Zoe. No wonder she looked frazzled lately. What did he mean by doing something for her?

My phone rang and I pulled it out of my pocket. Garrett's number flashed on the display.

"Ryn? Where are you?"

"At the café. The waitress is sick so I'm helping out today. What's up?"

"Bad news, I'm afraid. The district attorney is sending Hank's case to the grand jury in Denver. It's likely he'll be charged with first degree murder."

"Oh, no."

"No choice. Too much evidence against him and no alibi."

"Does he know?"

"Yes. An attorney has been appointed by the court. He's down there with him now."

I grimaced, knowing court-appointed lawyers doing *pro bono* work were sometimes less than diligent in cases like this. It made me more anxious than ever to find Sarge's killer.

"Garrett, do me a favor?"

"If I can."

"Can you do a background search on a kid named Derek Adamson? He lives in Denver. His father is an attorney. His firm is Adamson, Somebody and Schultz, I think. Derek's at the YMCA camp doing a community service stint for something."

"Is he a minor?"

"He's eighteen. You should be able to find something on him." Garrett was silent, so I continued. "I think he may be involved with something shady up here. And it may have something to do with Sarge's death. Garrett? Are you there?"

"I'm here. Look, Ryn. I'd like to help, but I'm kinda busy right now. Something important."

I couldn't believe something was more important to him than getting Hank out of that stinking jail. "Oh? Another case?"

"I can't really talk about it. But it could help exonerate Hank."

"So you *are* working on the case."

"Well, not exactly."

Garrett could be infuriatingly cryptic at times. I decided to change the subject. "Are we still on for tomorrow night?"

"Definitely. Come over around six."

"Okay. I'll see you then." We hung up and I sat on the patio watching another motorcycle club cruise into the lot. What was Garrett doing that made him sound so mysterious? And why couldn't he tell me about it? Whatever it was, I would find out over dinner the next night.

☙☙☙

By the time the café closed and we had cleaned up that night, I was ready for a relaxing poker game and some of Madam Gauzie's delicacies. Ashley had left for the cabin just as her father's silver Mercedes was pulling into the parking lot. Robert came into the café lugging his suitcase and gave Alma a hug and kiss. They talked quietly while Gil and I sat chatting at the poker table.

Madam Gauzie laid a tray of delicious-looking hors d'oeuvres in front of us, along with china plates from her tea set.

I watched Gil fill one of the delicate plates. "Are you sure you want us to use these, Madam G?" I asked. "Paper plates would do for us."

"No problem, dear. Somebody has to use them. Heaven knows I never entertain anymore."

While we waited for Alma and Robert, I asked Gil what he knew about the local drug culture, if anything. Having lived in Trout Fork for over twenty years, he knew pretty much everything that went on in the area.

"I'll tell you one thing," he said, "Legalizing marijuana is the worst thing that ever happened in this state."

"Oh? I thought it would generate funds for schools and other worthwhile projects."

He snorted. "They said the same thing about the lottery. The tax money isn't the issue. It's what the drug culture does to society, to the kids, to the crime rate."

I wasn't sure how legal pot smoking could constitute a "drug culture," but I let him continue.

"Pot is a gateway drug for too many people, especially teenagers who aren't ready to make good decisions about using it. The drug cartels know this, and they've flooded into the state. When the pot smokers tire of the moderate highs and look for something more, the cartels are right there to provide it—meth, crack, and heroin. Another thing is the homeless population which has exploded in the past few years. The cost for the cities to deal with all those people far outweighs the tax benefits."

"You seem to be pretty well informed about it."

"My buddies on the police force have nothing good to say about the miserable stuff and what they've had to deal with."

I remembered Gil's friends at his Fourth of July barbeque, three handsome young cops who helped squelch a potential problem with an unruly motorcycle gang.

"Something you might not know—it's such a new crop that there are no known pesticides for the bugs that attack the plants, so the growers have started making their own out of God knows what. The farmers whose fields are next to the pot fields are complaining that their crops are being contaminated by chemicals the pot growers are spraying all over the place."

"And those crops are going into the food supply like that?"

He nodded. "Yep. The idiot politicians didn't think about that, did they? All they saw was dollar signs." He paused and raised an eyebrow. "Ever smoke a joint, Ryn?"

"I tried it once in college. It made me act stupid and gave me a headache, so once was enough."

"That was what, about ten years ago? Well, the pot they're growing now is much more potent. The levels of THC are higher now than back then. It's the THC that's so dangerous to the kids. It affects how their brains develop."

That sounded pretty horrific, but I knew Gil's law-and-order stance was very conservative. He might be exaggerating. "I had no idea. Are you sure?"

"You're a journalist. Look it up. It will scare the hell out of you. I only wish I had known..."

I waited for him to finish his sentence. Then I noticed his eyes growing misty and remembered that his son was in jail in Canada for dealing methamphetamines and for killing a cop in a drug raid. For someone like Gil, whose reputation for law and order was well known, that must have been a terrible burden to bear.

Changing the subject seemed to be a good idea, so I said, "I'm going to ask Garrett if you can come to visit Hank. I know he'd be happy to see you."

Alma and Robert came to the table and pulled out chairs. "Sorry we're late," Alma said.

"No problem. Gil was filling me in on the marijuana situation in Colorado."

Robert reached for one of the hors d'oeuvres. "Legalizing pot has increased the case load at our firm. That's for sure. DUIs, illegal growers, robberies, burglaries, even murders."

"But I thought legalizing it would decrease the crime rate," Alma said. "That's what I always heard."

Robert picked up the cards Gil had dealt. "That's what they told us. But since legalization, the crime rate in

Denver has increased five times faster than the population growth rate. The cops warned this would happen, and it did. You'll always need money to purchase pot, whether it's legal or not, and once a pot smoker is hooked on it, the need for the addictive drug is a primary driver of marijuana-related crime. Add to that the numbing effect the drug has on the brain, and you can understand why the average pot junkie isn't working to feed his habit. He's more likely to be robbing a convenience store or panhandling on the street corners."

"How many cards do you want, Alma?" Gil said.

"Three, please."

Madam Gauzie passed around a tray of cheese and crackers. "Try some of this brie, Robert. I think you'll like it. You know, my Edgar told me the crew on his ship did their share of pot smoking. He said it relieved the boredom. That was until the end of the Vietnam War, of course. Then they were so busy taking care of refugees and shuttling them back and forth to Manila they didn't have time to breathe."

"I'll bet fifty cents," Gil said. "I know a lot of guys smoked weed in Nam. It was the only way they could get through the misery."

Robert threw a dollar onto the kitty. "Raise you, Gil. Well, the war's been over for over forty years. It's time we moved on."

"For some men, it's never over. Sarge was one of them. He battled his demons from that war until the day he died. Smoking the weed helped him forget."

Listening to Gil, I felt sad for Sarge and men like him. I also decided to make an effort to find out about the drug culture in this part of Colorado and whether there was any connection to Sarge's death.

CHAPTER 11

The next evening, I dressed casually for my date at Garrett's, looking forward to a quiet dinner in his peaceful cabin. I was just getting on my bike when Madam Gauzie came out of her antique store and hurried down the wooden walkway that connected the four stores.

She waved to me. "Yoo-hoo, Ryn. Wait a minute."

I smiled to myself as I watched her hustle toward me with agility uncommon in women half her age, the swish of her flowered skirt and jangling of her many necklaces accompanying the sound of her clogs resounding on the walk.

She wasn't even out of breath when she reached me. "You're going to Garrett's, aren't you?"

"Yes." I had told Alma I would be leaving work early to have dinner with Garrett. I felt a little guilty leaving her and Ashley alone in the café. Zoe hadn't been seen for two days. If it weren't for her old car still parked in the lot, I would have suspected she had taken off for parts unknown. Maybe she really was sick.

Madam Gauzie handed me a package. "Here. Give this to Garrett for Hank. It's some of my homemade fudge. Hank loves it."

"Thanks. I'll see that he gets it."

Lines of concern furrowed her brow. "And you tell Garrett to get busy and find out who killed poor old Sarge so Hank can come home." She gazed at the darkened store window of Hank's liquor store. "Tsk, tsk. Such a shame. Tell Hank Trout Fork needs him."

"I will."

"Oh, by the way. I'm having a little get-together in my cabin tomorrow night. Just a few of us—Alma and Robert, Ashley, Gil, and you and me. Invite Garrett. I'm making my famous Bo Luc Lac. Alma needs a break from cooking, don't you think?"

I had no idea what Bo Luc Lac was and didn't ask. "Definitely. That's very nice of you."

She noticed an older couple going in the front door of her store. "Goodbye, dear. Have a nice evening." With that, she trotted back down the walkway.

I couldn't help wondering how she could make a living in this out-of-the-way place. Did fishermen and Harley riders buy that many antiques?

I started the bike and pulled onto the road leading to Garrett's cabin halfway between Trout Fork and Pineland Park. Riding that road always brought me a feeling of tranquility as the bike maneuvered the curves and climbed the hills with agility and grace. Never did I feel more at peace than on that bike. The only thing missing on this trip was Jack in his basket in front of me, raising his nose to sniff at the wind rushing past.

I pulled into Garrett's driveway and parked next to his gray pickup. Strains of one of Mozart's operas wafted from the cabin, along with aroma of something scrumptious. I had to hand it to Garrett—he knew how to woo a girl.

He opened the door wearing a barbecue apron over his dress shirt and slacks and wielding a wooden spoon.

"Good evening, madam," he said with a slight bow. "Your table is ready."

I laughed at him. "Oh, you're the maître d' tonight?"

"Chef, waiter, host, you name it. Make yourself at home." He held the door open for me then headed back to the kitchen.

Making myself at home at Garrett's came naturally to me. Aside from Alma's, Garrett's cabin was the place I most associated with a feeling of homey-ness. The days I had spent there after the fire were incredibly special to me, so special in fact that I wondered if it was one of those fairy tale experiences that can never be repeated.

"Dinner is ready," he said. "Let me pour the wine."

I sat at the small table and admired the effort he had put forth. Candles glowed on the table, their flames reflected in the crystal wine glasses. A centerpiece bouquet of fresh flowers added to the atmosphere.

He stood next to me wielding the wine bottle with the expertise of a sommelier.

I looked up at him. His smile crinkled the corners of his blue eyes. "You're in a good mood," I said. "Any reason in particular?"

He bent down and kissed me. "I'm here with my best girl. That's reason enough."

Hmm. There's more to it than that. He hasn't looked this cheerful in weeks. Something is going on.

He went back to the kitchen and returned with two plates of chicken cacciatore with penne pasta and fresh spinach salads on the side.

"This looks wonderful, Garrett. You've outdone yourself."

He sat opposite me. "Here at Chez Easterbrook, we aim to please."

We chatted about nothing in particular as we ate and drank. Everything was so delicious and the ambiance so delightful, it was no wonder I felt at home. After we had finished the meal, we sat for another hour at the table enjoying the wine and watching the sun set behind the mountaintops. An owl hooted from a nearby pine tree.

"Would madam care for the dessert menu?"

"Madam is stuffed, thank you. Any more food and madam will be stretched out on your sofa."

"A delightful prospect."

"If I didn't know better, I would think you're trying to seduce me," I teased.

He grinned in that endearing way he had. "What makes you think you know better?"

I took my wine glass to the sofa and sighed as I plopped down.

Garrett went to the stereo and changed the Mozart CD to one of Debussy's sonatas. He came back to the sofa, sat next to me, and held up his glass for a toast. "To us."

We touched the glasses, and his eyes met mine over the rims. He put his glass on the coffee table and sat back, slipping his arm around my shoulders. "What about us, Ryn? I know what I want. Do you?"

There it was again, that unresolved question of our relationship. I knew what he wanted from me—some kind of commitment. I gazed at him and knew I couldn't put him off much longer. And I didn't want to. I opened up in a way I had never done before, spilling all my worst fears about serious relationships and marriage. I told him about my parents, the cold distance between them since little Davey's death, my brother's disintegrating marriage, Alma and Robert's conflicts, and the way it was affecting Ashley. I admitted to him my fear of being trapped in a similar situation. "The thought of ending up hating each other after a few years is just hideous, Garrett. I'd rather be alone."

"What makes you think we'd end up hating each other?

"I don't know. It's just that I see it everywhere."

"Look, Ryn. I know better than to rush you, and I'm certainly not proposing. I just want to know there's a future for us."

"Well, there isn't anyone else in my future. That I do know."

"I guess that will have to do," he said with a small smile, "for now." He nodded to the package I had left on the coffee table. "What's in the bag?"

"Some of Madam Gauzie's fudge. She wants you to give it to Hank."

"Speaking of Hank, I talked to him today. He asked to see me."

"How is he?"

"He looks much better. He's over the worst of the withdrawal symptoms."

"Alma will be glad to hear it. Why did he want to see you?"

He frowned slightly, and I knew what he was thinking, so I said, "Anything you can tell me, that is?"

He smirked. "You know I tell you everything, whether I should or not."

"Yes, I know that. So?"

"He's remembering more about what happened that night. It's coming back to him in bits and pieces. Sarge told him that night that he had overheard what he called 'that counselor' making a drug deal with someone in the woods near Sarge's campsite. A girl. He said it was the same two kids he saw having sex up there."

It must have been Derek and Zoe. I remembered Derek saying he could "do something" for Zoe. Did he mean supplying her with drugs?

"Was it Zoe?"

"He didn't know her name, but from the description, I think it must have been her. I don't think Derek is stupid enough to be dealing to underage kids. Anyway, Sarge confronted Derek and told him to knock it off or he would rat him out to the cops."

I whistled softly. "What did Derek say to that?"

"Hank doesn't know, but you can bet it wasn't pleasant. Derek knows he'd go to prison if he was found out. I told Hank I'd look into it, so I went back to the office and did some research on the kid. Know why he's at that camp?"

"Yeah. He told me he was on a community service assignment from the court. A 'youthful indiscretion' is what he called it."

"Indiscretion my eye. He was caught with cocaine in his car. He denied it belonged to him. His father's law firm represented him. The judge was lenient, his record was expunged because he was a juvenile at the time, and he got community service in lieu of a stint in the local juvenile facility. If he had been a couple of months older, he'd be locked up now."

My mind was whirling. "He must have killed Sarge to keep him quiet. He went to the campsite that night and waited until they both passed out. Then he hit Sarge with the rock and put it in Hank's hands to get his prints on it."

"We have no proof of that, but I am definitely going to bring him in for questioning first thing Monday morning. Even if he wasn't the one who killed Sarge, I may be able to get him to give up his drug dealer."

"Gil was telling us about the drug culture in the area. Are there a lot of dealers in Pineland Park?"

"Too many. We've been trying to crack down on them for months now."

We were quiet for a few minutes, sipping our wine and listening to the music. The cabin was an idyllic respite from the ugliness of the world outside, and I felt like never leaving.

But then the thought that Hank, who I was sure was innocent, was languishing in a stinking jail cell made me angry.

I took another sip of wine. "Garrett, I'd like to know more about the drug culture in this area. I mean aside from a law enforcement perspective. Do you think your buddy at the newspaper would talk to me?"

"Vince Bodmin? Sure. He'd like nothing better than to show off his newsroom to a pretty girl. Especially one from New York."

"What's his story anyway?"

"He moved here about five years ago from Iowa, somewhere near Des Moines. He's from Virginia originally. His father is a bureaucrat in DC. Vince got a job as an intern at the *Washington Post* right out of college, but it's been downhill since then. He's had a series of jobs at different papers. I hear he's hard to work for."

"Married?"

"Divorced. He has two grown sons living in California."

"What does he do when he's not working?"

"He's always working. Probably why his wife left him. I do know he makes trips to Cripple Creek regularly."

"To gamble."

Garrett nodded. "Why else would anyone go to Cripple Creek?"

"I think I'll pay him a visit Monday. He did invite me to come see his newsroom."

"Just be careful. He'll probably be happy to show you around, but I wouldn't ask too many personal questions."

"I'll be on my best behavior."

eↄeↄ

"Aren't you coming to the party? Madam G. is making something special." It was Sunday evening, and I was brushing my hair at the dresser in our room and watching Ashley in the mirror. She was sitting on her bed pulling a string back and forth for Jack and Sasha to pounce on it.

She rolled her eyes and said in mock seriousness, "Gee. Let's see. A party with my parents. Sounds awesome." She went back to playing with the cats.

"You need to give your parents a break. There are lots worse families you could be stuck in."

"I guess. Actually, Philippe is coming over to finish up his French lessons."

"Finish up? You've done all your assignments?"

"I wish. He's leaving tomorrow. His vacation is over, and he's heading back to Denver. So I'm on my own until school starts."

"Nice of him to spend his last night helping you out."

"Yeah. He's a good guy."

"Well, if you two get hungry, you know you're welcome to join us."

I left the bedroom and met Alma and Robert who were on their way out the door. Alma looked at me hopefully. "Isn't Ashley coming?"

"No. She's hitting the French books again tonight."

Robert smiled. "Good for her. I'm proud of her."

Alma punched him on the arm playfully. "Maybe you should tell her that once in a while."

We walked along the path to Madam Gauzie's together, enjoying the cool early evening air and the sounds of the pine forest. A group of five mule deer peered at us from among the trees. The three does and two fawns were poised on their thin legs, their large ears forward and focused on us. They watched us for a moment then moved off silently and disappeared in the brush.

Alma sighed and held Robert's hand as we walked. "I'm so glad Madam G. is doing this. She's a gem."

Madam Gauzie opened the door before we could knock. She wore a "kiss the cook" apron over a bright pink jogging suit and matching scarf trying up her gray hair. "Welcome, welcome," she gushed. "Come right in." She looked behind us and said, "But where's Garrett?"

"He said he's working on something. He sends his regrets."

"He works too hard. You can tell him I said so." She fussed over us, offering drinks, and making us feel at home. A table for six was beautifully set with her antique china and lovely linen.

Gil was already there sitting on the sofa, his large masculine presence looking out of place among the chintz and flowers of the cabin's décor. He looked up at us and forced a small smile. He got up and shook hands with Robert, and they small-talked while Alma and I offered what help we could in the kitchen.

"Absolutely not," Madam Gauzie declared, shooing us back to the living room. "Dinner is almost ready. Just relax and make yourselves comfortable."

Gil had returned to his place on the sofa, so I sat next to him. "Hey, Gil. How's it going?"

He nodded, seeming a little subdued, which was unusual for him. I wondered if he was missing Hank.

"Garrett told me Hank is doing better. He's over his withdrawal and seems to be coping pretty well."

He still seemed distracted. "That's good."

Alma and Robert were enjoying the view out the back window of the cabin, so I said quietly, "Anything wrong, Gil? Anything I can help with?"

His troubled eyes gazed at me, and he cleared his throat. "You've heard me talk about my son, Gil Junior?"

"Sure." All I really knew about him was that he was in jail in Canada. He and his motorcycle gang had been arrested for drug dealing, and the bust had gone wrong. A policeman had been killed, and Gil's son had been charged with murder. "Is he okay?"

"He called last night. His lawyer is appealing his conviction on some technicality. The kid thinks he might be able to get him off."

"Well, that's great, isn't it? What's the problem?"

His dark brows furrowed over his eyes, reminding me again of a bald eagle, the symbol of the country he loved and had served in the army. "The problem," he said, gazing at me with intensity, "is that he's guilty as sin. He killed that cop. A ten-year veteran with a wife and three little kids. And now my son, the one who made those kids orphans, is gonna get off? On a technicality? It makes me sick."

I touched his arm. The anger and sadness in his eyes were mixed with the understandable relief that, as a father, he must have been feeling. The conflict and guilt he was experiencing must have been overwhelming. "I'm sorry."

Madam Gauzie bustled in with a large bowl of what looked like stir-fried beef and plunked it on the table. "Come sit down, everyone."

Alma and Robert sat on one side of the table, Gil and I sat opposite them, and our hostess took her place at the head of the table. She chattered away as she dished out large servings of the beef onto plates and passed them around. Then she passed around a huge bowl of rice and another filled with a fruit and coconut salad.

Alma looked at her plate. "What did you call this, Madam G?"

"Bo luc lac. It's Vietnamese. My Edgar brought the recipe home with him when he was discharged from the navy all those years ago. I hope you like it."

I dug into the dish. It was delicious. "After this and Garrett's chicken cacciatore last night," I said, "I won't be able to get into my jeans. I'm going to need a new wardrobe by the end of the summer."

Alma and Madam Gauzie got into a discussion of international recipes, while Robert and Gil talked about politics and the military. Gil opened up to him about his son's legal difficulties, and while Robert admitted he wasn't all that familiar with the Canadian legal system, he offered to help in any way he could.

I listened to their conversations with warmth and affection, as well as a little twinge of regret that Hank wasn't here with us.

The evening flew by, and it was nearly eleven when we all said good night and headed home. As we got to the door of Alma's cabin, I gazed toward the cabin where Zoe was staying. The light was on in the living room. I wondered if she would be at the café the next day so I could go to the newspaper office. "Have you heard from Zoe?" I asked Alma as she was opening the door.

"Not a word. Why don't you go over and see if she's okay? I would go, but I don't want her to think I'm checking up on her or pressuring her to get back to work."

"Okay." I headed toward what used to be Zach's cabin, and as I got closer, an eerie feeling came over me. I hadn't been near it since that awful night earlier in the summer. At the front door, I raised my hand to knock, but then I heard voices and stopped. I listened and was sure I heard Zoe and a man's voice. They were laughing loudly, almost hysterically. They were clearly enjoying themselves. I decided she didn't need checking on, so I walked away quietly and headed back to Alma's.

Alma and Robert were sitting together in the living room, and they looked up as I came in.

"Well?" Alma said. "Is she okay?"

"I didn't talk to her, but I heard her laughing with somebody. So she's not sick."

Robert snorted. "It's probably that junkie."

Alma soothed him with a touch on his arm. "Let's not get started, Robert. I'll call her in the morning and make sure she'll be at the café."

"That's perfect," I said. "I want to go into town to-morrow anyway."

"Good night, dear. Sleep well."

I opened the door to the bedroom quietly and smiled at the sight of Ashley cuddled up with Sasha. I undressed and got into bed with Jack, who was waiting patiently for me. I gazed over at Ashley who was mumbling in her sleep and thought about her and Derek and Zoe. Aside from Derek's run-ins with the law, there was something distinctly discomforting about him. I hoped for all our sakes that he would be leaving Trout Fork soon.

CHAPTER 12

The next morning, I phoned the *Pineland Park Star* and asked to speak to the editor.

"Newsroom. Bodmin." Vincent Bodmin's gruff voice reminded me that I hadn't checked in with my own editor lately, a fact I had been trying to dismiss from my consciousness. I could almost envision Bodmin chomping on a cigar and dropping ashes all over his desk, although the stereotype was probably just in my imagination.

"Mr. Bodmin, this is Kathryn Lowell. We met about ten days ago. I was with Detective Easterbrook."

"Oh, yes. I remember. What can I do for you?"

"Well, I thought I would take you up on your invitation. To visit your newsroom?"

His gruffness dissolved into an almost sickeningly sweet demeanor. "I'd be delighted to show you around, Kathryn. When would you like to come in?"

"Anytime it's convenient for you. And it's Ryn."

"Come in about ten this morning, Ryn, and I'll give you the grand tour. Not that there's much to see. Not for a New York gal."

"Perfect. I'll see you at ten. And thanks very much."

I left the cabin and went through the back door of the

café. I asked Alma for a couple of hours off between the breakfast and lunch shifts. Monday mornings were light in the café anyway.

"You don't have to work at all today, dear," she said. "Zoe is back."

"Oh, good. How is she?"

She shrugged. "Seems fine to me. Have you eaten? I could make you some pancakes."

I thought about my ever-tightening jeans. "Thanks, but I'll just have coffee."

I went through the swinging door to the dining room, poured myself a cup of coffee, and sat at a table on the patio.

Ashley came by, and I told her about going to visit the newsroom. She seemed just a bit jealous. I knew she still had an interest in journalism as a career or at least a possible college major. "I wish I could go with you. Take some pictures, okay?"

"Sure. I'll be back before lunch."

Driving toward Pineland Park later that morning, I passed Garrett's driveway, and sweet memories of Saturday evening came back to me, especially Garrett's lingering kisses as we said goodnight and the temptation to spend the night with him. I felt my resistance weakening, and I was grateful he wasn't being insistent.

I had some trouble finding the office of the newspaper, which was situated in a nondescript red brick building on a side street. I parked in front of the building next to a black Lexus. I stared at the car for a moment. *Where have I seen that car before?* A painted sign sitting slightly crooked in a window announced *Pineland Park Star, V. Bodmin, Managing Editor.* I took a picture of it for Ashley.

I entered through an old wooden door with peeling paint to find a large, open room with a half dozen desks, only two of which were occupied. The two young women at the desks glanced up from their computer screens, but neither addressed me, even though they could see I was standing awkwardly at the door. I could almost hear their thoughts—*not my job to greet the customers.*

The door to a small office on the left opened, and Vincent Bodmin emerged waving a piece of paper. His voice boomed through the room. "Andrews! What the hell do you call this?"

One of the girls looked up, her face reddening. She spoke in a timid voice. "You mean my article?"

Bodmin, now standing over the girl, snorted derisively. "Article? Tripe, that's what it is. Pure, unadulterated crap." He held the paper by its edges as though it was contaminated with E. coli bacteria. Then he tossed the paper on her desk. "Rewrite it. And this time try to use at least a few interesting phrases."

The girl picked up. "Yes, sir."

Bodmin ran his hands through his hair. He was dressed exactly as I remembered him, as though he hadn't changed his clothes in weeks. His tie was still hanging lopsided from his wilted collar. His three-day old beard and bloodshot eyes gave him a distinctly harried look. He started back to his office, grumbling and growling. Then he noticed me and his demeanor changed completely.

He came to me grinning and extended his hand. "Miss Lowell—Ryn—I didn't see you there. Give me a minute to tidy my office and I'll be right with you." He went to his office and closed the door. I thought I could hear voices in there, but when he opened the door again, he was alone. He came to me, and I allowed him to usher me into his tiny office.

He moved piles of paper from the chair in front of his desk and dumped them on the floor. "Sorry about the mess," he said, "I don't get a lot of visitors. Please. Sit down."

I lowered myself carefully onto the rickety wooden chair and glanced around the room. Piles of newspapers adorned every surface, including the floor. A police scanner crackled on his desk, the dispatcher's voice breaking through the static intermittently.

"Thanks for seeing me," I said. "I hope I'm not interrupting."

He smiled obsequiously. "Not at all. Would you like some coffee?"

An ancient Mr. Coffee machine sat on a table by the window, the sunlight revealing the stains on the filthy glass pot.

"I'm good, thanks."

"I guess you've seen the newsroom. Not much to look at, is it?"

"Is that your entire staff, the two girls?"

"Except for our sports editor. He's out at the local high school interviewing the coach today. He's only part-time, though. So yeah, it's pretty much me and the two reporters." He waved his hand dismissively. "If you can call them that."

We chatted about circulation, advertising, the influence of the internet on news reporting, and the woes of small town weekly newspapers. I answered his questions about the magazine I worked for, the rigors of travel writing, and my experiences in New York. Finally, I said, "Mr. Bodmin—"

"Vince." There was that ingratiating smile again.

"Vince. I wanted to ask you about the drug culture in Pineland Park, in the whole the area really."

His brow furrowed. "For your column?"

"Not exactly, although it might be background if I were writing about this part of Colorado. I'm actually trying to find some information that might help solve the murder. You remember—the campsite near Trout Fork where we first met?"

His eyes narrowed. "Oh, yeah. What's that got to do with the local druggies?"

"Maybe nothing. What can you tell me about the situation here? Are there a lot of dealers? I've heard the new marijuana laws are causing them to bring in more of the hard stuff. Is that true?"

He looked up at the ceiling and made a steeple with his fingers. "Well, you know Pineland Park is right smack in the middle between Denver, the gambling towns, and the ski resorts. The gamblers do their share of drinking, and some get involved with the cheaper drugs. The wealthier ones who come through on their way to Vail and Aspen are mostly into snorting cocaine. As for the locals..." He spread his hands wide. "I guess what I'm saying is that we have our share, just like anywhere else. The cops do what they can to stop it."

I thought about Garrett and his fellow officers who he was afraid might be involved in the death of the busboy from Borelli's. "Speaking of the cops, have you ever heard anything about the local force?"

He squinted at me. "Like what?"

"Anything negative. Corruption, drugs, cops on the take, that kind of thing."

He hesitated. "Not really your beat, is it?"

I smiled in my most innocent manner. "No, but I guess every reporter is an investigative journalist at heart."

"Is that what you want to do?"

"Maybe. In college I investigated a town in upstate New York for a project. I uncovered some corruption and graft in the local police department, the town council, all the way up to the mayor's office. Seemed everybody was in on it."

"Well, you won't find anything like that here. We're a pretty conservative town for the most part."

He sat back and crossed his arms, giving me the distinct feeling the interview had come to an end.

I stood and shook his hand. "Well, thanks for your time. It was nice seeing you again."

He smiled once more, but this time it was one of those smiles that don't involve the eyes. Behind them was something I couldn't identify, but it wasn't good. My journalist's instincts began to warn me that something wasn't quite right here.

I left the building and mounted the bike. The black Lexus was gone.

༺༻

Riding back toward Trout Fork, I thought about that sad, stuffy little office and those two stressed out reporters who toiled daily in that atmosphere. Not for the first time, I felt grateful to have my job. I didn't make much money, and I'd never win a Pulitzer, but I was free and unencumbered. Hopefully, stuffy offices would never again be for me.

I had just pulled into Trout Fork when my cell phone rang.

I heard the voice of my editor. "Kathryn."

Uh-oh. He only calls me Kathryn when he's got a bug up his butt about something. "Good morning, Mr. Crenshaw. How are you?"

"Perturbed, Kathryn. I am perturbed."

"I'm sorry. Anything I can do?"

"Yes. You can explain what the hell you're doing out there. It's been almost two weeks since your last column.

And now I hear you're still in Trout Fork."

I wondered where he could have gotten that information. "Uh…yes, I am."

"I just got a call from the *Pineland Park Star*. The editor there tells me you're making inquiries that have nothing to do with your job. He called it unprofessional."

"Well, I—"

His voice was uncharacteristically edgy. "Enough, Kathryn. I want you to go to Boulder for your next column. Do you know where that is?"

"Yes, sir, northwest of Denver, but I can't—"

I thought I heard him open his desk drawer, no doubt reaching for his Rolaids. "You can't what?"

I took a deep breath. "I can't leave right now, sir. There's a situation here. A friend of a friend has been killed, and another friend is in jail. I know he's innocent. I want to help prove it."

There was silence on the other end. Then he sighed. "I'm afraid the time has come to sever our relationship. I'm going to have to let you go."

I couldn't believe what I was hearing. "But, sir, I—"

"It's no use arguing. I've made up my mind. Your column from the dude ranch is your last one. That check has been deposited to your account. I'm sorry it's come to this. You've done good work for me—when your mind isn't on other things. Good luck to you."

He hung up. I stood next to the bike like a statue, unable to move or think. My heart was pounding, and a sick feeling overwhelmed me. I was broke, thousands of miles from home, and now out of a job. The future yawned before me like a dark, bottomless cavern.

Still in shock, I wandered along the path next to the café toward Alma's cabin, which seemed like an oasis in a vast, dry desert. I went in, plopped on the sofa, and stared into the dark fireplace, not sure what to do next.

Jack must have heard me come in because he trotted out from the bedroom and hopped up on the sofa. He gazed at me with that quizzical look he gets when he doesn't know what the plan is. When I picked him up, he hugged my shoulder with his paws, nuzzling my ear and purring loudly. His furry warmth comforted me as I stroked him.

"Well, Jackie, I guess we're on our own from now on. Any ideas?"

All he said was *"Brrrt?"*

I put him down and went to the kitchen. After grabbing a quick lunch of leftovers from Alma's fridge, I went into town and spent the afternoon searching Craigslist and the Denver want ads for jobs but finding nothing promising. A couple of hours later, I came back to Trout Fork. Getting off the bike, I stretched my back, which was stiff from sitting at the coffee shop bending over my laptop. Knowing there was nothing like a jog through the woods to cure muscle aches, I went to the cabin and changed into my running clothes. I picked up Jack's leash and shook it at him.

"Come on, Jack. Let's go."

He opened one eye and regarded me placidly from Ashley's bed where he was stretched out next to Sasha. Mid-afternoon was his deep sleep time, so I knew there was no point trying to drag him outside.

I left the cabin and took deep breaths of the mountain air, hoping it would clear my head. Jogging along the creek, I was soon hypnotized by the rhythmic pounding of my footsteps on the trail, and the exercise helped wash away the fears and uncertainty about my future.

My phone rang, and I had a fleeting thought it might be Crenshaw calling to say he didn't mean it and would give me a second chance. But it was Garrett. I decided not to tell him I was unemployed.

He sounded rushed and got right to the point. "Ryn, do you have to work in the café tonight?"

"No. Zoe is back. Why?"

"Can you meet me at the station about six? Maybe we can go to the movies or something. Okay?"

I had no doubt this wasn't about the movies. Something was going on. Then I remembered he was supposed to bring Derek in for questioning that morning. "Sure. Did you interview Derek this morning?"

"What? Derek? Oh yeah, I did. See you later."

He hung up. It wasn't like Garrett to be brusque on the phone. Whatever was on his mind, it had to be important.

It was nearly five o'clock by the time I returned to the cabin. I showered and changed, fed the cats, and headed to the parking lot. I mounted the bike and turned the key. "Damn." The gas gauge read just under a quarter tank. I thought about my nearly-empty wallet and wondered how long a quarter tank of gas would last. I kicked myself mentally for allowing myself to get into this situation. It seemed I had been living on the edge of poverty for a long time, maybe too long. Maybe it was time to settle down. What was it that kept me moving? What was this compulsion I had to always be somewhere else? Madam Gauzie's words came back to me: "You young girls. Always looking over the rainbow." Is that what I was doing?

Halfway to Pineland Park, I glanced at my speedometer and realized I was driving way too fast. My thoughts were agitating me enough to lose control. *Stop it,* I thought. *This isn't helping.*

I pulled into the lot in front of the police station just in time to see a black Lexus leaving the lot. Its tinted windows prevented me from seeing the driver, but I was sure it was the same Lexus I had seen at the newspaper office.

Before I had a chance to get off the bike, Garrett hurried out the front door to me.

"Hi. Let's get a bite before the movies."

I got off the bike, hung my helmet on its hook, and grabbed my purse. Garrett was already starting the pickup before I had a chance to open the door. I slid into the front seat. "What's the rush?"

He backed out and pulled onto the highway. "Let's stop at Wendy's. We can eat in the car. Do you mind?"

This was unlike Garrett, who was usually fussy about where he ate. "Uh, no. I don't mind." I glanced over at him. His face was set, his eyes seeming to bore holes in the windshield as he drove.

After retrieving our order at the Wendy's drive-up window, we sat in the parking lot eating. He had said nothing, and I decided it was time to find out why he was behaving so strangely. Usually I waited for him to open up, but I was beginning to lose patience with that.

"So you interviewed Derek today. Anything interesting?"

"No. Nothing." More silence.

"Okay, Garrett. What's going on? And don't tell me it's nothing."

He looked over at me, his eyes projecting a mixture of fear and anger. "You went to see Vince Bodmin today, didn't you?"

"You're not going to give me a hard time about that too, are you?"

"Too?"

"Yeah. My editor in New York got a call from Bodmin complaining about my being unprofessional. I lost my job over it."

He looked thoughtful. "So that's what set him off."

"Set who off? What are you talking about?"

"Bodmin was in the captain's office again today. You must have spooked him big time."

I spread my hands at him. Garrett must have realized I was getting frustrated by all the secrecy.

"Okay, listen. Remember the busboy from Borelli's?"

"The one they found buried near Sarge's campsite? How could I forget?"

"Well, after they found his body, I went to Captain Williams to tell him what the kid said about a cop involved in a shakedown of the local business owners. I told him the kid said he saw a cop threatening Borelli. But Williams blew me off. Told me to forget about it. It was Detective Sloan's case, and I should let him do his job.

"Well, a couple of days after that, Vince Bodmin was in Williams's office, and I accidently overheard them talking. From the things they said, I realized it was Bodmin and Williams who were shaking down the businesses. Not only that, but they were talking about a shipment of cocaine they were expecting any day. To tell the truth, I'd been suspecting Williams was into something dirty for some time now. How else could he afford to drive a Lexus on his salary?"

"That's the captain's Lexus? The black one? I saw it in front of the *Star* this morning. Williams must have been there when I came in. Oh, no."

"What?"

"I asked Bodmin about drugs in the area. I told him about investigating the corruption in that small town in New York. I said the cops were involved in it."

Garrett tapped his fingers on the steering wheel. "No wonder Bodmin hustled over to the station. He must have gotten nervous about you asking questions and went right to Williams."

"Are you saying it was Williams that killed the bus-boy?"

"That's the way it looks."

"My God. Sarge must have seen Williams burying the kid. That's why he wrote the note to Gil reminding him about the army captain who did the same thing. Williams must have seen Sarge, followed him to his camp, and killed him. If only we could prove it."

"There's more. After I heard Bodmin and Williams incriminate themselves, I went to over to the police chief's office. The PC said he suspected something like this was going on, but he didn't know who he could trust in either of his precincts. He asked me to keep my eyes and ears open in hopes of building a case against Williams and Bodmin. So that's what I'm going to do. I'm to report to the chief whatever I find out."

"What a mess. But at least you know it's not one of your fellow officers. I mean the ones you work with in the field."

He looked disgusted. "No, but you know what they say about corruption at the top. It rots everything below it." He shook his head. "Wait. Did you just say you lost your job?"

"Yeah. Crenshaw told me to move on from Trout Fork. I said I couldn't leave yet, so he canned me."

Garrett slipped his arm around my shoulders and pulled me close to him. "We're a pair, aren't we?"

"Yeah, we are. Oh, to hell with it all. Let's go see a movie."

We found a small art theatre which was showing a Japanese film, the plot of which escaped me. I soon grew tired of reading the translations and gave up trying to figure it out. I just enjoyed being close to Garrett in the dark, feeling his arm around me.

"Let's go to my place for a nightcap," he said as we left.

I gratefully agreed. His cabin was so cozy that I could think of no better place to hide from the world's evil.

We drove along the winding road out of Pineland Park, each of us lost in our own thoughts. We crested a hill and started down toward his driveway. Suddenly, the pickup seemed to be hitting the curves a little too fast.

"Garrett, slow down," I said, grabbing the handle above my door. I looked over at him and saw the fear in his eyes. He was stomping on the brake pedal over and over, but the truck kept speeding up as it flew down the hill. Garrett gripped the wheel with both hands, desperately trying to muscle the truck to keep it on the road. We slewed downhill through the curves, going faster and faster, the truck's tires squealing around each bend.

"The brakes are failing," he shouted. "Grab the emergency brake!"

I grabbed the brake lever between the bucket seats and pulled it up as hard as I could, but it slowed our speed only marginally. The lever vibrated violently in my hand and seemed to be fighting me, pulling me as hard as I was pulling it. My heart was pounding as I used all my strength against the brake.

We careened around another curve to see a yellow van coming right toward us. The driver must have seen we were out of control, and he pulled onto the shoulder to barely miss us, his tires spraying dirt everywhere.

The curve was too sharp and the hill too steep for Garrett to hold the pickup on the road. The truck screamed across the two lanes, and we left the pavement and crashed through the brush off the left side of the road.

The soft dirt slowed us down a bit, but we were still going too fast.

I put my hands onto the dash in front of me and closed my eyes as we headed for a clump of trees. The truck struck a tree on the left side with a loud crash and the sickening sound of metal being shattered and bent. I was thrown hard against my seat belt and then slammed back against the seat by the airbag deploying. But we were stopped. There was no sound except the hissing of steam escaping from the radiator in the mangled front of the truck.

I looked over at Garrett. A tree was embedded into the door on his side. He was slumped forward, held by his seat belt. His eyes were closed and blood was pouring from his head.

CHAPTER 13

Garrett! Garrett! Are you all right?" I reached for him and he groaned. *Thank God he's alive.* Vapor from the deployed airbags filled the cab, along with the smell of gasoline.

I heard footsteps running toward the truck and the creaking sound of crunching metal as the door on my side was torn open. A man's bearded face peered in at me. "Are you okay, miss?"

I felt nauseated and disoriented. "I—I think so. But my friend—"

The man took out his phone, and I heard the distinct three beeps that signaled a call to the emergency services. He described the accident to the operator, who told him to keep us from moving, which was fine with me. And Garrett was definitely in no shape to be going anywhere.

The man looked at Garrett's side of the truck and saw the tree embedded there. "The fire department will have to get your friend out. Why were you going so fast around that curve?"

I leaned back and my head swam. "The brakes—"

Garrett groaned again. The blood from the cut on his head wasn't flowing as fast as before. Or did it just seem that way because I wanted it to be true?

The bearded man spoke to me in a soothing voice. "What's your name, honey?"

When I didn't answer, he continued talking to me quietly, but I had no idea what he was saying. All I could do was hold Garrett's hand, pray he would survive, and try to make sense of what had just happened.

The sound of sirens in the distance came closer. Flashing red lights reflected on the cracked windshield. Then the bearded man's face was replaced by a young man in a yellow coat and fireman's helmet. He asked me questions, but all I could say was, "Help him. Please help him."

His strong hands helped me out of the pickup and gave me into the care of another rescuer who led me to the back of an ambulance. Lights were flashing everywhere, providing enough light to see the scene. A path of crushed bushes and small trees marked our descent from the road, the same path the rescue vehicles followed to get to us.

I looked back at the pickup as several men carefully lifted Garrett through the passenger side door and laid him on a board. They placed his neck in a brace and strapped him to the board. Then they brought him to the ambulance where they put us on side-by-side stretchers. Garrett was conscious and began calling my name.

"I'm here. I'm okay."

He mumbled something incoherent and groaned again. The last thing I saw of the scene was the bearded man looking at me. He smiled and nodded as the door of the ambulance closed.

As we sped toward the hospital, siren screaming, the two EMTs worked on us quickly and efficiently. They took my vital signs and assured me I would be okay, but the ones attending to Garrett didn't say much. I heard one talking on a phone, saying something about a possible fractured clavicle and concussion. Then he said our ETA was five minutes.

I kept trying to look over at Garrett lying on the stretcher next to me, but the EMTs were in my way. I reached over and tugged on the coat of one of them. He turned to me.

"How is he?" I said.

"It's not too serious. You were both very lucky. What's your friend's name?"

"Garrett Easterbrook. He's a detective with the Pineland Park Police."

"Do you know anything about his medical history?"

I was embarrassed to say I knew nothing about it.

"It's okay. The precinct will have his records."

We pulled up to the hospital where Garrett and I were wheeled in and placed side-by-side in a curtained room in the emergency area. The doctors asked him a series of questions he had difficulty answering, such as his occupation, the date, and who the president was. When he answered "Jimmy Carter," I must have looked horrified, because the doctor smiled and assured me that kind of confusion was common with concussions. He said that it would pass quickly.

The rest of the evening was a blur of tests, questions, forms to be filled out, and nurses constantly taking my blood pressure. At one point, they wheeled Garrett out of the room for an MRI.

The adrenaline that had flooded my system was subsiding, leaving me with a pain across my chest that the nurse explained as coming from the seat belt. I gratefully accepted a shot of something to ease the pain and promptly fell asleep.

I don't know how long I slept, but I woke to see Captain Williams and Detective Sloan leaning over Garrett talking softly to him. Williams was saying, "You just take as much time as you need, Detective. There's no hurry to come back. Sloan can handle it."

You hypocrite, I thought. *You'd like nothing better than to get rid of both of us.*

Detective Sloan noticed I was awake. He smiled at me. "You're a lucky young lady. You both could have been killed."

Williams turned to me, all solicitous and concerned. "Miss Lowell, how are you feeling?"

"Okay. How's Garrett?"

Garrett reached for me and took my hand. "I'm fine. Don't worry about me."

The nurse bustled in and helped us sit up. "You two are being released in a few minutes. Do you have a ride home?"

"We'll take them home, Nurse." Williams said Then to us he said, "We'll wait for you at the front entrance." The two men left the room.

We signed some forms, and the nurse gave me an instruction sheet. "Your friend has a concussion and a dislocated shoulder. Does he have anyone to look after him?"

"I'll stay with him for a few days."

"Be sure he keeps that sling on. And watch for any of the signs on this sheet that the concussion might be worsening. Here are the pain meds the doctor prescribed. If he needs more, let us know. He needs to follow up with his own doctor. Any questions?"

I shook my head, watching Garrett, who didn't seem to know we were talking about him.

"Just wait here for the wheelchairs that will take you out."

When she left the room, I sat next to Garrett on his bed and smoothed his hair away from his face. The cut on his head had been bandaged, but his left eye was beginning to swell. His left arm was in a sling. He had that far-away look in his eyes that signaled a concussion. "Hey," I said softly. "How are you?"

He tried to focus on my face, but his eyes kept moving around the room. "Let's get out of here." He stood and wobbled a little.

I steadied him just as the nurses came in and helped us into the wheelchairs. I felt fine except for the pain across my chest, but they insisted I not walk out on my own.

The black Lexus was parked at the front entrance. Garrett was helped into the front seat. I slid into the back and stroked the soft leather seat.

So this is how the crooks live, I thought. *Well, we'll just see about that.*

Williams prattled away at Garrett as he drove, making inane comments about how lucky we were and how Garrett needed to be more careful when he drove. I was sickened by his fake concern.

We pulled into Garrett's driveway, and Williams started to get out.

"That's okay, Captain," I said as I helped Garrett out of his seat. "We can manage."

"If there's anything you need, Miss Lowell, don't hesitate to call." He said good night and drove off. As I stood watching him, the nausea I had felt in the hospital returned, but it had nothing to do with my physical condition.

I helped Garrett change out of his bloody clothes and get into bed. He looked small and helpless as he lay there gazing up at me, his left eye swelling and turning black and blue. "How are you going to get home?"

I kissed him on the forehead. "Don't worry about me. I'll make myself at home in your guest room. Now try to get some sleep. I'll leave the door open. Here's the pain pills and some water. Call me if you need anything else."

He gave me a small smile and closed his eyes. "Thank you," he mumbled. "I'm sorry."

I felt a rush of affection and sympathy for him. Leave it to Garrett to apologize for something not at all his fault.

I went back to the living room and plopped on the couch. My adrenaline rush had subsided, leaving me with the aftermath—fatigue and soreness, especially where the seatbelt had cut across my chest and shoulder. I fished in my bag for my phone. "Hi, Alma," I said when she answered. "I'll be staying at Garrett's tonight."

"Ohhh," she said. I could picture her raised eyebrows and grin.

"It's not what you think. We were in an accident on the way home from the movies."

I heard her gasp. "No!"

"We're okay. Garrett is banged up. I'm just a little sore."

"Oh, thank God." I could hear Ashley in the background saying, "What? What is it?"

"I need a favor."

"Anything. What can I do?"

"My bike is at the police station and Garrett's truck is out of commission. Can you come here in the morning to take me to the station?"

"Of course, dear, but it will have to be early. Before I open the café. Say about six-thirty?"

I groaned inwardly at the thought of dragging my aching body out of bed that early, but it couldn't be helped. "That will be fine. I'll see you in the morning. Thanks, Alma."

I leaned back and went over the events of the evening. All the sights and sounds of the accident were imprinted on my brain, and thinking about them made me a little dizzy. I waited for a few minutes then got up to check on Garrett who was asleep. Then I went to the guest room and curled up under the comforter. My last thought was how much I missed Jack's furry warmth cuddling with me.

Garrett was still asleep when I checked on him early the next morning. I could see he had taken a dose of the pain meds sometime during the night. He groaned slightly as he turned over. His eye had swollen shut and was turning shades of yellow and blue. I found some paper in the kitchen and wrote a note explaining where I was and that I would be back soon. I propped it up next to his water glass, pulled the blankets up to his chin, and left quietly.

Alma was waiting in her car in front of the cabin. The early morning air was chilly, and I was glad she had the heater running. I slid onto the seat and flinched as I pulled the seatbelt across my sore chest.

"You look awful," she said, her brows furrowed.

"I feel awful. But I'm glad to be alive."

Alma turned the car around and headed down the drive. "What the heck happened?"

I told her everything I could remember about the accident, the hospital, and Garrett's injuries.

"What I don't understand is how his brakes could suddenly fail. Garrett takes such good care of that truck."

"I've been wondering about that myself." I decided not to let Alma in on Garrett's suspicions and the situation with Williams and Bodmin. She would only worry. So I changed the subject. "How's Jack?"

"Fine. He slept with Ashley and Sasha last night."

"I'm going to need to stay with Garrett for a few days. Then I'd like to work at the café, if it's okay. I know Ashley will have to stop working when she starts school tomorrow. I can cover for her."

She peered at me. "Of course, dear. But what about your job?"

I sighed. "I don't have a job. I got fired." I explained the situation with Crenshaw and his ultimatum.

"I'm sorry to hear that. But I'm glad you'll be around for a while."

"Me too," I said, not wanting to let her know how terrified I was to be out of a job and dependent on other people, even people I loved and trusted.

"Oh, by the way, that detective was in the café last night."

"Sloan? What for?"

"He was with Sarge's brother-in-law. They talked for quite a while."

We pulled up in front of the police station. I opened the door and said, "I'll come back to get some clothes and pick up Jack. I'll start work tomorrow. Thanks for the ride."

"Give my love to Garrett."

I put a couple of dollars' worth of gas in the bike and headed back to Trout Fork. I slowed down as I passed the site of last night's accident. A queasy feeling came over me as I peered down the hill at the crushed bushes. I wondered what happened to the man in the yellow van who had stopped to help us. Maybe I could find him through the police report and thank him.

By the time I had collected Jack and my things and tied them onto the bike, it was nearly nine o'clock. I hurried back to Garrett's to find him sitting up, his legs over the side of the bed. He looked better, although still a bit groggy.

He smiled up at me then winced and reached up to gingerly feel his eye.

"Good morning. How do you feel?"

"Not too bad. Hungry."

"That's a good sign. I'll make us some breakfast."

I helped him into a bathrobe and watched him totter toward the bathroom. Then I went to check the fridge, hoping he had done some shopping lately. I found eggs and some leftover ham. I stood at the stove scrambling the eggs when Garrett shuffled in and put his arm around my waist.

"You should do this more often."

"What, get into an accident?"

"You know what I mean. You look right at home in my kitchen."

I ignored the implication. "Go sit down before you fall down."

He tottered to the table and spotted Jack sitting on the sofa. "Jack is here. Does that mean you're staying for a while?"

I brought the food to the table and sat with him. "Unless you'd rather hire a live-in nurse."

He smirked. "Definitely not." He dug into his eggs. "Umm…this is great."

We ate in silence for a while then I said, "Alma told me Sloan was in the café last night with Howard Milner. What's that about, do you know?"

"Probably interviewing him about Sarge. Now I wonder—" He was cut off by his cell phone ringing in his bedroom. "Can you get that for me?"

I went to his room and answered before it had a chance to go to voice mail. A deep male voice said, "Garrett Easterbrook, please."

I took the phone to Garrett and started clearing the table. I heard him say, "Yes, sir. I'm fine. Just a dislocated shoulder. I'll be back to work in a few days."

I frowned at Garrett and shook my head.

Garrett listened for a while, interjecting only "yes,

sir" every few seconds. Then he hung up and gazed thoughtfully out the window.

"Was that Williams?"

"No. It was the chief. He said I'm to lay low, as he put it, for a while. He has someone else he trusts keeping an eye on Williams while they build a case against him and Bodmin for racketeering."

"Did he say who?"

"Sloan."

I pictured the paunchy detective trudging up the hill toward Sarge's campsite and then pulling out of the station in his beat-up Ford. He seemed to be everywhere at once.

Garrett put down his coffee cup and squinted at me with his one good eye, which seemed to be having difficulty focusing. His face registered pain and fatigue.

"I think you should go back to bed." I got up, took his arm, and helped him toward his room, somewhat surprised he didn't offer any resistance.

After downing one of the pain pills, he settled back against the pillow. "Thanks," he mumbled. "You're…" His voice trailed off and his breathing became heavy.

I kissed his forehead. "Big, tough cop," I whispered as I pulled the blanket over him. He was sound asleep.

I tiptoed out of his room and pulled the door half closed. Jack was gazing at me from the sofa with his quizzical expression. I sat beside him and stroked him while I tried to piece together events and how they related to Sarge's murder. Williams and Bodmin were into some pretty nasty stuff, but were they really killers? Williams was the prime suspect for the death of the busboy. That's why Sarge was trying to remind Gil about the army captain who was involved in drugs and killed one of his men. Did Sarge confront Williams with what he knew? Did Williams get Bodmin to kill Sarge to keep him from talking? Bodmin was certainly an odious character, but somehow I couldn't see him as a murderer.

And what about Howard Milner? Now that Sarge was out of the way, Howard and his wife were sole owners of the house. Howard could access the equity in the house to pay off his gambling debts. But was that enough of a motive to kill his brother-in-law?

Then there was that note with the word "wind" written on it, as well as the crushed fingers. What did they have to do with Williams or Bodmin or Howard? Nothing that I could see. What was it that we were missing?

CHAPTER 14

Garrett slept most of the day while I cleaned up the cabin and spent several hours searching the internet for jobs. One of the things I loved about being at Garrett's was the internet connection. Trout Fork was still in the technological dark ages, so whenever I needed to search the web, I had to go somewhere closer to town. When I closed my laptop after finding nothing, I wondered why I wasn't all that disappointed.

Jack had settled himself in the guest room and seemed to be right at home. I felt perfectly at home myself. I even enjoyed cleaning and organizing the kitchen. Toward evening, I searched the cabinets for something I could cook for dinner and found some pasta that would go nicely with the leftover ham. I cooked the pasta then made a sauce of butter, flour, milk, and mozzarella cheese and poured it over the ham and pasta. I found some Italian spices in the cabinet to add to the mix.

I had just put it in the oven and was preparing a salad when Garrett wandered out from the bedroom, still in his bathrobe.

His hair was ruffled and he needed a shave. He sat on a stool at the counter dividing the kitchen from the dining room and yawned.

"Good morning," I teased.

He looked out the window. "Is it morning?"

"No. Just kidding. How's the shoulder?"

He fingered the bandage over his eye. "Not as bad as this. I just looked in the mirror and didn't recognize myself."

His eye was partially open, although the whole area around it was swollen and multicolored.

"You're a sight for a sore eye," I quipped.

"Funny. What are you cooking?"

"Mac and cheese with ham."

"Smells great."

There was a knock at the door. Garrett and I looked at each other. "Are you expecting someone?" I asked.

"No."

"Should I answer it?"

"Wait a minute." He went to his jacket draped over the sofa and took his revolver out of its holster. He unlocked it and held it behind him. "Okay." His action both comforted and unnerved me. I was never comfortable around guns.

I opened the door a crack and saw Detective Sloan standing on the stoop. I opened the door all the way.

"Hi. It's Miss Lowell, isn't it?"

"Ryn. Come in, Detective."

He stepped into the room, his bulk seeming to dwarf the furnishings. He watched Garrett put his gun away. "Dude. You look like hell."

"Thanks. What brings you out here?"

"The chief asked me to check on your truck, so I went over to the garage. The brake line was cut nearly through. There was just enough brake fluid to last a few minutes."

Garrett grimaced. "Just until we hit the hills."

I gasped as the realization hit me. Someone had tried to kill one or both of us. I stared at Garrett, but he didn't seem all that surprised. The timer on the oven started buzzing.

"Have you had your dinner?" Garrett asked.

Sloan sniffed the air. "Not yet."

"Come and sit down."

The two men settled into chairs at the small table while I brought the casserole and salad then took my place next to Garrett. I was still reeling from what Sloan had just told us. I thought back to the previous evening. Someone must have tampered with the brake line while we were at the movies. That would mean they followed us from the station to the theatre.

I watched them eat and chat about the doings at the station, seemingly blasé about the fact that someone had tried to kill us last night. It was then I realized that cops exist in an alternate reality, one in which the worst of human nature is accepted as commonplace. It was hard to reconcile Garrett's love of opera and Romantic poetry with that side of him. No wonder he seemed an enigma to me at times.

When we finished polishing off the casserole, Sloan leaned back and patted his ample stomach. He eyed me admiringly and said to Garrett, "You two shacked up or what?"

Garrett gave him a stony stare. "Ryn is helping me out for a couple of days. That's all."

"Too bad. She's some cook. Not bad looking, either." He winked at me, but seeing that neither of us was amused, he patted my arm. "Don't mind me, honey. I'm a little rough around the edges. I don't mean anything by it."

I went to the kitchen and brought the coffee to the table.

"Someone told me you were interviewing Howard Milner today," Garrett said. "Get anything out of him?"

Sloan leaned forward. "Little Howie's a piece of work. I told him I was trying to find out who killed his brother-in-law. At first he was very cooperative, playing the grieving relative. Then I told him I knew about his gambling debts, and he looked like a scared rabbit. He admitted he wanted Sarge to sign over the house so he could pay off his gambling debts. Turns out he was in really deep to a bookie in Las Vegas. Lucky for him that bookie got whacked about a year ago. Now he's in trouble with a loan shark who has ties to the mob out there. He's sweating it big time. What really pissed him off—" He glanced at me. "—er, annoyed him is that it was Sarge who referred him to the bookie. Said they were old army buddies."

"Marines," Garrett said.

"Oh, yeah, that's right."

"Pretty convenient the bookie turning up dead," I said, half to myself.

"Convenient and weird."

Garrett put his coffee cup down. "How so?"

"They found him in a park with his skull cracked open."

"What's weird about that?" I asked.

"Nothing, but whoever killed him broke all his fingers. After he was dead."

Garrett and I looked at each other, and Garrett's eyes widened slightly. "Are you sure?"

"Yep. Look it up. It's all in the Las Vegas PD database. It's just like this case, and the only common denominator is Howard Milner."

Garrett gazed out the window. "So you're thinking Milner killed his bookie, got in trouble with the loan shark, and got desperate. Then he killed Sarge to get his share of the house to pay off the shark. Is that it?"

Sloan nodded. "That's the way I see it."

"Then what about Williams and Bodmin? We know they're shaking down businesses and distributing cocaine. I'm sure they killed the busboy, and we know Sarge saw them because he was trying to warn Gil about it with that note."

Sloan shrugged. "Maybe the three deaths aren't related."

"I would buy that except for the crushed fingers on both Sarge and the bookie. That has to mean something."

"Like I said, the only thing both had in common was Howard Milner. He has to be involved." He got up from the table. "Well, I'll be off. Thanks for the meal."

We walked him to the door. He turned to Garrett. "Check in with the chief. He wants to hear from you when you're up to it."

After he left, Garrett and I stood silent for a moment. Then he went to the stereo and put Mozart's *Don Giovanna* on. He shuffled to the sofa where he sat staring at the fireplace.

I sat beside him. "Garrett, you need to tell the police chief that someone cut the brake line on your truck, someone who hoped we would be killed in a wreck on those hills."

He kept staring at the fireplace. "Umm."

"Who would want to get rid of us and why?"

"Someone who thinks we're getting too close to the truth."

"Do you think it's Williams or Bodmin?"

He was silent. I knew he was thinking about Sloan's revelations and trying to make sense of it all, so I decided not to disturb him. I left him to ruminate and went to clear the table. Then I fed Jack and headed to the guest room to get ready for bed. I was tired and had to be at the café before seven the next morning.

After about an hour, he appeared at the door to my room. "I'm sorry I'm ignoring you. After all you've done for me."

I laughed at his comical appearance—swollen face, grubby bathrobe, two-day beard. In spite of it all, he looked adorable. "That's okay. Do you need anything?"

He rubbed his hand across his chin. "What I really need is a shower and a shave." He grinned at me. "I don't suppose you'd want to help with that."

I got up and unbuckled his sling. "Sorry," I said, patting his shoulder. "You're on your own there. I'm sure you can manage. It's your left arm that's injured and you're right-handed."

"Damn. You're too sharp for me."

"Call me when you're out of the shower, and I'll help you into the sling."

He went back to his room, and soon I heard the shower running. I leaned back on the bed and thought about what Sloan had told us. Was it really Howard, that mousy, hen-pecked little man, who was at the bottom of this? Could he really have killed two people? Something was missing, something we didn't know or hadn't considered, something that linked the murders of the busboy, the bookie, and Sarge.

Or maybe Sloan was right and they weren't linked at all. It was the broken fingers that linked Sarge and the bookie, but the busboy's fingers were intact. I had believed the editor and the police captain were responsible for the busboy's death, and Sarge was caught up in it because he saw the busboy being buried. But Sarge was also linked to the bookie by the fingers. And now we find out the two men were in the Marine Corps together. Was breaking a victim's fingers some kind of message I wasn't familiar with? Maybe Garrett could find out.

I heard Garrett puttering around in his room, so I went to his door and knocked. He was sitting on his bed trying to put his left arm into the sling and groaning each time he moved.

I sat next to him and helped him into the sling. "Why didn't you call me?" He had changed into clean pajamas, but still hadn't shaved. "Maybe you should grow a beard for real. You'd look pretty hot."

"But then I'd have to beat off all the women."

"Yeah, I'm sure that would be tough on you."

He grinned and pulled the covers back. "Sure you don't want to join me?"

"I'm sure." I helped him get into bed and lie back. "I have to leave early for the café. I'll be back after lunch. Text me if you need anything."

"Okay." He was already drifting off. "Good night."

I left early the next morning without eating. I was hoping to avoid waking Garrett by puttering in the kitchen. Jack followed me to the front door, looking up at me with his inquiring eyes.

I bent down to stroke him. "No run today, Jack. Maybe when I get back."

Driving to Trout Fork in the early morning light and air, I felt exhilarated and very much at peace. It felt so good to be back on my Honda, zipping around the curves. Leaning into one curve and cresting the hill, I had a momentary thought about the brakes. Did Hondas use brake fluid? If so, where was the brake line? Could it be tampered with? I had no idea and thought I'd better call the Honda dealer when I got back to Garrett's cabin.

It was six-thirty when I pulled up in front of the café. Ashley was standing at the school bus stop dressed in a new outfit and carrying a new backpack that looked heavy. She grinned and waved to me. I could see she was excited to be going back to school after a summer filled with drama.

"Good luck with your French class," I called, and she gave me a thumbs-up.

I went around the corner of the café and through the back door. Alma was busy preparing for the breakfast rush. "Ryn! Thanks for doing this. Zoe is late, as usual. Didn't Ashley look adorable in her new outfit? Get the dining room prepared, would you? And sweep the patio?"

I hugged her. "Good morning to you, too," I teased.

She rolled her eyes. "I'm sorry. Good morning. Have you had breakfast? How's Garrett?"

I decided not to tell her the accident was caused by a severed brake line. "He's getting better, and no, I haven't eaten. I'll grab something before we open."

"There's fresh bagels on the counter. Help yourself." She slammed a plate down. "Where the hell is Zoe? That girl will be the death of me."

Just then Zoe burst through the back door, her hair disheveled and her normally bright eyes bloodshot.

"Nice of you to join us," Alma said.

Zoe mumbled, "Sorry." She followed me through the swinging door and headed for the coffee machine. She stood there weaving slightly, her hands trembling as she poured herself a cup.

"You and Derek have a rough night?" I asked.

She shook her head. "He left yesterday. Back home to Denver to pack. He's heading for Stanford this morning."

She looked genuinely sad, and my heart went out to her. "I guess you'll miss him." *Or maybe you'll miss the dope he's been providing.*

"I'm thinking about going out there."

I couldn't believe my ears. "To Stanford?"

She nodded. "I can find a job out there. I've always wanted to go to California."

I hesitated. Then I decided to offer my opinion, whether or not it was wanted. "Zoe, following him out there is a monumentally bad idea." She squinted at me, but I continued. "He's moving into a whole new world, with new friends and experiences. Academics, activities, things he's never experienced, things you can't be part of. When young people go off to college, most want to distance themselves from their former lives. That means they leave their old friends and even their family members behind." She looked both sad and resentful, but I continued. "Trust me. I've been through it. He's moving on. You should, too."

She stood there drinking her coffee. I decided to confront her about the drugs I knew Derek had been giving her. "Besides," I said, "Derek isn't a good guy. He's into some bad stuff. You know that, don't you? Look what he's done to you. You look awful."

She nodded silently as tears began flow down her cheeks. "I wish I never met him," she blurted out. "I know he's bad for me. But I…"

"But you're crazy about him."

She nodded again, sunk in the misery familiar to every young woman who had ever fallen for the wrong man. "I knew it was wrong. But he made it seem so glamorous, so hip. He made me feel like a loser for refusing, so I did it. Then I did it again. Pretty soon we were partying every night. It was like I couldn't stop. You know?"

"What was it? Cocaine?"

She nodded again, her eyes averted. Clearly she was embarrassed by it. "You know what really eats at me? He'll probably do the same thing out in Stanford, only with other girls." She shook her head sadly. "It's so wrong."

"Yes, it is. Getting you involved with it was very wrong. And he needs to be stopped before he hurts other people." I watched her reaction and saw she was truly remorseful. "Zoe, do you know where he was getting the cocaine?"

She sighed. "All he said was it's some cop high up in the police department."

"In the Pineland Park Police?"

"Yeah. That's all I know."

I thought a moment. "Would you be willing to talk to my friend, Detective Easterbrook, about it? He's pretty sure he knows who it is that's been selling the dope, and he wants to stop it."

She pulled away, her eyes suspicious. "Talk to a cop? I don't want to go to jail."

"You won't. If you're not using, and you don't have any of the drugs now, you aren't guilty of anything except past bad judgment. But you might be able to help prevent Derek from hurting anyone else."

"I don't know. Maybe. I'll have to think about it."

Alma came to the window between the kitchen and the counter. "Are we ready to open, girls?"

"Almost," I said. I patted Zoe on the shoulder. "I know you'll do the right thing." I watched her walk away and begin to wipe the tables. I took a broom and headed for the patio.

As I swept the leaves and flower petals from the patio floor, I wondered whether Derek could be linked to Sarge's murder. Even if Williams and Bodmin were guilty of operating a drug ring, and Derek was buying from them, that still wouldn't get Hank out of jail. We just had to find Sarge's killer, and I was sure the death of the bookie in Las Vegas and his broken fingers was the key.

I worked steadily until midafternoon. Then I told

Alma I was going to check on Garrett, but I would be back before dinner. I drove back to Garrett's, parked the bike, and opened the front door. All was quiet, so I thought he might be taking a nap. I tiptoed to his bedroom and peeked in to see him sitting up in bed with his laptop on his lap and Jack curled up beside him. Garrett was scratching between Jack's ears.

I sat on the bed beside him. "How are my boys doing?"

"We're just fine. I think he likes me." He patted Jack's head. "Don't you, buddy?"

Jack looked at me with half-closed eyes then snuggled closer to Garrett.

"I guess I've been replaced in his affections. You look like you're feeling better."

"I am. I haven't had to take any more pain meds today."

"I had an interesting talk with Zoe today. She admitted Derek got her started on cocaine."

Garrett's eyes smoldered. "That creep. I'd like to wring his scrawny neck."

"Too late. He and his neck left town yesterday. He's going off to college. I asked Zoe if she knew where he was getting his drugs and she didn't, but she said it was from a cop high up in the Pineland Park PD."

Garrett looked pained. "Williams. I knew it, but I didn't want to believe it. Is Zoe willing to tell the chief what she knows?"

"I'm not sure. She's pretty skittish about getting in trouble. I told her if she isn't using and doesn't have any drugs, she can't be charged. I asked her to come and talk to you. She said she'll think about it."

Garrett shook his head. "This will be a black mark on the department."

"Maybe, but I think people will be glad to know corruption isn't tolerated. That counts for a lot with the public."

"I guess." He looked down at the computer screen. "Listen to this. Remember Sloan told me to look up the file on the bookie in Las Vegas?"

I nodded. "Anything interesting?"

"Very. Not only did he have his fingers broken, just like Sarge, but they found a piece of paper on the body with one word on it."

"Let me guess—'wind.'"

"Nope. This time the word was 'frequent.'"

"Frequent? What could that mean?"

Garrett shrugged. "The guy was a frequent gambler? A frequent snitch? A frequent drug user? Who knows? And that's not all. He was killed on August seventh last year."

"So?"

"Sarge was killed on August seventh this year."

I stared at him. "Two murders on the same day a year apart, both with broken fingers and both with a note on the body containing a single word."

He nodded. "One thing is for certain. Sarge and the bookie were killed by the same person and probably for the same reason. We find the motive, we find the killer."

CHAPTER 15

Garrett was beginning to look sleepy, so I left him and Jack to take their nap together and wandered out to the kitchen. I made a ham sandwich for Garrett's dinner and left it in the fridge. I didn't think he was quite ready to fend for himself just yet. Besides, I was enjoying the idea of taking care of him.

I cleaned up the kitchen and puttered around the cabin for a while. Then I tiptoed into Garrett's room to leave a note on his nightstand telling him about the sandwich. I smiled as I added a little heart at the bottom of the note, even though I felt a little silly doing it. Something about Garrett tended to bring out the silly in me.

I drove back to Trout Fork just in time to see Ashley getting off the school bus in front of the café. She hurried over to me as I was parking the bike. She was hauling her heavy backpack and began to talk, breathlessly and non-stop.

"Oh, my God! School was so awesome. I saw all my friends. There's this new guy who ate with us at lunch. His family just moved here from Atlanta. He wears glasses and has the cutest accent. His name is Gerry, short for Gerald. And he's *in my French class.* Can you believe it?"

"So how did that class go?"

"It was awesome! The teacher, Monsieur LaSalle, started speaking to us in French right away, and I was one of the only ones who could answer all his questions. Thank God for Philippe. He used to speak French to me really fast, and I hated it, but it was the best thing ever. Monsieur LaSalle even complimented me on my accent. I'll have to write to Philippe and thank him."

"I'm sure he'd like that."

She stopped to take a breath and looked at me curiously. "Hey. Mom said you and Garrett were in an accident. You guys okay?"

"Garrett has a dislocated shoulder and a cut over his eye, but he's getting better. I wasn't hurt."

"How long will you be staying with him? Sasha is missing Jack."

"Couple more days. I'll probably come back here this weekend."

Ashley rolled her eyes. "Just in time for the next installment of the Robert and Alma show. Have you heard the latest?"

"No. What?"

"Dad wants Mom to marry him again."

I put my arm around her shoulders. "Well, that's great, don't you think?"

"Except he wants her to sell the café and the cabins and for us to move back to Denver with him. That would mean I have to transfer to a school up there. I'd hate that."

"What did your mom say?"

"She went all radical feminist on him. She's all like 'why do I have to uproot my life? Why don't you move your practice down here?'"

"Would he do that?"

"He said that was ridiculous. Then she said something like he thinks his career is more important than hers and wasn't that always the way with men."

"I'll bet that went over big with him."

She rolled her eyes and moved her backpack to her other shoulder. "I don't know. I went to my room and closed the door. I was like 'whatever.'"

Poor Ashley. My heart went out to her. It just didn't seem like her family situation would ever resolve. I knew that feeling. "Well, maybe they'll work it out."

We walked into the café together, and Ashley went to the kitchen to see Alma, while I started preparing the dining room for dinner. I went to check the patio and found Zoe sitting at one of the tables staring into space. She looked at me with those sad green eyes. "I've been thinking about what you said. About talking to your cop friend about Derek."

"Oh?"

"I was thinking that Derek has his whole life ahead of him, so if I can do anything to keep him from ruining it, I should do that, shouldn't I?"

"That's a good way to look at it. Sometimes hurting people is the best way to help them."

"Yeah. Okay. I'll talk to the cop."

"Good. I'll set up a time when he's feeling a little better."

She headed into the dining room then stopped in the doorway and turned back to me. "Know what else I've been thinking? I might want to stay here for the winter. Maybe learn the restaurant business from Alma. Maybe that's something I can do someday, have a place like this of my own."

"I think that's a wonderful idea."

I watched her walk away. I was happy for her, but a cold feeling came over me as I realized she would be taking from me the only job I had at the moment. If I wasn't working at the café, I would also have no place to stay. I couldn't ask Alma to put me up and not pay rent or work for her. Just as I had feared, my nomadic lifestyle had finally caught up with me. The prospect of having no choice but to return to New York to start again loomed over me, and it gave me a slightly sick feeling in the pit of my stomach.

The dinner rush could hardly have been called a rush. It was nearing the end of summer, and once school started, the number of tourists always fell off dramatically. Tonight it was mostly the locals. Howard and Estelle Milner came in. They were still renting a cabin from Alma, making me wonder what was keeping them in Trout Fork this long. Didn't she say they would stay around until Sarge's killer was found? Now that Hank's case was before the grand jury, there didn't seem to be any reason for them to remain.

Gil and Madam Gauzie came in and sat together at the table near the window. I waited on them, leaving Zoe to take care of the Milners.

Gil searched my face with concern. "Hey, Ryn. How's Garrett? Alma said you were staying with him for a couple of days."

"He'll be fine. His shoulder just has to heal so he can take the sling off. Jack is keeping him company."

Madam Gauzie looked sideways at the Milners. "I see Mrs. Pruneface and her husband are still here. Like ghouls. Just waiting for the execution."

"Execution?"

"Yes. Poor Hank's trial."

"I doubt he'll go to trial in less than a year." Gil said. "You know how those smarmy lawyers are, dragging it out forever to collect their fees."

I wondered if Gil had heard any more about his son's release from prison on a technicality. But I decided if he wanted me to know, he'd tell me. I also wondered how Gil would react to the news that a police captain was involved in extortion and drug dealing, once it was proven. "Gil," I said, "You have friends in the Pineland Park Police Department, don't you?"

"Yeah, you met a few of them at the barbeque. Remember?"

"Oh, right. Nice guys. Did they ever say anything to you about their boss, Captain Williams?"

"Like what?"

I was reluctant to tell him what Garrett and I suspected. "Oh, nothing. Never mind. What can I get you to eat tonight?"

He regarded me with a furrowed brow for a moment. "The tuna melt for me with fries. And iced tea."

"Madam G?"

"Hmm?" She seemed to be distracted watching Estelle, who was deep in conversation with her husband. "Oh, I guess the chicken salad. Is it fresh?"

"Alma made it this afternoon."

"That will be fine."

As I passed the Milners on the way to the kitchen, I noticed that Estelle was talking quietly but vehemently to her husband, bearing in on him. I heard the words "gamble" and "debts" and thought again about his bookie and the connection to Sarge.

But I still couldn't picture mousy little Howard cracking someone's head open with a rock then breaking all his fingers. But he was the only one with a motive to kill them both.

The bookie was leaning on him to repay his debts, and Sarge's death finally gave him access to the equity in the house in Albuquerque.

After the café closed, I went to the kitchen to tell Alma I was leaving. She was scouring the grill, her face redder than normal, either from the exertion or her thoughts about her husband.

She looked up when I came in. "Leaving, dear? Be sure to give Garrett my love. I'm so glad he has you to look after him. Does he need any food? There's plenty of leftovers in the fridge."

"Thanks, but we have more than enough to eat at the cabin. I saw Ashley this afternoon. She seems pretty happy about school." I wasn't sure whether to bring up the subject, but I said, "She'd hate to have to leave it."

She stopped what she was doing and eyed me. "She told you, didn't she?"

"She did mention something about Robert wanting you to move back to Denver."

Her eyes searched mine. "Am I wrong to not want that? To not want to give up what I've built here to be the lawyer's wife and just go to cocktail parties with the other wives? I don't think I could stand it."

"Robert asked you to marry him again, didn't he?"

She nodded, wiping her face with her apron. "You know, I still love him, even after all these years. But do I love him enough to uproot our lives, Ashley's and mine? I just don't know. I think maybe too much time has passed." She seemed both sad and angry.

I gave her a hug. "I'm sure you'll make the right decision. See you in the morning."

I left her and went out to my bike. The motor purred to life, and I pulled slowly out of the lot, enjoying the feeling of freedom the bike always afforded me. I thought about Alma and Robert and their dilemma, grateful once again that I was single.

Jack greeted me at the door of Garrett's cabin, meowing and rubbing on my legs. I picked him up and put him on my shoulder, stroking him as he nuzzled my ear. "Did you miss me, Jackie?"

"Yes, he did." Garrett was seated at the table in his bathrobe working on his laptop. "He's been looking for you all day."

I joined him at the table with Jack still on my shoulder. "You're looking pretty perky. But where's your sling?"

"I took it off. I can't do anything with it on." He saw my concerned look. "It'll be fine, Nurse. As long as I don't lift my arm, my shoulder won't dislocate again. How are things in Trout Fork?"

"The usual dramas. Alma's trying to decide if she wants to go back to Robert, Ashley is freaked out about having to leave school if that happens. The Milners are still there. Don't ask me why. Let's see, what else? I was thinking about asking Gil if his buddies from your precinct know anything about Williams, but I decided not to."

Garrett looked at me with wrinkled brow at the mention of Williams. "I'm glad you didn't say anything. I spoke to the chief today. He said they're closing in on Williams and Bodmin and their protection racket. He wouldn't want you to say anything that might get back to Williams and spook him."

"Did the chief say anything about your brake line?"

"Only that if it was Williams or Bodmin, or one of their thugs, who cut the line, it's because I was getting too close when I questioned Borelli about what his busboy told me. The chief is pretty sure it was Williams who killed the kid, but he has to build a case before he can arrest him. I think Borelli is the key. If we can get him to talk, if he agrees to testify against Williams and Bodmin, that will pretty much wrap it up."

"Does he think Sarge was killed because he saw Williams burying the kid?"

"Not after I told him about the Las Vegas bookie

with the crushed fingers. He said in Sarge's case, we're looking for someone not connected with Williams and Bodmin."

"So if Williams and Bodmin had nothing to do with Sarge's death, that leaves us back at square one. No suspects. No motive. Nothing."

He tapped on his keyboard. "Not exactly. I've been searching police databases all afternoon. It's been a hit-and-miss operation, but I finally found something. A case in North Carolina with similarities to Sarge and the book-ie."

"No kidding?"

"A doctor in Durham, a surgeon, killed in the middle of the night in the parking lot at the hospital. He was hit from behind, and then his fingers were smashed and a note left at the scene."

"What's the word this time?"

"Operation."

"Do they have any suspects?"

He peered at the screen. "One—a Geoffrey McDaniels, whose wife was operated on by the surgeon. She died on the operating table during a routine hysterectomy. Her husband went ballistic and blamed the surgeon for botching the operation. Swore he'd get even."

"Did they arrest him?"

"Not enough evidence. And the case is starting to go cold."

"When did it happen?"

"Two years ago…on the seventh of August."

I put Jack on the floor where he continued to rub on my legs. "August seventh? The same as Sarge and the bookie."

"Yep."

I thought about the three murders. "Garrett, do you think this is a serial killer? I mean, could there be dozens of victims killed on August seventh with notes and smashed fingers?"

"Let's hope not. I'd really like to find out more about this guy in North Carolina who lost his wife. Has he had any dealings with the Las Vegas bookie? With Sarge? Has he ever been in Colorado?"

"I have an idea. If you can get his phone number, I'll call him and pretend to be selling real estate or something. I can find out if he's ever been in Colorado or Las Vegas. If he has, he may have known Sarge and the bookie. What do you think?"

"That's not exactly ethical. And even if you do get some information that implicates him, if it's based on what you find out while you're pretending to be someone you're not, it may not be admissible in court."

I shrugged. "Well, it was just an idea."

He smiled at me. "It's worth a try." He wrote down the husband's name on a slip of paper and handed it to me. Then he yawned. "I think I'll turn in. Thanks for making the sandwich." He grinned at me. "I saw your note. Does that little heart mean what I hope it means?"

I got up from the table. "Let's get you into your sling. We can talk about hearts some other time."

He yawned again. "You're a slippery little thing, aren't you?"

I followed him into his bedroom and helped him take off his bathrobe and put the sling on over his pajama top.

He headed toward the bathroom. "I can take it from here, Nurse."

"Sleep well."

After Garrett was in bed, I sat on my bed with Jack and opened my laptop. I searched the social media sites for Geoffrey McDaniels in Durham, North Carolina. He had a Facebook page on which he had posted rants about the doctor who he claimed had "butchered" his wife during an operation. The posts were old and stopped abruptly in August, two years ago. I guessed he had been visited by the police after the doctor's body was found and got scared of incriminating himself. He had even posted something apologizing to the doctor's family. I wondered how sincere that was.

Researching a little further, I found his address and phone number. It was too late to call tonight, but I would try first thing in the morning. North Carolina was two hours later than the Colorado time zone, so I could call before work.

I closed my laptop, took a shower, and got ready for bed. I filled Jack's food and water bowls, cleaned his litter box, and checked on Garrett one last time. He was sound asleep and snoring like a buzz saw. A fleeting thought caused me to wonder whether sleeping with him would be difficult for someone who was easily awakened by noise. Like me.

The next morning, the bright sun coming in the window woke me. I rolled over, heard Jack grumble in protest as I moved him, and stared at the ceiling. I lay there inhaling the pine smell from the trees outside the open window and listening to the birds chirping their morning joy. The peaceful feeling of that scene was short-lived, replaced by the cares of an unsolved murder, a friend stuck in a smelly jail cell, and my own situation—unemployed and homeless.

I left the guest room, sat at the table, and pulled out the slip of paper with Geoffrey McDaniels's number on it. I dialed and waited. A gruff voice answered, and I began the spiel I had invented. "Mr. McDaniels, this is Maria with Western Vacation Consortium. How are you today?"

"Fine."

"I'll only keep you a minute. The reason we're calling you today is to let you know about a once-in-a-lifetime opportunity we're offering on condominiums in some of the country's most fabulous resorts, specifically in Vail, Colorado and Las Vegas, Nevada. We got your name from a list of people who might be interested in a condo in one of those areas. Tell me, sir, have you ever been to Vail or Las Vegas?"

I heard him hesitate and hoped he wouldn't just hang up on me, which is what I do when called by a telemarketer. But he said, "I been to Las Vegas, but that was twenty years ago. Never been in Colorado."

"You're not a skier, I take it?"

"I'm not anything. I have MS and I'm in a wheelchair. So I don't travel, and I'm really not interested in condos. Sorry." He disconnected.

I felt sorry for him and a little foolish. If he was telling the truth, he couldn't have been in Trout Fork three weeks ago. Although he may have had a motive to kill the surgeon, he had no connection to Sarge. And if he hadn't been in Las Vegas for decades, he had no connection to the bookie. Garrett and I were sure we were looking for one person responsible for all three murders. We had to find something to link the three victims to one another.

CHAPTER 16

Zoe seemed distracted and thoughtful as we worked together in the café most of the day. Then toward the late afternoon, she came to me and said she would come to Garrett's that evening to talk to him about Derek and what she knew about his cocaine suppliers. I thanked her and called Garrett. He was delighted.

After dinner, we cleaned up the café as quickly as we could and said good night to Alma.

Then Zoe got into her old car and followed me to Garrett's. As we parked in front of the cabin, I saw her hesitate a moment in the car. Hoping she wasn't changing her mind, I got off the Honda and opened her car door. "Everything okay?" I asked.

She grimaced. "I don't know if this is a good idea. I don't like talking to the cops."

"Don't be nervous. Garrett is a regular guy. Oh, be prepared. He looks a little scary right now with his black eye."

I held the door of the cabin open for her, but she hesitated. "Come on in. He doesn't bite."

Jack trotted out of the guest room to greet us, and Zoe backed up when he came near her. "Pretty kitty," she said. "I wish I wasn't so allergic to cats."

"That's Jack." I picked him up and moved him away from her. "I named him after Jack Kerouac."

"Who?"

"You know, the travel writer."

"Never heard of him." She sighed. "There's so much I don't know. I wish I had paid more attention when I was in school."

I took Jack to the guest room. "I'll be right back."

I closed the bedroom door to keep Jack in just as Garrett emerged from his room wearing sweat pants and a T-shirt with his arm in the sling.

I introduced him to Zoe, and he smiled and shook her hand.

She winced a little as she examined his swollen face and multi-colored eye. "Ouch," she said. "That looks painful. Sorry to hear about your accident."

He gestured toward the sofa. "It's not as bad as it looks. Have a seat."

Zoe and I sat on the sofa with Garrett opposite us in his comfy overstuffed chair. I could feel Zoe's nervousness, so I tried to put her at ease. "Can I get you something, Zoe? Something to drink."

"No, thanks," she said. She sat tensely with her arms around her midsection. Her green eyes were wide as she stared at Garrett, and she kept reaching up to pull at her strawberry blonde bangs.

He smiled at her again. "I appreciate your coming to talk to me, Zoe. I want you to know that this is an informal interview. I'm not recording it and I won't make an official report. But I understand you have some information that may help us solve some of the drug crimes in this area, possibly even a murder."

Zoe flinched and wrinkled her brow at Garrett. "I don't know anything about that murder."

"No matter. Just tell us what you can about your

friend, Derek. The two of you partied with coke, is that right?"

Zoe swallowed and nodded.

"Where did he get the stuff? Did he tell you?"

She looked imploringly at Garrett. "I don't want to get him in trouble. But I hate to see him ruin his life, ya' know?"

"Yes, I know. But the best way to help him is to make him face what he's been doing. Don't you think?"

She nodded again. "He's never had to face anything. He's always been able to charm his way out of things. Or depend on his father."

"Let's start with the cocaine. Who supplied it?"

"I don't know any names. I only know it's a Pineland Park cop high up in the department."

"Just try to remember what he told you."

"One night we were snorting, and I got scared of what would happen if we got caught. He just laughed. 'Not gonna happen' is what he said. 'I have connections.' That's the word he used—*connections*. I told him the cops don't care about connections if they bust you with coke."

"What did he say to that?"

"He laughed again and said, 'They'd care about these connections 'cuz it's their boss I get it from.' I said, 'You're lying' and he said, 'No, really.' Then he laughed again."

Garrett leaned back in the chair. "But he never gave you the name."

Zoe shook her head. "I didn't want to know. The whole thing freaked me out." Her eyes found Garrett's. "I mean, if you can't trust the cops, who can you trust?"

I saw that familiar sadness in Garrett's eyes. "Indeed," he said. "One more thing, Zoe. Did Derek ever say anything about a cop, or someone else, threatening the businesses in town?"

"No, nothing like that."

"Did he ever mention a busboy who worked at Borelli's, the Italian restaurant?"

She shook her head. "Nope. Who's that?"

"Never mind. What about Sarge, the old man killed at the campsite up the hill from the café? Did Derek ever mention him?"

She hesitated a minute, glancing at me. "Well…"

I touched her arm. "Go head, Zoe. Don't be afraid."

"That old guy, the one who got killed? He saw us in the woods one night. We were partying pretty hard. As we were leaving, the old guy came out from behind a tree. Scared the crap out of me. He was all in Derek's face. Said he would turn him in to the cops if Derek didn't stop what he was doing."

"What did Derek say?"

"He grabbed the old guy by the collar and told him to mind his own business if he knew what was good for him. Then he like pushed him away, and we left. The old guy just stood there watching us leave. That's the last time I saw him."

Garrett said, "When was that? Do you remember?"

She shrugged. "I don't know. A few days before the old guy died, I think." She looked at Garrett, alarmed. "Wait a minute. You don't think Derek killed that old geezer, do you? I mean, why would he?"

Garrett gazed into the fireplace, which told me he was far away, and I knew the interview was over. I put my arm around Zoe's shoulders. "You've been a big help. And you were very brave to come here. If Garrett has any more questions, I'm sure he'll call you."

We stood up together, and I walked her to the door. She opened the door then turned to me. "What will happen to Derek? Will there be trouble for him?"

I glanced back at Garrett who was still in his trance-like state. "I don't honestly know. He's in California now, so it's up to the police what they want to do with the information."

She seemed relieved. "Okay. Whatever happens, I've decided I'm not going to follow him to Stanford. I'm staying here, at least for the winter."

"I'm sure Alma will be glad to hear that. Thanks for your help. Drive carefully."

I closed the door and stood there a moment. Then I went back to the bedroom to open the door for Jack, who was meowing and scratching at the door. He gave me one of his disgruntled looks, strolled past me, and hopped up on the sofa, where he began to nonchalantly groom himself. I sat beside him and tried to stroke him, but he moved away from me as if to punish me for having the effrontery to lock him in the bedroom. I laughed at him. "Now, Jackie, don't be like that."

Garrett seemed to come out of his reverie when he heard my voice. He looked around. "Is she gone?"

"Yep. Just now. Garrett, you don't think Derek had anything to do with Sarge's death, do you?"

"No. The scams Williams and Bodmin were running and the busboy they killed had nothing to do with Sarge either."

That was a bit of a shock. I had assumed they were all tied together. "How do you know?"

He got up from the chair, retrieved a yellow legal pad from the table where his laptop was, and came to sit by me on the sofa. "I checked with the police departments in Durham and Las Vegas today to get background information on the doctor and the bookie. I knew there had to be something linking them to Sarge. I've found things that convince me Sarge's death is not related to anything going on here—not Williams or Bodmin, not drugs, and not the busboy." He turned over a page on the yellow pad. "Listen to this. The three victims—Sarge, the doctor in North Carolina, and the bookie in Vegas—were all murdered by the same person. I'm sure of it. All were killed on August seventh, all had those cryptic notes found near the body, and all had their fingers broken or crushed."

"We already knew that."

"Right. But what we didn't know until today is that all three of them were in the Marines, and all were deployed to Vietnam at the same time. In fact, they were in the same squad."

This was amazing. "So the three must have known each other."

"Of course. Their squad of ten Marines was posted to the US Embassy in Saigon, what's now called Ho Chi Minh City, until 1975 when the last of the US personnel finally left Vietnam. After the war, their unit was posted to guard the embassy in Switzerland then eventually sent back to Camp Lejune in North Carolina. All three left the service after their tour of duty. One stayed in the area, went to Duke University, then got his MD. Well, you know what happened to him."

My mind was spinning. Here was the link we'd been searching for. Were we finally going to find Sarge's killer? "Ten men in the same Marine unit, and three of them have been murdered. Do you think one of the other seven Marines killed Sarge and the other two?"

Garrett tossed the yellow pad on the coffee table and stretched. "That seems the most likely scenario. One of them may have had a grudge against the three, maybe for something that happened back then, a grudge he's held onto all these years. Whatever it was, maybe he decided to even the score."

I thought about the police report that said the scene indicated anger or revenge. Surely this was the explanation. "Okay. Where do we go from here?"

"I have a friend in the Veterans Administration in Denver. I'm going to ask him to find the whereabouts of the remaining Marines from that squad. They need to be warned that their lives may be in danger." He stretched again and yawned.

He reminded me of a little boy who had stayed up too late. "You look worn out. How's the shoulder?"

"Not too bad. Just a little stiff." He got up from the sofa. "I think I'll turn in."

I watched him walk toward his bedroom, a little unsteadily, it seemed. I cleaned up the kitchen and turned out the lights. As I started toward the guest room, Jack trotted after me. I bent down to pet him as he arched his back under my hand. "Have you forgiven me for locking you up?"

He said, "*Brrrt,*" and hopped up on the bed.

In the shower I stood under the hot water, letting it massage my neck and shoulders while I went over all that Garrett had told me about Sarge's Marine unit. It was hard to believe that after suspecting the police captain and Sarge's brother-in-law, the killer could have been someone from Sarge's past.

I was just coming out of the bathroom when my cell phone began ringing. It was nearly ten o'clock. Who could this be? I answered and heard an unfamiliar male voice say, "Kathryn?"

"Yes?"

"It's Dan. Dan Blanchard. From New York?"

I recalled my mother telling me that Dansby was in Vail and might be calling me.

"Dan. It's good to hear from you. I understand you're in Colorado, too."

"Yeah, I live in Vail now. My mother gave me your number. So I thought I'd get in touch. I hear you're some kind of writer?"

I felt a twinge of embarrassment. "Well, I was, but I just lost my job. Now I'm waiting tables at a café."

He chuckled. "That must be a shock to your parents."

"You could say that."

"I sympathize. I've been a serious disappointment to my father. He likes to remind me of the expensive education I'm wasting."

"Yale, wasn't it?"

I heard him sigh. "Yeah. Getting a degree in finance was never my idea."

"So what are you doing now?"

"I work in a ski shop in Vail during the summer, and I'm a ski instructor in the winter. Ever been to Vail?"

"No. I was supposed to write an article on the ski resorts for my magazine, but that was before I got fired."

"You should come for a visit. It's a beautiful area. Where did you say you were?"

"A little place called Trout Fork." I gave him the names of the roads that formed the intersection in front of the café.

"Oh, I know that place. In fact, I'm going through there tomorrow on my way to Denver. If you're going to be around, I'll stop in. That's if you don't mind."

"That would be nice. Mid-morning is the slowest time at the café. It's called Alma's, the only one in town. You can't miss it."

"Great. I'll see you around ten."

We hung up and I sat back, trying to remember what Dansby Blanchard looked like. I hadn't seen him since high school graduation. I could only recall him as being skinny, with thick glasses, protruding front teeth, and unruly, dirty blond hair. It was hard to imagine him as a ski instructor.

My phone alarm buzzed and vibrated next to my pillow the following morning. I turned over and flung back the blankets, causing Jack to grumble as I disturbed his sleep.

One of the things I had loved about being a travel writer was making my own hours. What a delightful break that was from working in the office at the magazine.

How I had hated having to rise at dawn in New York, stumble half-awake through my morning routine, and join the throngs in the subway all trying to get to their offices at the same time. Once on the road, I had lived for myself, made my own itinerary, and kept my own schedule. I didn't realize how ideal it was. Now here I was once again a slave to the alarm clock, only this time it was to wait on strangers in a tiny café in the middle of nowhere.

I stroked Jack's soft orange fur. He didn't know how lucky he was. No matter where I lived or worked, he seemed content just to be with me. Why couldn't I find that kind of easy contentment with whatever life sent my way? What was it that kept me always moving along, looking for something I couldn't identify?

Jack jumped off the bed and stood by the door, staring at me patiently with his amber eyes.

He darted toward the kitchen when I opened the door. I padded after him in my pajamas and filled his bowl with cat food, trying not to wake Garrett. I tiptoed to his bedroom door which was ajar and saw him on his back with his good arm behind his head. He was snoring again.

I dressed and left the cabin quietly. It was nearly six-thirty, the time I was supposed to be at the café. Normally, I would race along the winding road to Trout Fork, but this morning I decided to slow down to enjoy the sensations of riding a motorcycle. I left my helmet on its peg behind me, allowing the mountain air to caress my face and blow through my hair. The golden morning sunlight through the trees cast dappled shadows across the road. I crested the last hill before Trout Fork to see the cloudless crystal sky spread out before me like a vast ocean of blue.

I rode slowly down the hill and pulled up in front of the café just as Madam Gauzie and Gil emerged from their stores and headed down the wooden walk. Gil said, "Morning, Ryn" and kept walking toward Alma's, but Madam Gauzie stopped and stared at me, her hands on her hips. "Don't tell me you're riding around on that thing without your helmet," she admonished. "Tsk, tsk. What would Garrett say?"

I laughed. "He'd probably give me a ticket. The morning is just too beautiful. I couldn't resist. It's only this one time."

"I hope so. One accident is enough excitement for the summer, don't you think?"

I hadn't told her, or anyone else in Trout Fork, about the tampered brake line on Garrett's truck. "Yes, more than enough."

We went into the café together. Zoe was already there, making several pots of coffee. She smiled at me as I entered the kitchen through the swinging door to find Alma piling pancakes on a plate in front of Ashley.

Alma looked up. "Morning, Ryn. Pancakes?"

I slid onto the stool next to Ashley. "No, thanks. I'll just have some juice. Hi, Ash. How's school going?"

She stifled a yawn. "Okay. I just wish it didn't have to start so early. It takes me two classes before I'm really awake. How are things at Garrett's? Are you coming back soon? Sasha misses Jack."

"Pretty soon, I think. Garrett's healing fast." I was surprised at how much the thought of leaving Garrett's did not appeal to me. I was beginning to feel more at home there than was probably good for me.

CHAPTER 17

Zoe and I easily handled the limited breakfast crowd that morning. As I watched her, I realized she had an excellent work ethic and a real knack for dealing with the public. She joked with the local fishermen who like to flirt with her, and she handled the elderly tourists with a great deal of grace and patience. I frequently heard her asking Alma questions about food preparation. If she was serious about someday owning her own restaurant, she couldn't find a better mentor than Alma.

At mid-morning, she came to me. "There's a hottie on the patio asking for you."

I wonder who that is. It can't be Dansby Blanchard, I thought. *He's anything but a hottie.* "A hottie?"

She headed toward the kitchen and said over her shoulder, "Totally. If you don't want him, send him my way."

My curiosity propelled me out the door to the patio where I stopped and looked around. There were three motorcyclists, an older couple, two fishermen, and a solitary young man sitting alone. *That must be Mr. Hottie,* I thought as I approached his table.

He stood quickly when he saw me. "Ryn! Good to see you."

I stared at him, dumbfounded. Was this the skinny, acne-plagued teenager I remembered from New York? He was indeed a hottie—tall, well-built, and tanned with long light brown locks, piercing light blue eyes, and a radiant smile that lit up his face.

"Dan?" I managed to stammer.

He smiled and gave me a friendly hug then ushered me into a chair at his table, which was a good thing because my knees had suddenly gone weak. "I—I didn't recognize you. It's been a long time."

He laughed an easy, melodic laugh. "I guess I do look different. Amazing what contact lenses and a good orthodontist can do. You look just the same, though. You always were cute."

A slight warmth crept up my neck, making me suddenly feel fifteen again.

Zoe came out to deliver an order to the fishermen. As she passed our table, her eyebrows went up, and she grinned at me.

"So," Dan said, "how long have you been in Colorado?"

"Just a few months. I wrote an article about this area for the magazine. Then I traveled around a little and wrote a few more articles. That was before I got fired."

"Lousy spelling?" he said with a grin.

"No. My editor told me to move on from Trout Fork, but I said I couldn't leave just now. I have a friend who's in jail for a crime he didn't commit, and I want to stay here and try to help clear him. He said that wouldn't work for him. Then he fired me."

"Sorry to hear that. So what's the plan going forward? Waitressing?"

"I hope not. Right now I guess I'm between jobs. How about you? How did you wind up in Vail?"

He took a sip of his coffee and smiled, his perfect white teeth gleaming. "Totally by accident. I had a two-week vacation from the firm, so I decided to just take off. I've always wanted to see Colorado. I did a little skiing in the Poconos during college, but when I saw the Rocky Mountains, I was hooked. I pulled into Vail one day, looked around, and said to myself, *Goodbye, New York.* That was three years ago. I've been here ever since. Best decision I ever made."

"Your parents must miss you."

He shrugged. "I've been back a couple of times to visit. I think my mother is okay with me chucking Wall Street to become a ski bum, as she puts it. My father is another story. I doubt he'll ever accept it. Can't blame him, though. He did put me through Yale with the stipulation that I would join the firm."

As he talked I studied his eyes and expression. He was so different from Garrett—his personality free and breezy where Garrett's was serious and intense. I couldn't help comparing the two men.

"I guess it takes a while to figure out where we belong in life," he continued. "Just because we major in something in college doesn't mean we're stuck in that field forever, does it?"

"I guess not. Although my major was journalism, and it's the only thing I've ever done. I love writing. I just couldn't stand working in an office."

"Another refugee from the rat race, eh? Ever think about changing jobs?"

"Writing is all I've ever known. I don't know what else I could do."

"There are all kinds of job openings in Vail. You should spend some time there. It's paradise."

"I can't ski. I tried it once, but I fell down a lot. It was cold and wet and totally unappealing."

"There's plenty of other things to do in a ski resort. I think you'd be great in hospitality. You know, hotel and resort management? You have the perfect look, and you're personable, too. You'd have no trouble finding a job. Good managers make six figures in a place like Vail."

I had to admit, it sounded more appealing than serving burgers and chili. Then there was the fact that Vail was only a couple of hours away, far enough to put some distance between me and Garrett while I decided if we had a future together. "I'll think about it."

"So tell me," he said. "Have you ever been married?"

My hesitation must have given him the impression I was offended by his question.

When I didn't answer, he said, "I'm sorry. I didn't mean to pry."

His eyes and smile put me at ease. "Marriage is a very scary thing to me. I mean look at all the awful marriages we see. They're everywhere."

"Yeah. If your parents were half as miserable as mine, well…"

I sighed. "I guess I can't blame mine after what they went through with my little brother. That couldn't have been easy."

"I remember my parents talking about that. He drowned, didn't he?" He seemed genuinely sorry.

I nodded. "How about you? Anyone special in your life?"

He smiled. "As a matter of fact, there is a girl. We met in Vail. Her name is Kira and she's…well, just about perfect."

"That's great, Dan. I wish you the best."

"What about you? Is there a man in your life? Or are you keeping your options open?"

Before I could answer, I heard Zoe's voice from inside the café. "She's on the patio, Garrett."

Garrett appeared in the doorway and scanned the patio, his eyes quickly finding our table. I could tell from his expression that he wasn't pleased to find me sitting with a handsome young man.

I waved to him, doing my best not to look like I was trying to hide something. He approached the table, giving Dan his skeptical detective look. I introduced them and asked Garrett to have a seat.

"Detective, huh?" Dan said. "That must be interesting."

"Yeah," Garrett said shortly, still watching the two of us analytically.

Dan must have felt the tension. After a few minutes of pleasantries, he stood and picked up his check from the table. "I'll pay for this inside. Good to see you again, Ryn. Give me a call if you decide to visit Vail. I'll show you around. Nice to meet you, Garrett." He flashed that brilliant smile of his and strolled toward the door.

Garrett's eyes followed him. "How do you know him?"

"He's a childhood friend from New York. He lives in Vail now."

"What's he doing in Trout Fork?"

"My mother knows his mother, so she gave her my phone number to give to Dansby."

He snorted. "Dansby? What kind of name is that?"

I was beginning to be just a little irritated with him. "It's a family name."

"Oh, so that means he's rich."

"His family is rich, but he left them and the whole New York society scene behind."

His lip turned up just enough to express his disdain. "Then I guess you two have a lot in common."

I was finding Garrett's jealousy irritating. I changed the subject. "How did you get here?"

"They brought my truck back this morning. They had to put a new door and fender on it, but it runs good as new."

"Can you drive with your shoulder?"

He stretched his left arm in front of him and rubbed his shoulder. "It's fine. Just a little stiff. I should be able to go back to work Monday."

I wanted to tell him not to rush it, but I knew now that he was feeling better, he'd be getting antsy at home.

Zoe came out of the dining room with an order for another table. "That fat cop is here again. He's looking for Garrett. I told him you're out here. You want to order something, Garrett?"

"Just coffee, thanks."

Detective Sloan's bulk appeared in the doorway. He saw us, nodded, and waddled toward the table. He dropped into Dan's vacant chair with a grunt, wiping his sweaty face with a dingy handkerchief. His wrinkled, wilted shirt was sweaty, his ancient tie stained with what looked like ketchup. "Whew. Hot, ain't it?"

Garrett leaned forward. "What brings you to Trout Fork?"

"Looking for you. I went to your place first. Figured you'd be out here. Got some news for you."

Zoe brought Garrett's coffee and set it on the table. I felt guilty sitting there when I was supposed to be working, but I was desperate to hear anything that might pertain to Sarge's death. "Is it busy in there, Zoe?"

"Nope. Take your time." She smiled pleasantly. How much more relaxed and at peace she appeared since Derek had left.

"Get me a chocolate milk shake to go, will you, honey?" Sloan said to her.

Garrett wrinkled his brow at him. "You need to lay off the calories, Sloan. Or you'll never make it to retirement."

Sloan grunted again. "You sound like my wife."

"So what's the news?" Garrett asked.

"We arrested Vince Bodmin. Dragged him right out of his newspaper office this morning. You should have heard him squeal about his First Amendment rights and all that crap."

Garrett sipped his coffee. "What's the charge?"

"Racketeering. That restaurant owner got fed up with paying for protection. He came to the police chief's office and ratted him out."

"You mean Borelli?"

"Yeah, that's him. He gave the chief the names of other business owners he knows that have been paying for protection, too."

"What about Captain Williams?"

"He wasn't arrested. Yet. The chief told me to keep an eye on him. Make sure he doesn't leave town before the arrest warrant is issued for him. But he's in it up to his neck."

"I knew it," Garrett muttered.

"At first Bodmin tried to tell us he was working alone. Then we told him we were charging him with killing the busboy, and he folded like a cheap suit. Spilled his guts big time. He said he had nothing to do with that, that it was Williams who killed the kid. Then Williams told him that old guy, Sarge, saw him burying the kid, so he had to get rid of him before he talked. Williams knew where Sarge was camped and followed him back to the campsite."

I exhaled slowly. "So it was Williams who killed Sarge."

"Not according to Bodmin. Williams told him that when he got there, Sarge was already dead and someone else was there burning the old guy's stuff in the fire. Williams didn't know who the guy was and didn't care. He just split."

"What about Hank?" I asked.

Sloan shrugged. "Dunno. Maybe Williams thought he was dead, too."

How ironic. Hank's one major shortcoming, his excessive drinking, must have saved his life that night. He was passed out and no threat to the killer, whoever he was.

"What happens now?"

Sloan pulled out his handkerchief to wipe his forehead again. "Williams should be in custody this afternoon. We'll have no trouble linking them both to the drugs, and some other things, too. Extortion, money-laundering, you name it, they were into it. They have a couple of goons working for them who roughed up anyone who got out of line. One of them probably cut the brake line on your truck. Once you started asking questions at the restaurant, they knew you were getting too close."

Garrett shook his head. "A police captain. It makes me sick."

"At least we got them." Sloan hauled his bulk off the chair. "I'd better get back. I want to be there when the boys from the police chief's office come for Williams. I want to see the look on his smug face. I always hated that arrogant SOB."

Zoe brought the milk shake. He took it and handed her some money. "Keep the change, honey." He looked at Garrett sideways. "You coming back to work or what?"

"I'll be there Monday. We still have a murder to solve."

I watched Sloan cross the patio and amble toward the parking lot. It was a relief to know Williams and Bodmin had been caught, but that wouldn't help Hank. Until we could find Sarge's killer, Hank would remain in jail, the number one suspect. I watched Garrett gaze off into space. "Do you think Captain Williams is telling the truth? That he didn't kill Sarge?"

"I do. It's the part about the burning of Sarge's stuff that convinces me. Williams had no reason to do that."

"Sarge must have gone back to the camp to write to Gil about that army captain. The killer must have been waiting for him."

"Seems so."

"And we still have no idea who it was."

"I'm waiting to hear from my buddy at the VA. That Marine unit from Vietnam is the key. One of the guys in that unit, or someone they knew, is responsible. I'm certain of it."

I found it hard to believe something that happened more than forty years ago could have resulted in three murders. But if there was one thing I'd learned as a journalist, it's that human behavior can't always be explained rationally.

Garrett finished his coffee and put some money on the table.

"Are you going home?"

"Not yet. I want to check in at the station. Some of the younger guys might be feeling a little down. Maybe I can help."

I realized how deeply Garrett's love for law enforcement went and how this scandal was affecting him.

He got up to leave. "You coming back to my place after work tonight?"

"I may want to stay for the poker game. I haven't talked to Ashley in a while. I'd like to see how she's doing in school."

He gazed down at me with his one good eye. "Did you invite Pansby to join the game?"

I couldn't help being irritated with his attitude. "It's Dansby, and no, I didn't invite him. He did invite me to visit him in Vail, though. He said I could probably find a good job there."

"Well, you'll just have to go and do that. Can't miss an opportunity to take off again."

He must have known from my expression that he had hit the sore spot between us and walked away before I could respond. I sat there for a while thinking about Dan and all the fun we'd had growing up. Maybe after this business with Hank was straightened out, I'd take him up on his offer to visit Vail and scope out the employment possibilities. I couldn't see myself working in the café much longer. As much as I loved the people in Trout Fork, I knew that without a challenging and fulfilling job, I'd be miserable.

We closed the café a little earlier that night. Business was slow and Alma said we all needed a break anyway. Robert was down for the weekend again. He came in from the cabin with his arm around Ashley. They were chatting about school. Apparently, he had given up the idea of Alma selling the café and moving to Denver.

Madam Gauzie came in with her usual trays of hors d'oeuvres which she plunked down on the card table. She was even more outlandishly dressed than usual this evening.

She had taken to wearing neon colors lately and sported a flowing, lime green caftan with a bright yellow scarf holding back her unruly gray hair. Pink running shoes completed the ensemble. As bizarre as her outfit was, no one seemed to notice. I admired her ability to cast aside convention and dress to suit herself.

Gil sat quietly at the card table. He picked up the deck of cards and began shuffling absent-mindedly. I sat next to him and began to load some hors d'oeuvres onto a small plate. "Can I fill a plate for you, Gil?

"Not really hungry, thanks."

"How are things at the bait shop?"

"Same as usual."

"Fishing pretty good this year?"

"Yeah." He kept shuffling the cards. Clearly something was eating at him. He was usually more talkative, especially about fishing. He stopped shuffling and looked at me. "How's Hank doing? Does Garrett know?"

"Garrett hasn't been to the station since the accident. He went in this afternoon, though. I'll ask him how Hank is getting along."

He nodded. "Damn shame, him being locked up when he's innocent. And there's guilty men going free all the time." He shook his head. "Something's wrong with this system."

"No system's perfect. But they get the criminals more often than not. Did you hear about the police captain at Garrett's precinct?"

Gil looked up from his cards. "No. What about him?"

I told him the whole sordid story about Captain Williams. He seemed genuinely upset. "What's happening to this country? You can't trust anyone these days. If the cops are corrupt…"

"It's not all the cops. Garrett is a straight arrow. And there's those three buddies of yours. And that Detective Sloan. They're all good guys."

"Yeah, but the few bad apples give all of them a bad rap."

I knew that was true, especially when the bad ones were at the top. How distressing it must have been for a law-and-order guy like Gil. "Have you heard from your son?" He didn't answer, and I wondered if I was treading on his personal space.

After a moment he sighed. "Yeah. The case to dismiss the charges against him is going forward. His lawyer says he should be out by Christmas." He turned to me, his eyes full of pain and confusion. "He wants to come here. I don't know what to tell him. He's my son, but how can I have him here knowing what he did to that cop and his family..."

His voice trailed off. I laid my hand on his arm, unable to offer any advice.

Alma and Robert came to the table together and pulled out the chairs. Ashley sat next to her father at the table, although she never played poker. Alma was beaming, her face alive with the joy of having her family together again. Even with their unresolved issues, the three of them seemed delighted to be together.

Gil dealt the first hand while Madam Gauzie chattered away in the background, flitting here and there with her homemade goodies.

She layered my plate with more hors d'oeuvres and said, "Ryn, I guess you knew Sarge's sister and brother-in-law have left Trout Fork. Good riddance, I say. That woman was such a pruneface. I swear she could curdle milk by just looking at the cow."

We all laughed. Even Gil cracked a smile.

"Now Madam G," Alma said with a small smile. "That's no way to talk about Sarge's sister."

"No disrespect meant to Sarge, I'm sure. But I mean seriously? How do people like that stand their own company? I sure feel sorry for that husband of hers."

Ashley took a piece of chocolate from the plate and

said to me, "Speaking of Sarge, are the police any closer to finding his killer?"

"They've eliminated several possibilities. Garrett is looking into Sarge's background in the Marines. There have been two other similar murders of men in his squad."

She furrowed her brow. "Wow. That's weird, huh?"

"Yeah." I wasn't sure how many details I should relate to them. I decided to wait until Garrett had something definite regarding the Marine unit. He should know something fairly soon. Hopefully, whatever he found out from his friend in the Veterans Administration would lead to an arrest and Hank's homecoming.

CHAPTER 18

I went back to Garrett's that night to find him asleep with Jack lying at the foot of his bed. Garrett looked so adorable sleeping that I forgave him for his snarky remarks about Dan. I had to admit to myself that I was actually a bit flattered by his jealousy.

In the kitchen I noticed that Garrett had fixed dinner for himself and fed Jack, whose cat food and water bowls were full. If he was able to do for himself now, there was really no reason for me to stay on at the cabin. I should pack up and go back to Alma's, but I was beginning to feel at home here and hated to leave. At the same time, that feeling made me uncomfortable.

I went to my room, sat on the bed, and opened my laptop. I pulled up my favorite job search sites and perused the entries. Nothing. Was it disappointment I felt? Or relief?

Jack trotted in and stood next to the bed staring at me. I patted the mattress by my side. "C'mon, Jack. Up here." He hopped up and rubbed on my hand as I stroked his silky orange fur. "What do you think? Should we go back Alma's or stay here a few more days?"

He gazed at me with his wide inquisitive eyes. "*Brrrt?*"

"You're no help." I headed for the shower.

ℰↄℰↄ

Garrett was still asleep when I left the cabin early the next morning, desperate for a cup of coffee. Pulling into Trout Fork, I was grateful to see no other cars in the lot beside those of the residents. At least I'd have time for breakfast before the café opened.

I parked the bike and went in the back door of the café to find Alma humming to herself as she turned over the pancakes on the grill. She smiled as I came in. "Sit down, Ryn, and have your breakfast. Bacon?"

"Yes, please. I'm starving."

She plunked a plate of pancakes and bacon in front of me, along with butter and syrup and coffee. *No hope for getting into those jeans now,* I thought.

Alma slid onto the stool beside me. She sipped her coffee and watched me eat.

I dug into the pancakes and broke one of my mother's cardinal rules—talking with my mouth full. "How are things going with you and Robert?"

"You know, I think there may be hope for that man."

"How so?"

"Well, he's given up the idea of us moving back to Denver. And he's actually talking to me like I'm an equal. He's offering advice on legal matters regarding the stores and the cabins, things like avoiding paying more in taxes than I should and making the most of my investment."

"Is he still talking about remarrying?"

She blushed slightly, her normally ruddy cheeks turning even redder. "Yes. I think it might work out this time. Ashley is delighted with the new Robert. He's become more of a friend to her, instead of the tyrant he's been lately."

I laid my hand on her arm. "I'm delighted for you both."

Zoe came in looking perky and happy. "Good morning," she beamed. "Anything I can help you with, Alma?"

"Nothing special, dear. Have some pancakes?"

Zoe headed for the door to the dining room. "No, thanks. I'll just get started out here." She pushed through the swinging door.

We watched her leave. "I don't know what's gotten into that girl," Alma said. "It's like she's become a new person."

I suspected her new attitude had plenty to do with getting away from Derek and the drugs, but Alma didn't need to know that. "I think she's found a new direction in life. Did she tell you she's talking about going into the restaurant business?"

Alma seemed surprised. "No, she didn't. So that explains it. She's been looking over my shoulder and asking a lot of questions lately. Well, good for her. Now that I know that, I'll do what I can to help her."

"Better watch out or someday this place will be called Zoe's Café," I teased.

About mid-morning, Garrett came in and sat at one of the patio tables. He gestured to me to join him and, after checking with Zoe, who was happy to take care of the few customers in the place, I sat with him. His eyes were bright and his complexion had a healthy glow.

"You're looking much better. Even the swelling around your eye has gone down."

"I feel great. What a beautiful day."

We sat in silence taking in the sights and sounds of the Colorado morning. Magpies flew from treetop to treetop above while a gray squirrel scampered along the patio railing, stopping to investigate the flowers cascading from Alma's planters. A warm breeze wafted off the creek across the street, ruffling the umbrellas.

"Garrett, since you're doing so well, I think it's time for me to move back in with Alma."

His face darkened. "There's no rush. You're welcome to stay as long as you like. I'm enjoying the company."

"And I've enjoyed being there. But you don't need me anymore. You're going back to work Monday, so Jack and I will move back here then."

"If you must."

"I think it's time."

He pulled his little black notebook from his pocket. "I thought you'd like to know what I found out from my buddy at the VA." He turned the pages slowly. "He looked up the ten Marines from Sarge's squad. We know the three that are dead—Sarge, the North Carolina doctor, and the bookie from Las Vegas."

"Right. That leaves seven."

"Five, actually. Two of them died years ago, both from cancer."

"Could he trace the other five?"

"Yeah. It's all right there in the government database. There's nothing remarkable about any of them. I thought we'd hit a dead end until he told me about their assignments in Saigon at the end of the war. I told you that squad was assigned to protect the US embassy. Well, the three murdered men were part of a four-man helicopter crew aboard one of the Chinooks."

"Chinooks?"

"The helicopters they were using to evacuate the Americans and South Vietnamese from the embassy grounds. They ferried them out to the ships waiting in the South China Sea. I remember reading about that. Thousands of desperate Vietnamese crowded into the embassy compound trying to escape the North Vietnamese army as it was closing in on Saigon. Those people knew the NVA would kill anyone even suspected of cooperating with the Americans. The US helicopters got thousands of them out, fifty or sixty at a time, but there was a limit. When the copters stopped flying, thousands more were left to face the approaching Communists. There was panic and chaos that last day."

"Good Lord. I had no idea." The picture on Madam Gauzie's table suddenly came to mind. "You know what? Madam Gauzie's husband was involved in that evacuation. He was in the navy, stationed on one of the ships where those helicopters were landing. He and his shipmates took care of a whole bunch of Vietnamese."

Garrett nodded. "That sounds about right. But here's the thing. Remember my buddy told me Sarge and the other two dead men were part of a four-man helicopter crew? Well, the fourth Marine is still alive. He lives in Littleton."

My mind began spinning. Three of the four men in one helicopter crew had been murdered. Surely the fourth was in danger, and he lived in South Denver, just an hour north of Trout Fork. "My God, Garrett, that means—"

"Right. That man is in danger. We need to warn him."

"Do you know how to contact him?"

"I already have. My buddy knows him personally. He gave me his number, and I spoke with him this morning. I asked if I could come up to see him tomorrow. He was a little reluctant at first. Said he wants to forget everything that happened in 'that hell-hole,' as he put it. But he agreed to see me around eleven." He gave me a little sideways glance. "I don't suppose you want to—"

"Of *course* I want to come with you," I nearly shouted. "Do you know what this means? Whoever killed Sarge may still be in the area, just waiting for a chance to kill the fourth man."

"Something must have happened with that crew that made them a target for whoever is doing this."

"Maybe they were into something illegal?"

Garrett shook his head. "According to the VA records, these were stand-up guys. Decorated Marines with good conduct medals and all sorts of commendations."

"Well, one of them became a bookie. He couldn't have been all that stand-up. Maybe the four were into gambling or drugs or something illegal over there."

Garrett watched one of the magpies strut across the patio. "You know," he said slowly. "We need to talk to Hank again. He was close to Sarge. Maybe he can recall anything Sarge may have said about that time in Saigon."

"Good idea. I can bring him some more of Alma's chili."

"Meet me at the station after work. Let's make it around eight. That way Williams will be gone. I don't want him involved in this."

"You mean he's still around? I thought he was going to be arrested."

"Sloan said it will be Monday. He's licking his chops."

Garrett left, and I sat at the patio table enjoying the summer breeze. I was thinking about Sarge and his helicopter crew, wondering what had happened so long ago that could have resulted in violent deaths of three of them.

My cell phone vibrated in my pocket. I pulled it out and stared at the display. It was a local number. Although I didn't recognize it, I decided to answer anyway.

An unfamiliar deep male voice said, "Miss Lowell?"

"Yes?"

"This is Harrison Cosgrove."

That name sounded familiar, but I couldn't quite place where I had heard or read it. "Yes?"

"I'm the owner and publisher of the *Pineland Park Star.*"

Now I remembered. I had read that name on the masthead of the *Star*. I couldn't fathom why he'd be calling me. "Oh yes, Mr. Cosgrove. What can I do for you?"

I heard him chuckle. "Well, I was hoping we could do something for each other."

"Oh?"

"I suppose you know I recently lost my editor, Vince Bodmin."

You mean that drug-dealing slimeball who's on his way to prison? "Yes. I did know that."

"Well, I'm looking to fill his position. Quickly. And I'm in a bit of a bind." I didn't respond, so he continued. "I understand you have a journalism degree from Columbia, and you're an experienced writer and editor. I was hoping I could interest you in applying for the job."

I was speechless. Was this really happening?

"Miss Lowell. Are you still there?"

I cleared my throat. "Yes, I'm here. I'm flattered by the offer, Mr. Cosgrove…"

"Call me Harry."

"Harry, but I'm not really qualified to—"

"You were managing editor of the *Spectator*, weren't you? The Columbia student newspaper?

How the heck does he know that? "Well, yes, in my senior year, but—"

"Those Ivy League university papers are bigger than most of the small town papers in America. Did you know that?"

"I didn't, actually."

"I looked it up. The Columbia *Spectator* has a staff of over a dozen. Compare that to the little staff of the *Star.*"

I remembered the two harried-looking girls in the *Star*'s newsroom.

"You *are* out of a job, are you not?"

"Well, yes, but—"

"Then it can't hurt to at least apply for the editor position, can it?" Clearly this was a man used to getting his own way, a type-A, take-charge kind of guy. "I'll tell you what. Come into the office on Monday, and we can talk about it. About nine? What do you say?"

"I can do that."

"Wonderful. I look forward to seeing you."

"One question before you go. How did you hear about me? How do you know so much about me?"

He chuckled again. "It was Detective Easterbrook who put me onto your trail."

I might have known. Anything to keep me in the area. "Oh? He never mentioned you."

"Garrett and I go way back. From our days in Denver. He was on the force up there, and I covered the police beat for the *Denver Post*. Nice guy, Garrett. He speaks very highly of you. Well, goodbye, Miss Lowell. I'll see you Monday."

I disconnected and sat staring at the phone. A newspaper editor? Me? I thought back to my time at Columbia. I had enjoyed working on the paper, assigning stories to the writers, helping them craft articles, correcting their grammar, coaching them as they developed their writing. But that was college. This would be the real thing. I wasn't sure it was what I wanted. But then again, like the man said, I was out of a job. And I had to admit the newspaper business was more appealing than waitressing. Besides, with winter coming on, there wouldn't be enough business in the café to justify Alma having two waitresses. Taking the job at the paper would give me a regular salary, enabling me to afford a place of my own.

A couple of cyclists came onto the patio, the cleats on their bike shoes tapping on the concrete floor and jolting me out of my reverie. I took their order and went to the kitchen to hang the ticket on the wheel.

Alma peered at it. "Garrett's looking better, isn't he?"

"Definitely. He feels better, too."

"That's wonderful."

"We're going to see Hank tonight. Do you have any more chili I can bring him? You know how he loves your chili."

"There's some in the freezer that I've been saving for him. I'll thaw it so it will be ready tonight. Tsk, tsk. Poor Hank. Will he ever get out of that awful jail?"

"As a matter of fact, we may be closing in on something that will help. Garrett found out some things about Sarge's time in Vietnam that might have something to do with his death."

"Really? Well, that's encouraging."

"That reminds me. I need to take tomorrow off, if you can spare me. Garrett and I are going to Littleton to interview one of Sarge's Marine buddies."

"Sure, honey. Ashley can cover for you. And when you come back, have Garrett join us for dinner at Madam G's. She's having us all over again tomorrow night."

"I'll tell him. Thanks."

芝芝芝

I met Garrett at the police station that evening, and after heating the chili in the microwave, we descended the familiar staircase to the cells in the basement. The dank smell was just as I remembered it.

We found Hank stretched out on his bunk, his arms behind his head, staring at the ceiling. He got up beaming when we approached. "Ryn. I'm glad to see you."

"Hi, Hank. How are you doing?"

"Much better, thanks, but I'd rather be in Trout Fork. What's that I smell?"

I handed him the chili. "Alma sent more of your favorite."

"God bless that woman."

He sat on the bunk and dug into the chili. "Mmmm. Alma's the best. How is she doing?"

"She's fine."

"How about Ashley? Does she like school?"

I was struck by the bonds the residents of Trout Fork had forged over the years. Here was Hank in jail and about to be tried for murder, yet he was still interested in the everyday lives of his friends.

"She's enjoying school a lot this year. She has some really hard classes, but she's doing well."

He nodded as he chewed. "Tell them I miss them. Gil, too, and Madam G." We stood quietly until he finished. He wiped the inside of the bowl with his finger and sucked the last morsel off it. He sighed and put the empty bowl aside.

Garrett moved closer to the bars. "Hank, I was hoping you might be able to remember more about Sarge and the things he talked about."

Hank shook his head sadly. "I told you. I was out of it that night."

"How about other times when Sarge talked to you about his past. Specifically about his time in Vietnam. Did he ever mention the other Marines in his squad?"

Hank thought for a moment. "You know, it's funny.

He was a Marine through and through. He loved the Corps and was very proud of it. He had some great stories about his buddies and the pranks they pulled while they were guarding the embassy in Saigon. Two years they were there after the troops were pulled out in seventy-three. But he never liked to talk about the evacuation at the end."

"Why? Do you know?"

"All I know is there was something that happened during those last days that shook him up. He never said what it was. I didn't like to pry, but whatever it was, it ate at him until the day he died. He drank a lot and then smoked pot when it became legal. If you ask me, he was trying to forget."

"Did he ever mention any of his buddies by name?" Garrett said. "Or anything about them after they left the Corps?"

"Nope. I don't think he ever contacted any of them either. He just wanted to forget it all, I guess."

We chatted with him for a while about the folks in Trout Fork. Hank mentioned that his lawyer seemed hopeful that if they went to trial, he would be acquitted for lack of evidence. I could tell from Garrett's expression that he wasn't as confident. As we left the station, he said, "Hank's lawyer is blowing smoke. Hank is looking at life in prison."

"Oh, Garrett. We just have to find the real killer and get Hank out of here." I stopped and grabbed his arm. "Wait a minute. How do we know that fourth Marine isn't the killer? Maybe he had something against the other three for whatever happened in Vietnam, whatever it was Sarge didn't want to talk about."

"I thought of that. But that man is totally blind. He lost his sight years ago. He couldn't possibly have committed those murders. No, he's definitely in danger of being the fourth victim."

CHAPTER 19

I woke abruptly Sunday morning and looked at the clock. Eight-thirty. *Oh, no. I'm late for work. Why hasn't Alma called?* In a panic, I threw off the blankets, uncovering Jack in his usual position by my side. He looked me through one sleepy eye as though I had lost my mind. It was then I remembered it was Sunday, and Alma had given me the day off.

I could hear Garrett puttering in the kitchen talking to himself as he made coffee. I pulled a sweatshirt over my pajamas and went to the kitchen. He was standing at the sink gazing out the window, so I approached quietly, hoping to surprise him. Of course he heard me coming and turned his head just as I came up behind him to put my arms around his waist.

He pulled me close against him. "Good morning, sleepy-head. I was beginning to wonder if you were still alive in there."

I snuggled my face on his back and breathed in the smell of him—strong, masculine and comforting. "I'm alive. Very much so."

He turned around and wrapped me in a tender embrace. Then he gave me a long, lingering kiss. I felt as though I wanted to wake to this every morning for the rest of my life. It also occurred to me that I must have a serious case of morning breath. But he didn't seem to mind.

We stood like that for a few minutes. Then Jack came into the kitchen and began rubbing on our legs, yowling for his breakfast in that insistent way he had.

"I'll feed the beast," Garrett said. "You get dressed. We have to be in Littleton at eleven."

I headed for the shower, the feeling of Garrett's lips still tingling on mine. By the time I changed and came back to the kitchen, Garrett was pouring coffee into a travel mug. He handed it to me and propelled me to the door. "Do you want a donut to go with this? There's one left."

I resisted the temptation to make a crack about cops and donuts. "No, just the coffee."

We got into his pickup and headed north on the county road. As we sailed through Trout Fork, I saw Robert's silver Mercedes in the parking lot. "Robert is here again," I said. "Did I tell you that Alma's thinking of remarrying him?"

"Mmm," Garrett said with a nod. "I hope it works out for them this time."

"So do I, if only for Ashley's sake. She needs a strong male influence in her life at her age."

Garrett gazed over at me, his one good one eyebrow raised. "What about you? Did you have a strong male influence in your life?"

I was surprised at the question. Garrett was usually reluctant to ask me personal questions about my past. "I had male influences, but I don't know how strong they were. My father and I were close when I was younger, but after my little brother died he sort of shut down emotionally. He became a workaholic, and my older brother followed suit."

"Lots of people bury their grief in work. Maybe that's the only way your father could cope."

"The only other strong male in my life was my journalism professor, Dr. Stangel. Some of the students called him 'Dr. Strangle' because he was such a tough cookie. He was the adviser for the student newspaper and kind of took me under his wing." I turned to him. "That reminds me. I got a call from your friend Cosgrove."

"Oh?"

I could see he was doing his best to look innocent. "Yeah. Seems he's heard a lot about me from a mutual acquaintance."

He grinned at me. "Who could that be?"

"I wonder. He knew all about my journalism background, my work on the *Spectator* at Columbia. He offered me Bodmin's old job at the *Star*."

He didn't seem the least bit surprised. "Are you going to take it?"

"I haven't decided. I'm going to see him tomorrow."

A small smile played on his lips, but I think he knew better than to pressure me. "Harry's a good guy. You'll like working for him. That is, I mean, if you…"

I couldn't help laughing at him. "Right."

The trip to Littleton took a bit more than an hour, and we arrived at a small, older house on the outskirts of town. The yard had a neglected, unkempt look, the grass unmowed, and the paint peeling off the siding.

Garrett stopped the truck on the street and turned to me. "I do the talking. You listen. Deal?"

I gave him a mock salute. "Aye, Captain. What's his name?"

"Arnold Rimsky."

We picked our way among the broken concrete of the weed-infested sidewalk to the house. Garrett opened the battered screen door and knocked. We heard slow, shuffling steps coming from inside. Then a hand tentatively opened the door slightly.

"Mr. Rimsky, I'm Detective Easterbrook," Garrett said. "We spoke on the phone yesterday?"

The door opened wider, revealing an elderly man with thinning gray hair and a pale wrinkled face. He wore dark glasses and carried a red-tipped cane. "Oh, yes. Come in." He shuffled backward a few steps and led the way into the room, swinging his cane before him. He settled into an armchair, its flowered upholstery faded to a dingy gray.

He motioned toward a couch with his cane. "Have a seat. Sorry I can't offer you anything. I get my food from Meals on Wheels, and they don't deliver on Sundays."

I felt terribly sorry for this wreck of a man, a shadow of the virile Marine he must have once been.

"Quite all right, Mr. Rimsky."

His face was turned up as though looking at the ceiling, a common pose for the sightless. "What can I do for you?"

"I was hoping you could provide some information about your Marine squad," Garrett said. "The one that guarded the embassy in Saigon at the end of the war. Do you remember those days?"

He grunted. "I may have lost my sight, Detective, but there's nothing wrong with my memory. What do you want to know?"

"I'm investigating the death of one of your squad mates, Richard Horner."

"Horner's dead?"

"Yes. He was murdered. We're trying to find his killer, and we believe it may have something to do with the last days of the evacuation of the embassy in Saigon."

"My God," the man whispered. "Somebody killed him?"

"Yes. I'm sorry." Garrett gave the man a few moments. "What do you recall about those days, specifically the helicopter you and the other three Marines manned?"

He sighed and ran his hand across his stubbly chin. "It was a hell of a time, I can tell you that. We must have made thirty trips between the embassy compound and the ships. Night and day those birds flew, stopping only long enough to fuel up. Those pilots, they were the heroes. I don't know how they did it."

"I'm interested in the four-man crew on your Chinook. What was your job?"

"We loaded the Americans from the embassy, their families, and some of the locals—the Vietnamese who worked at the embassy and their families—onto the birds and shuttled them to the ships waiting in the South China Sea. Then they sailed to Manila, and the American personnel were reassigned to various parts of the world. The Vietnamese stayed in the camps there for a while then many were brought to the US. They were the lucky ones. Not everyone got out."

"What happened to the ones who couldn't get out?"

"They stayed in Vietnam, I guess. Poor bastards. I remember the final trip we made. We could see the last eleven Marines on the roof waiting for the last bird to pick them up. Down below the locals were breaking down the gates and storming the building, trying to force their way to the roof. The Marines on the roof had to use tear gas to keep them out of the stairwells. God, it was chaos." He ran his hand across his forehead. "Complete chaos."

My heart went out to this man who was still haunted by forty-year old memories of that horrific time.

Garrett waited a moment then said, "Does crushed fingers mean anything at all to you?"

The man was silent, but his face was stricken. Suddenly a sob caught in his throat. "How did you know about that?"

Garrett leaned toward him. "About what?"

"About what we had to do."

"What? What did you have to do?"

His voice became strained and desperate. "They gave us no choice, you know. If we hadn't done it, they would have overwhelmed the copter. As it was, we loaded more than the maximum capacity. Those birds were supposed to carry fifty people, but we loaded sixty, sixty-five. But still more of them hung onto the ramp when we tried to raise it. You know, those Chinooks have the loading ramp in the rear. They hung onto that ramp even as we were trying to take off. We had to make them let go. So we used our rifle butts on their fingers."

"Did you all do that? You and Horner and the others?"

The old man nodded, tears beginning to stream from his sightless eyes. "They gave us no choice. We had to. It made me sick. But if we took off with them hanging onto the ramp, they would have fallen to their deaths."

"I understand."

The man wiped his nose with a grimy handkerchief. "Do you? Ever been in a war, Detective?"

"No, but I can imagine—"

"I don't think you can. Not having to do what we did then. I remember turning around after we pulled up the ramp and seeing their faces, the ones on the copter. The horror of what we had just done to their countrymen, the shock in some of their eyes, the anger. I'll never forget those faces. Never. There was this one kid who got separated from his family. We pulled him on board, but then the rest of his family got shoved aside for an American diplomat from the embassy and his family. By the time they got on board, we were overloaded and had to pull up the ramp. That kid got hysterical, pointing at his family and screaming at us in Vietnamese. But there was nothing we could do."

"What happened to that kid? Any idea?"

"Dunno. He was unloaded onto one of the ships with the rest. I guess he wound up in the Philippines. There was so much sadness. I can't even think about it anymore."

Garrett gave him a few moments to compose himself. "Is there anything you can tell me about the other two men on the helicopter?"

"There was a Lieutenant Lopez and a guy named Devlin or Deverin, something like that. I lost touch with them after I left the service. Why? Do you know anything about them?"

"We know Lieutenant Lopez settled in North Carolina and became a doctor. Ronald Devlin lived in Las Vegas. Unfortunately, both were murdered, we believe by the same person who killed Richard Horner."

The shock on the man's face was evident. "You mean someone's killing off that crew from the helicopter? One by one?"

"It appears so, yes. It can't be a coincidence that three of the four in that crew were murdered."

"So that's why you're here, to find out if I'm the one doing it?" He waved his cane in the air. "Well, you can see that would be impossible."

"Actually, I've come here to warn you. If the killer is trying to settle some old score relating to that helicopter, you would be a natural target, the last target."

The man sighed. "I appreciate your concern, Detective, but my life is hardly worth saving. I mean, look around."

I took in the depressing surroundings. I could see the man's point.

"Nevertheless," Garrett said, "I can talk to the Little-ton police and ask them to keep an eye on your place, at least until we find whoever's responsible for the deaths of your crewmates."

The man shrugged. "Suit yourself. It makes no never mind to me. Those three guys are the lucky ones, if you ask me. This is no life for a Marine."

Garrett stood and reached out to shake the man's hand. "We won't take up any more of your time, Mr. Rimsky. If you think of anything else, don't hesitate to contact me. You have my number."

He waved his hand in the air until he made contact with Garrett's. "Sure. Thanks for coming."

The ride back to Trout Fork was quiet. I could feel that Garrett was as depressed by the visit as I was. We left the freeway and turned onto the county road that headed south along the river. The scenery was a welcome relief from the traffic and congestion in the city.

Garrett must have felt it too, because he pulled into one of the picnic areas along the road. He stopped the truck and pointed to the sign for the trailhead. "Let's take a walk along the river."

We got out and started down the trail. The South Platte flowed gently downhill, the water murmuring as it cascaded over the rocks. Garrett reached for my hand as we walked along. Neither of us spoke, almost as though we were hesitant to break the spell of the beauty around us.

At one point, we stopped to sit on a fallen tree near the edge of the creek. Garrett picked up some rocks and tossed them into the water, listening to the *plop* they made as they sank. A speckled trout leaped out of the water, soaring through the air then diving deftly back into the water.

Garrett sighed. "Hard to believe."

"What's that?"

"The beauty and peace in parts of the world. The ugliness in other parts."

I nodded. There wasn't much I could add. Garrett was displaying the side of him that loved opera and the Romantics. I often wondered how he made that work with his chosen profession. It was just one more thing about him I didn't yet understand.

As though switching from one Garrett to another, he turned to me. "Our killer was on that helicopter. He, or she, watched what those Marines did and never forgot it."

I nodded again. "Had to be. But how the heck do you trace sixty Vietnamese out of the thousands who were evacuated over forty years ago?"

CHAPTER 20

We left the idyllic scene along the river and headed back to Trout Fork, stopping for lunch at Alma's. As we sat at a table on the patio, Zoe came by to take our order. She told us that Dansby had been in the café that morning asking for me. The storm cloud that passed over Garrett's eyes must have been as obvious to her as it was to me, so she said, "Maybe he was just passing through…or something. I'll get your order." She moved off quickly.

Garrett's stony stare followed her. "What does Pansby want?"

"No idea. Maybe he was just coming back from Denver and decided to stop in for breakfast. And it's Dansby."

"Hmmph."

I reached for his hand across the table. "Garrett, there's no need to be jealous of him. You should know by now how I feel about you."

His eyes met mine. "How would I know that? You never want to talk about us. We just tiptoe around it. Every time I bring it up, you change the subject."

"I don't know what you want."

"Of course you do. I want a commitment." He leaned

in closer and his hand tightened on mine. "I love you, Ryn. That's all I know. This last week with you staying with me has shown me what we can have together. But I always feel like you're just waiting to be on your way out the door."

I wanted so much to tell him how much he meant to me and that I knew there was no one else for me. I wanted to say I couldn't imagine life without him and wanted to stay in his safe little cabin with him and Jack forever. But fear shot through me like a lightning bolt, and I couldn't get the words out. I just stared at him until he sat back, clearly frustrated with me.

"Yoo-hoo. There you are, you two." Madam Gauzie had marched through the door from the dining room, her gray hair tucked under a floppy fuchsia hat. She came to the table and put one hand on each of our shoulders. "Now remember that tonight is my little soiree. You two simply *must* attend. I won't take no for an answer." She looked closely at Garrett. "My goodness, dear, you are certainly looking well. Ryn's ministrations have done wonders. Well, I must get back to my store. See you both tonight." Without waiting for an answer, she turned and hurried from the patio.

Garrett stared after her. "How does she make a living selling antiques in this place? I mean, who buys them?"

Grateful he had changed the subject from our relationship, I said, "It's a mystery. In fact, she's a mystery. I mean, why does everyone call her Madam Gauzie? Why not Missus Gauzie? And what's her first name? Does she even have one?"

Zoe brought our lunch, and we ate in silence. My mind was spinning with unanswered questions, and none of them involved Madam Gauzie's first name. I had no idea what Garrett was thinking about, whether it was his revelation about his feelings for me or the four Marines on that helicopter. So much of Garrett was still a puzzle to me. They say we only put our best side on display to others. What if what I knew about Garrett was only part of him? Was that the reason I was reluctant to open myself up to him?

We finished lunch, and Garrett motioned to Zoe for the check. "We should go. I have work to do, and you probably want to pack."

"Pack?"

"Aren't you moving back to Alma's tonight?"

"Oh. Yeah." The thought of leaving Garrett's cabin overwhelmed me with feelings of regret and relief, all at the same time. No wonder he was frustrated with me. I was frustrated with myself.

We spent the afternoon in his cabin carefully avoiding one another. Garrett sat at the kitchen table typing on his laptop, while I tidied up the guest room Jack and I had called home for the last week. When I opened my battered suitcase and started folding my clothes into it, Jack eyed me curiously, but he didn't pace and meow like he usually did when it was evident we were about to be on the move again.

I tried to create some enthusiasm. "We're going back to Alma's, Jack. You'll be with Sasha again."

He usually perked up at the sound of Sasha's name, but this time he just curled up, lowered his chin onto his front legs, and closed his eyes. Maybe it was just the afternoon blahs so common to cats. Or was my traveling cat finally growing tired of moving?

I made two trips out with my suitcase, laptop, and Jack's basket and secured them on the bike. Garrett seemed not to notice. When I left the guest room for the last time with Jack on my shoulder, Garrett looked up.

I stood over his shoulder and stared at the screen. "What are you working on?"

"Typing up my report on our visit to Rimsky. I want to put down the details before I forget them. The more info I can give to my buddy at the VA, the easier it may be to track down the killer."

"Will he be able to find all those people from the helicopter?"

"If he can't, he'll know someone in the government who can. Those people didn't just disappear. Someone knows where each of them was settled after the war." He looked up at me. "On your way?"

I nodded, half expecting him to add the word "again."

He stood and stroked Jack. "See you later, Buddy."

Jack rubbed his head on Garrett's hand.

"Thanks for everything," I said.

He kissed my cheek. "You're the one who should be thanked. You've been nurse, housekeeper, cook. I couldn't have done without you."

"Take care of your shoulder." I started for the door then turned back to him. "You'll be coming to Madam Gauzie's dinner, won't you?"

"I wouldn't miss it. Drive carefully." He went back to the table, and I shut the door behind me.

I drove slowly to Trout Fork, enjoying the late summer breeze and golden glow of the sunlight through the trees. Jack curled up in his basket instead of sitting up sniffing the wind like he usually did. I wondered if there was something wrong with him. He hadn't had a visit to a vet in years, due to my financial circumstances. Maybe it was time for a checkup.

We pulled into the lot in front of the café, and I began unloading the bike. I took Jack and his basket to the cabin first. The front door was open as though they were expecting me, so I went in and opened Ashley's bedroom door. She was on her bed with Sasha amid a pile of books, and both looked up at us.

Ashley grinned and got up to help me. She took Jack from me and put him down with Sasha, who greeted him with a playful swat with her paw. Jack ignored her. He hopped off the bed and onto my bed where he curled up on the pillow with a sigh.

Ashley's eyebrows rose. "What's up with Jack?"

"I don't know. He's feeling a little poopy today, I guess. He's been like that all day. I need to get my suitcase."

I brought in my laptop and suitcase, tossed them on the bed, and began to unpack. "How's school going?"

"Not too bad. A lot of work, though. It seems all I do is study."

"How's the French?"

"Good. I aced the last test. Now it's chem that's giving me fits."

"I know. I was lousy at chemistry. I couldn't get interested in the periodic table and all those formulas. Yuck."

"I know, right?"

"Is your dad down this weekend?"

"He was, but he went home early. Some big case that he's preparing for."

"How about your mom? Still hearing wedding bells in the future?"

She shrugged. "Who knows? I've stopped worrying about it. I'll deal with it when it happens…if it happens. Have you seen Hank lately?"

"Yeah. We saw him yesterday. He's doing okay, I guess. He asked about you and how you're doing in school. He said he misses everyone in Trout Fork." Her question made me feel guilty at not having spent more time thinking about Hank and how I could help get him out of that awful, smelly jail cell. The accident and Garrett had consumed so much of my time and mental energy that Hank's situation had been put on the back burner. That simply had to change. After all, wasn't that why I had returned to Trout Fork?

I finished hanging up my clothes, put the suitcase under my bed, and sat on the edge of Ashley's bed. "Have you heard from Derek at all?"

"No. Why?"

"Did you know that police captain is going to be arrested for drug dealing? I was just thinking that Derek might be called back to town to testify against him."

"Whatever."

Apparently both she and Zoe had gotten over the Derek blues. How resilient teenagers could be. One day's major drama could be the next day's distant memory.

"So what does that mean for Garrett? Will he get a new captain?"

"I guess. He hasn't mentioned it. He'll be at Madam G's tonight. You can ask him." *What does it mean for Garrett?* I wondered. I knew Garrett's need for things to be neat and orderly with no loose ends. I had no doubt he wouldn't like the state of flux his station would be in starting tomorrow. Maybe that was why he pressured me for a commitment. He just didn't like unresolved situations. Clearly he had picked the wrong girl to fall in love with.

Ashley and I spent the rest of the afternoon reading. At about five o'clock, we heard Alma come in from the café and head for the shower. Ashley and I dressed casually, then the three of us left the cabin and walked along the path toward Madam Gauzie's. Alma carried a covered casserole dish from which delicious smells were emanating.

"What's in the dish, Mom?"

"Some of my chicken Kiev," Alma said. "Madam G. told me not to bring anything, but I hate to have her do all the work."

We knocked and opened the door to Madam Gauzie's cabin. Garrett was already there talking to Gil.

"But where's Robert?" Madam Gauzie asked.

Alma carried her dish to the table. "He had to go back early. He has to be in court in the morning."

"Oh, too bad. Well, let's sit down, shall we?"

We all came to the table heavily laden with numerous dishes and sat down. There were two empty chairs. I assumed one was for Robert, but the other one? "Are you expecting someone else, Madam G?"

"I've decided to leave a place for Hank at my table. Just so we don't forget him."

"Not a chance," Gil said. He turned to Garrett. "Any closer to getting him out of jail?"

Garrett accepted a bowl of vegetables from Gil, spooned some onto his plate, and passed it to me. "Actually, I think we may be closing in on whoever killed Sarge."

"Really?" Alma said, her eyes wide.

Garrett nodded. "Ryn and I met a man today who helped us link Sarge's death with two other murders. Turns out the four of them were in the Marines in Vietnam together, crewmates on a helicopter that airlifted refugees from the embassy compound in Saigon the last days of the war. We believe the killer may have been on that helicopter. He must have seen something—"

I gave him a warning glance. The others didn't need to hear the gory details of what their friend was forced to do all those years ago.

"Good heavens," Madam Gauzie said. "Imagine that."

Garrett seemed to enjoy being the center of attention.

"It's bizarre. So long ago, so many miles away, and someone from that time comes here to kill. You would think he'd have had enough of war and killing. There's still a lot we don't know and things we can't yet piece together."

"Like what?" Gil asked.

"Like the notes found on each of the bodies that had the words 'wind,' 'frequent,' and 'operation.' We thought at first the word 'operation' referred somehow to the Marine who became a surgeon after the war, but no. We don't know what they mean."

"I know what they mean," Madam Gauzie said, chewing slowly. "You were talking about Vietnam. Well, the code name of the evacuation of American personnel from Saigon was Operation Frequent Wind."

We stared at her. "Are you sure?"

"Of course I'm sure. My Edgar was part of it." She got up from the table, crossed to the sofa, and brought back the picture album. She turned the pages to the picture of her husband and his smiling buddies and set it in front of Garrett. "See? Here's my Edgar with his shipmates from the USS Kirk. They were part of Operation Frequent Wind."

Garrett stared at the photo. "What did he tell you about those days?"

"Edgar rarely talked about it, but one night he had a nightmare and woke up sweating," Madam Gauzie said. "That was the night he told me about one memory that haunted him for years. There was a boy who came in on one of the copters alone and crying hysterically. The boy—he was about ten years old, I think—was the son of an interpreter who worked at the American embassy in Saigon. He had gotten separated from his family. Isn't that awful?"

"That poor child," Alma said. "Whatever happened to him? Was he reunited with his family?"

"Edgar never found out. The boy was taken to the Philippines with the rest of the refugees and left in the American camps there. I believe most of them were resettled in the US, but where the boy was taken is anyone's guess. Edgar said that poor boy's face haunted him for years. Of course, he was just one of many terrified children that dreadful day."

My mind was trying to put together all the pieces. Edgar had told the same story we heard today from the fourth Marine. Could that little boy have grown up to be our killer?

Garrett had put down his fork. "If that kid, or someone else in that helicopter, is responsible for the murders, that would mean he was here in Trout Fork just recently."

Alma shook her head. "We haven't seen any Vietnamese around here all summer. No Asians at all, in fact."

"You're forgetting Philippe," said Ashley, who had been listening quietly. "He's Vietnamese."

"I thought he was French," Alma said.

"His mother was French. His father was Vietnamese. His mother was descended from the French ruling class who colonized Vietnam. She met Philippe's father there. He was educated and spoke both English and Vietnamese. He was an interpreter at the US Embassy during the war. At least that's what I thought Philippe said. He was speaking French, so I might have gotten some of that wrong."

Garrett and I stared at her. Then we looked at each other.

"Oh, come on," Ashley laughed. "Philippe? He's not the killer. He wouldn't hurt a fly."

I visualized Philippe, that polite little man I had met on the trail the day he fussed over Jack and volunteered to tutor Ashley in French. A more unlikely murderer I couldn't conceive of.

"Of course he wouldn't," Alma chimed in. "But you know he works for the government, in the VA office in Denver. If anyone could get information about Operation Whatsit, it's Philippe. I'm sure he'd be glad to help."

The group broke up around nine, and Garrett walked me back to Alma's. He had been very quiet all evening.

"Garrett, do you think Philippe could be the murderer?"

"Well, he could be the boy on the helicopter. He's the right age. Now that I know he works at the VA, I can get more information about him from my buddy there. I'll call him first thing tomorrow."

"Damn," I said.

"What?"

"I promised to meet with Harrison Cosgrove at nine tomorrow about the editor job."

"Have you decided to take it?"

"I haven't even thought about it. Listen, I'll stop in at the station on my way. Wait for me before you call your friend at the VA, okay?"

"Of course. I wouldn't do anything without my assistant detective."

I turned to go into the cabin. "Very funny."

"You know," he said, "you have all the instincts of a good reporter. You'll make a great editor."

CHAPTER 21

The next day, I parked my bike in front of the police station just in time to see Captain Williams in handcuffs being escorted out of the building by two plainclothes officers who I assumed were from the office of the police chief. Williams was impeccably dressed as usual, although his demeanor didn't match his clothing. His shoulders were slumped and his eyes downcast. He didn't look at me as he passed.

Detective Sloan stood watching them, his bulk leaning heavily against the station doorway, a look of smug satisfaction on his face.

The men put Williams in the back seat of a patrol car and drove off slowly, leaving the captain's black Lexus standing forlornly in the parking lot. I had the sensation of sadness as I watched one of the community's guardians brought down to the level of the criminals he had sworn to guard against. *How fragile is the structure that separates law enforcement from the chaos that can swamp us in a moment.* I had a fleeting thought about a great series of articles on the subject, although such a series was completely out of the question for a travel writer. Maybe I could incorporate it into the novel I'd been writing for years.

I found Garrett in his office. "Oh, good. You're here," he said. "Sit down."

I sat in the chair opposite the desk.

He pulled the desk phone toward him and dialed a number. He hit the Speaker button and we listened as it rang. A male voice answered. "Benefits Department, Grayson."

"Grayson. It's Garrett Easterbrook."

"Easterbrook. This is getting to be a regular thing. My wife will wonder what's going on between us."

"Cute. You've been a big help, and I really appreciate it. I have one more favor to ask."

"Just one?"

Garrett winked at me. "Just one. I'm looking for some information about one of your coworkers, a Philippe Tran. Know him?"

"Sure, I know Tran. Works in Family Affairs. Good guy. Why are you after him?"

"He may be connected to a case I'm working on. What can you tell me about him? Specifically his background. I know he's Vietnamese. I need to know when he came to the US and anything about his family. I know you guys do a pretty thorough check before you hire someone."

There was silence on the other end, and Garrett held up crossed fingers. Then the man said, "You know I always like to help the cops, but this feels like ratting out a coworker."

"Look, Grayson, this guy might be involved with the deaths of three Marines. Coworker or not, you'd want to know that, wouldn't you?"

More silence, then a sigh and the sound of tapping on a keyboard. Garrett raised his eyes to the ceiling and mouthed, "Yes!"

"It says here Tran was born in 1965 in Saigon. His

father was an interpreter at the American embassy there. He came to the US in 1978 after spending three years in a refugee camp outside Manila. He left the Philippines and settled near San Francisco with a Vietnamese family who sponsored him. He eventually attended San Jose State. Got a degree in Government and came here to work for the VA after college. He's been here ever since." He snickered. "We call those guys 'lifers.'"

"What about his family in Vietnam?"

"Father, mother, sister, brother. Nothing was heard from them after Saigon fell. All assumed killed by the Communists, like so many that cooperated with the Americans. Geez, I had no idea."

"Anything in there about the date August seven?"

We could hear him scrolling through pages on his screen. "Nothing that I can see. He does take his vacations the same time every year—first two weeks of August. Been doing that for years."

"Give me his address, will you?"

Grayson dictated Philippe's address in Denver. Garrett wrote it down and I made a mental note of it.

"Thanks, Grayson. I owe you one."

"Anytime. Come up one of these days, and we'll have a beer. Better yet, we'll get tickets to a Rockies game."

"I'll do that." Garrett disconnected the phone and looked at me. "It all fits. Philippe Tran is our murderer. He was on that helicopter with the four Marines. He watched them use their rifle butts on his parents' hands as they tried to board. He probably made a mental note of their names and ranks from the ID badges on their uniforms. I wouldn't be surprised if he got a job at the VA with the intention of tracking them down. When he had the chance, he did just that and killed them, one by one. I have no doubt Rimsky will be his next victim, next year on August seventh."

"But why did he choose August seventh? Why August seventh?"

"I don't know, but I can guess. Somehow Tran got word that his family was killed on that date, either years later from the Americans or through someone who had contacts in Saigon. I don't know what else it could be."

I sat stunned and sickened by the whole scenario. "So that little boy on the helicopter grew up, came to America, and vowed vengeance against four Marines who were just doing their job."

"War is hell."

"What do we do now?"

He stood, came around to my chair, and lifted me by the elbow. "*We* don't do anything. I'll give the information to Sloan, and he'll try to find evidence against Philippe. You will go to your interview with Cosgrove." He ushered me to the door of his office and kissed me on the cheek. "Give him my regards."

I passed Detective Sloan on my way out of the station. He was chatting with the desk sergeant, and they appeared to be having a good laugh about the captain being arrested. How much interest did Sloan really have in finding Sarge's killer? Would he be willing to dedicate the time and energy necessary to connect Philippe to the other two murders?

It was just past nine o'clock when I pulled up at the office of the *Star* and parked the bike. I entered the building and noticed the same two young women at their desks staring at their computer screens. Both looked up and smiled at me. The one Bodmin had called "Andrews" got up and went into the office where I had interviewed the former editor. Perhaps it was my imagination, but there didn't seem to be the same agitated feeling about the newsroom I had sensed before.

Through the door of Bodmin's office, I could see a man I assumed to be Harrison Cosgrove seated at the desk, nearly hidden behind a pile of newspapers. He looked up and saw me through the door. He got up and quickly came to me, his hand extended. A more unlikely-looking newspaper owner I couldn't imagine. He was young, barely in his thirties, I guessed, with flaming red hair, deep green eyes behind horn-rimmed glasses, and clear pale skin with a blanket of freckles across his nose. He wore jeans and a T-shirt with scuffed running shoes and no socks. Either he was going for the casual look to impress the employees, or he had no interest in fashion whatever. Either way, his appearance accorded perfectly with the relaxed atmosphere in the room.

He flashed a boyish grin. "Harry Cosgrove, Miss Lowell, thanks for coming."

I shook his hand. His handshake was warm and firm. "It's Ryn. Thanks for inviting me."

"My pleasure. Can I get you anything? Coffee?"

"Sure. Cream, no sugar."

He addressed the girl who was still in his office. "Moira, two coffees, please. Oh, this is Moira Andrews, one of our reporters. Meet Ryn Lowell, hopefully your new editor."

The girl was tall and thin with curly black hair and hazel eyes. She said, "Hi" and smiled at me shyly. I liked her immediately.

He gestured toward the other girl. "And that's our other reporter, Lindsey Malone." The pudgy blonde girl looked up from her computer screen and nodded, her expression wary.

Cosgrove took my elbow and directed me toward the office. "I'd show you around, but there's not much to see.

Just the newsroom and the two offices. One's a storage closet really. This will be your office."

"Well, I haven't really—"

He laughed heartily. "I know, I know. You're just here on inspection." He gestured to the same chair I had occupied when I interviewed Bodmin a week ago, although it seemed like months. I sat and watched him. As a journalist, I had developed a sixth sense about people. I couldn't help being attracted to his buoyant personality and confident, upbeat manner, especially compared to my former editor in New York.

He pushed the stack of newspapers aside and tossed three folders across the desk to me. "These are the paper's three employees, the two reporters out there and the part-time sports editor. Of course, if the paper grows, you can hire more." He laughed again. "That is, if you take the job."

He explained more about the inner workings of the paper and his vision for it, as well as what he expected from a managing editor. "Look, Ryn, Vince Bodmin has let the paper slide over the past few years." He rolled his eyes. "No doubt his other activities took precedence. But this area is growing rapidly and needs a comprehensive daily newspaper with a greater community impact. For one thing, more of a crime beat. Also, more human interest, more national news, more politics, more everything. Most of all, I want to move from a weekly to a daily paper. I want to rebuild the paper from the ground up, and I need someone like you to spearhead it. What do you say?"

"You realize my only newspaper experience was at Columbia. I've been working for a magazine since I left college. Wouldn't you want to hire someone with more experience?"

"You mean someone like Bodmin? Stuck in the past,

doing things the way they were done twenty years ago? No. This paper needs new blood, fresh ideas, and a younger approach. Someone tech savvy. I want the paper to have an online presence, too. Guys like Bodmin just see the internet as a nuisance."

We talked for nearly an hour. His enthusiasm was infectious, and I had to admit he made it sound very attractive. The salary was generous, as was the amount of freedom I would have to shape the coverage. When I asked if I would have to sign a contract, he said we could try the arrangement on a temporary basis. If we both agreed, we could talk about a long-term contract at that time. "How about six months?" he asked.

I was tempted to take the job then and there. I certainly didn't have any other offers on the table, and the alternative—going back to New York—was not an option. And then there was Garrett. Living and working near him for six months would give me plenty of time to decide whether we had a future together. "It certainly sounds appealing. Can I take just a day or two to decide?"

"Sure, sure. But we need to move forward on this, so let me know quickly, okay?"

I got up from the chair and shook his hand again. "I will. Thanks very much."

I left the building and straddled the bike. Before I made any commitments I had one thing I just had to do, and that was make sure Philippe Tran was arrested and Hank was back in Trout Fork with the people who loved him. I had decided my next move before I had even left the police station. I was going to Philippe's house in Denver, whether to confront him or just poke around, I wasn't sure. I only knew I had to do it. I typed his address into my phone's GPS and headed north.

The clouds were just beginning to gather as I entered the northern suburbs of Denver two hours later. The weather report had said the late afternoon thunderstorms so common in Colorado were expected. As much as I loved my Honda, riding in a rainstorm was distinctly uncomfortable. Colorado thunderstorms could be brutal, often accompanied by hail and high winds. I had gotten caught in the rain on the Western slope weeks before and had to pull under a highway overpass to wait it out. Riding on a winding mountain road in a blinding downpour was to be avoided. I only hoped I could find something linking Philippe to the murders and get back to Trout Fork before the skies opened up.

I found Philippe's street and left the bike near a park a block from his address. His was a middle class neighborhood, complete with trees and manicured lawns gleaming emerald green in the mid-day sunshine. I assumed Philippe would be at work at the VA this time of day. I looked briefly up and down the street and, seeing no one, I slipped around to the side of his house, stood on tiptoes, and looked in several windows.

The interior of the house was much like the outside—neat, orderly, and well-kept, with rather spare and sterile-looking furnishings. There was a wooden fence surrounding the property with a gate accessing the back yard. I glanced around one more time then pushed the gate open slightly and waited, just in case Philippe had a dog guarding the property. But there was no sound from the back yard other than birdsong from the treetops.

I pushed open the gate and stood transfixed at the scene before me. In direct contrast to the interior of the house, the entire back yard was landscaped into a luxurious, shaded garden. Exotic shrubs and exquisite, fragrant flowers lined the colored-rock walkway that wound through the garden. A gentle breeze stirred several wind chimes, adding soft tinkling music to the scene, while basil and coriander from an herb garden scented the air.

I strolled quietly along the rock walkway, wending my way toward the centerpiece of the garden, a shimmering pond in which green lily pads and white flowers floated. Shadowy sunlight dappled the yard, creating moving images cast by the tall shrubs. The whole atmosphere spoke of peace and tranquility.

Approaching the pond, I saw a small Buddha carved from what appeared to be jade. In front of the statue were four glass containers with candles burning in each one. The glasses sat on small square tablets of stone embedded in the ground. I squatted down and moved one candle holder to read the writing: "Tran Quang Dinh. August 7, 1975." The other three tablets all had the name "Tran," followed by two other names and the same date. Knowing that family last names always came first in Vietnamese, I realized these must be the names of Philippe's parents and siblings. I stood and considered the tablets. Surely they weren't buried here. This must be some kind of shrine of remembrance for his family.

A soft breeze moved the wind chimes just above the pond again. But their lovely sound was interrupted by a woman's voice from the yard next door. "Good day, Philippe. Having lunch at home today?"

"Hello, Mildred. Yes, I thought I'd take a break from the office."

I recognized Philippe's voice from our conversation on the trail weeks ago, but this time that voice sent a shiver of fear through me. I tried not to panic as terrified thoughts filled my mind. *He must be at his front door. What if he sees me? How can I explain it? Would someone who has killed three people hesitate to kill me? How can I get out of here?*

I quickly scanned the area for a place to hide. Some tall shrubs near the back fence seemed the only alternative. In seconds I was crouched down behind them, my breath coming fast and my heart racing. Thank God I had the sense to park my bike down the street. Now if only I could get to it. I thought about making a dash to the side gate and prayed he wasn't looking out the back window. But before I could move, the back door of the house opened and Philippe came out carrying a metal watering can. I watched him through the wide fronds of the shrub I was crouched behind.

He moved among the flowers and bushes, pouring water on them and mumbling to himself. He was agonizingly slow as he followed the walkway from the house to the pond, where he stopped in front of the tablets. Then he started back toward the house. Suddenly he hesitated and turned to look back at the shrines, his eyes narrowing.

Fear shot through me at the thought that I might have forgotten to put the candle holder back when I moved it to read the writing on the tablet. I squeezed my eyes tightly shut and willed my breathing to become slower and quieter. *God help me if he finds me here. He could kill me and bury me in this garden and who would ever know?* Memories of Garrett's eyes, his gentle voice, and the warmth of his embrace flooded through me. I would do anything if only I could live to see him again.

Philippe stood for a moment staring at the pond then moved slowly back to the house. In minutes, he returned with a food tray that he placed on the small table in the shade of his patio. He sat and methodically ate and drank, gazing around at his garden. When he finished eating, he pulled out his cell phone and a small slip of paper. He dialed a number from the paper then crumpled it up and tossed it on the tray.

"Mr. Rimsky?" I heard him say. "This is Philippe Tran from the VA. How are you, sir? Fine, fine. Mr. Rimsky, the reason I'm calling is to let you know there are some additional veterans' benefits you may be entitled to. Yes, sir, that's correct. What we need from you is just a couple of signatures." He was silent for a moment. "I'm aware of your condition, sir, which is why I'd be willing to come to your house to get those signatures. Would today at four be convenient? I could stop over on my way home from the office."

I couldn't believe my ears. Here was the killer making an appointment with his next victim. But why now? Why not on August seventh like the rest of them?

"Yes, sir," he continued. "I have your address. Fine, sir. I'll see you then." He hung up and sat gazing toward the pond. I had the eerie sensation that he was staring right at me, although I was well hidden. After a while, he stood and took the tray back into the house. Then I heard the front door slam, followed by the sound of a car engine starting. I heard the car drive down the street, but I stayed crouched in the garden for another hour, fearful that he might be waiting outside for me.

Pulling out my phone, I dialed four-one-one and got the number of the Veterans' Administration in Denver. I listened through the list of prompts then was connected to Philippe Tran's office. When he answered, I said I had the wrong number, apologized, and hung up quickly. Now I knew it was safe to leave the garden, so I hurried to get back to my bike. Passing the shrine, I noticed that I was right. I hadn't put the candle holder back, and Philippe must have seen it.

CHAPTER 22

I gunned the engine of the bike and flew out of the neighborhood at top speed. I stopped at the first coffee shop I came to, ordered a latte, and sat at an outside table. Ominous storm clouds were darkening the sky, and a strong breeze was coming from the West. I pulled out my phone and dialed Garrett's number. When I told him I had been at Philippe's house, his voice hardened. "You what?"

"Now before you start the lecture, listen to me. Philippe is going to Rimsky's house this afternoon. I'm sure he's going there to kill him."

"How do you know that?"

"I overheard him talking to Rimsky."

"Even if Philippe is planning to kill him, wouldn't he do it on August seventh, like the other three?"

"I think he knows we're on to him. I'm sure he knows someone was in his garden today. I moved something while I was looking around, and he noticed it was out of place. I think that's why he called Rimsky and made an appointment to go to his house this afternoon. He's afraid he's been found out. I think he's determined to finish the job before he gets caught."

"That makes no sense. If he thinks he's about to be caught, wouldn't he leave town or hide out somewhere?"

"I don't know. I can't read his mind. All I know is he's going to Rimsky's at four, and we have to be there to stop him."

"Okay. Where are you?"

I gave him the address of the coffee shop.

"Stay there. I'll get Sloan, and we'll meet you there. Do not, I repeat, *do not*, go to Rimsky's by yourself. Understand?"

"Yeah, yeah. Hurry, Garrett. It's one-thirty now, and it'll take two hours to get here."

"Don't worry. We can use the lights and siren if necessary. Just don't move."

I hung up and thought about Philippe while I sipped my latte. I had no doubt he was going to try to kill the fourth Marine from the helicopter, yet he was so calm and deliberate about it. I also thought about the statue of Buddha and the tablets. Was there some kind of mystical meaning to the shrine, and did it have anything to do with the revenge murders of three, possibly four, people? I was completely ignorant of Buddhism, but I knew someone I could ask.

I dialed information again and asked for the number of the college where I knew Duane, the motorcyclist I had met earlier that summer, was a member of the faculty. I smiled at the memories of the rides on his Harley as he taught me how to drive a motorcycle. It was Duane who had explained the effects of oppressive religion on the psyche and how it could lead even to murder, as in the case of Zach Wayland.

I asked the switchboard to connect me to the Philosophy and World Religions department and soon heard Duane's voice.

"Ryn! What a surprise. How's your Honda?"

"It's great. Listen, Duane, I'd love to chat, but I'm in a bind, and I really need your help."

"Anything I can do."

"I need to know something about Buddhists."

"Like what?"

"I have a Buddhist…acquaintance…and he has some kind of shrine in his garden. There are stone tablets with the names of his parents and siblings and candles on each. What's that all about, do you know?"

"Are his family members still living?"

"No. They were all killed in Vietnam at the end of the war. He was the only one to survive."

"It sounds like he's built wind tombs. It's a Vietnamese tradition where a family member sets up graves and gravestones for those whose bodies can't be found or recovered. Someone lost at sea, for instance. Wind tombs are empty graves where the family members can mourn and remember. They're also called séance graves and wind graves. Not at all uncommon."

"I understand. Let me ask you this. Is vengeance allowed in Buddhism?"

"No. In fact, Buddhists believe two wrongs don't make a right, and revenge is never an excuse for violence."

I couldn't reconcile that with what I knew Philippe had done. "Even if the revenge is for family members?"

"Well, that brings up an interesting point. The Vietnamese have been ingrained with a belief in ancestor worship. That was introduced into Vietnamese culture by the Chinese two hundred years before Christ. If your friend is considering avenging his family members, he could be torn between his reverence for them and the Buddhist doctrine of nonviolence."

"If someone was struggling with those things, could it lead him to murder?"

He was quiet for a moment then said, "If the circumstances were such that he couldn't accept the fate of his family members, then yes, it's possible."

I thought about that traumatized ten-year old boy on that helicopter all those years ago watching his family's fate being decided by four seemingly heartless Marines. No wonder he was driven to revenge.

"Thanks, Duane. You've been a big help."

"Anytime. Are you still in Trout Fork?"

"Yes. Come by one of these days. We'll take a ride through the mountains together."

"Definitely."

I hung up and looked at my phone. Two o'clock. I ordered a sandwich and bought a copy of the Denver daily newspaper to peruse while I ate. I found myself taking note of things I usually didn't bother with like the masthead and editorial pages. I even scanned the ads, wondering how much they cost and how they affected a newspaper's budget. Before I knew it, I realized I had pretty much decided to take the job at the *Star*. It surprised me that I made the decision so quickly. Maybe that scare in Philippe's garden that brought Garrett to mind had really been the deciding factor. I just had to be where Garrett was, and this job would let me do just that.

I picked up my phone again. *No time like the present,* I thought, as I dialed Harrison Cosgrove's number. When I told him I had decided to take the job, he seemed delighted.

"Wonderful, Ryn. When can you start? How about tomorrow?"

I laughed at his enthusiasm. "I'll need a few days. Can it wait until next week?"

"Sure. I'll be in touch."

Well, that was that. I was going to be staying in one place for at least six months, and that was a first for me. I hadn't stayed put that long since I left New York. The thought was both comforting and frightening, comforting in that I would stay in touch with my adopted family— Alma, Ashley, Madame Gauzie, Gil, and, hopefully, Hank. Frightening because my relationship with Garrett would either flourish and end in marriage or peter out completely. I wasn't sure which of those two scenarios scared me more.

The weather finally stopped threatening and burst upon the area with a frightening intensity. I scurried inside the coffee shop just as the skies opened and the deluge began. Lightning bolts slashed down, followed instantly by cracks of thunder that seemed to split my eardrums. The wind kicked up to hurricane speeds, blowing tables, chairs, and umbrellas across the patio while the soaked employees tried to corral them into a corner. Then the hail started, tiny ice balls falling lightly at first, but increasing quickly until golf ball-sized chunks bombarded everything in sight, bouncing three feet into the air as they hit the cement patio floor. Rivers of hail-choked water rushed down the street toward the clogged sewers, temporarily halting traffic in both directions.

I stood transfixed at Nature's furious power. I'd heard about Colorado's violent summer storms, but this was the first one I'd experienced. Then, almost as quickly as it had started, it was over. The hail stopped, and the clouds traveled before the wind, trooping off eastward in long, darkened columns. A rainbow appeared, and sunshine bathed the area in an eerie orange glow.

Those who had sheltered with me in the coffee shop began to filter out to the parking lot, some checking the damage to vehicles parked nearby. A few had cracked windshields and most had an array of small dents in the roofs and hoods. One woman strolled by me on her cell phone, talking to her insurance agent. An older man stared at his laptop's screen and said to no one in particular, "They got it really bad south of here. A couple of roads are closed due to flooding."

I moved closer to the man and looked over his shoulder at the map of road closures highlighted on the screen. The road from Trout Fork to Denver was flashing an ominous red. If Garrett and Sloan got caught on that road, they would have to backtrack and find a different route. They might not make it up here by four o'clock.

I dialed Garrett's number, but it went to voice mail. I left a frantic message. "Garrett, are you stuck in the storm? I'm afraid you won't get here in time, so I'm heading for Arnold Rimsky's place. Meet me there instead of the coffee shop. And hurry!" My phone's display told me it was three-thirty. I could only hope that Philippe had also been delayed by the storm.

I dashed to the bike and used my sleeve to dry the seat. I noticed there were dents on the gas tank and one small crack in the windshield, but for the most part, the bike was untouched. I turned the key and the soaked engine sputtered to life. I drove as quickly as I could toward Littleton, avoiding the freeway which was bound to be a parking lot. The back roads were relatively clear, and I drove faster than was really safe. I could hear Garrett's voice in my head warning me of the dangers of motorcycles.

I turned onto Rimsky's street, glad to see no car in front of his house. I stopped the bike down the street and waited. I kept checking my phone to see if Garrett would text me, but nothing. Four o'clock came and went. I breathed a sigh of relief. Maybe Philippe was delayed by the traffic or maybe even had decided to cancel.

Several more minutes went by. Then a white car turned onto the street and passed me slowly. I shuddered. It was Philippe. I watched him park in front of Rimsky's house and move up the sidewalk, picking his way through the cracked concrete just as Garrett and I had done. He rang the doorbell and waited. He rang again.

Just as I was hoping Rimsky might be sleeping, the door opened and Philippe stepped into the house. I thought for a moment he looked my way as he entered, but decided it was my imagination.

I dialed Garrett's number one more time in desperation. I hung up when it went to voice mail. What do I do now? Wait here until it was too late for that helpless, blind man? But what could I do? I had no idea what kind of weapon Philippe had. Then I thought about Sarge. Wouldn't I have intervened to try to save him? I knew I couldn't just sit there and do nothing. I left the bike and hurried to Rimsky's house. I pounded on the door, my heart in my throat.

The door was opened by Philippe, whose smile and charming manners shocked me. "Miss Lowell. How nice to see you again. Do come in. We've been expecting you, haven't we, Arnold?"

Arnold Rimsky sat in his usual chair, but his tense body language told me he wasn't fooled by Philippe's courtesy. It was then I noticed that Philippe was holding a pistol with a long slender piece of metal attached to it. A silencer. He waved it toward the sofa where Garrett and I had sat just the day before.

"Please have a seat."

I complied and sat at the edge of the sofa, not sure what would happen next. "Are you okay, Mr. Rimsky?" I asked the blind man.

He nodded, his sightless eyes searching the ceiling. I was young, healthy, and strong, and I was terrified. What was that vulnerable old man feeling?

Philippe moved to Rimsky's chair and stood over him, the pistol pointed at the man's head. His voice was calm and deliberate. He could easily have been talking about the weather. "I was just explaining to Mr. Rimsky here that I remembered him from those last days in Saigon. We shared a ride on a helicopter that day, didn't we, Arnold?"

Rimsky didn't move. He appeared to be numb with fear.

"Arnold assures me that he remembers that day well. I've had to inform him that his crewmates have all been accounted for."

I was appalled by his unnerving composure. "Accounted for? Is that what you call murdering three men?"

Philippe remained calm but kept the pistol pointed at the blind man. "Murder is such an ugly word."

"So is revenge," I shot back.

The blind man put his hand over his heart. "'Vengeance is mine, saith the Lord.' That's what the Good Book says."

A look of disgust crossed Philippe's face, the first visible crack in his stoic armor. "What does your Book say about a man who worked tirelessly for years for you Americans at your embassy, only to be shoved aside when you decided to abandon us to the Communists? What does it say about Marines who crush the hands of those fleeing for their lives? What about two innocent children left to die?"

Rimsky spread his hands out to implore him. "I've tried to explain that to you. We had no choice. If we had brought more people on board, that bird would have been overloaded, and we all could have been killed. We had to make your parents let go of that ramp, for their own safety. Don't you understand?"

There was no pity in Philippe's expression, and I wondered if his other three victims had also tried to explain what happened that day. If they did, it had clearly been to no avail. Reasoning with him would have no impact.

I knew what I had to do. I got up and moved slowly toward him, keeping one eye on his pistol. I held my hands out in front of me. "Philippe, I know why you killed Sarge and the other two men. I know why you're here—to finish avenging your family. It's something you just have to do, isn't it?" A few steps closer. "I saw the wind tombs in the garden."

His eyebrows rose at my use of the term. "I knew someone was there. When I saw your motorcycle down the street, I thought it might be you."

"Yes, I was there. That's the reason you called Mr. Rimsky, isn't it? Why you couldn't wait until next August seventh."

He nodded with a half-smile. "My mission is almost complete. One more task."

I moved a few inches closer to him, keeping his eyes on mine. "What's the note going to say this time? You've already used Operation Frequent Wind."

He smiled again and pulled a piece of paper from his pocket. "See for yourself."

I took the paper. It had one word: "*Accompli.*"

I handed it back to him. "French for 'finished.' There's just one problem, though. What are you going to do about me? I had nothing to do with your family. I wasn't even born when Saigon fell. Killing me won't avenge anyone. It's just senseless, insane destruction."

He seemed genuinely surprised. "Oh, my dear. What makes you think I would harm you? No, no, no. That would be barbaric. Not my intention at all."

"What then? You kill this old man, and then what happens? We sit down to dinner together?"

"I expect the police are on their way. Surely you didn't come here without alerting them. I'll just wait for them to take me away. It's the only fitting ending, don't you think?"

I moved still closer to him. I expected to see dilated eyes or some other indication of insanity, as I saw in Zach's face, but he seemed as normal as when I met him on the trail that day when he called Jack *mon petit chat*.

"Please don't come any closer. I don't want to hurt you, but I can't let you stop me either. You do understand."

I felt unusually calm. "Yes. I understand. But you have to understand that I can't stand here and watch you put a bullet in this man's head."

"Well, we are at an impasse, aren't we?"

I moved suddenly between him and the man in the chair, which caused Philippe's gun to be pointed at my chest. His expression was almost sorrowful as he knocked me to the floor and pressed the pistol to Rimsky's head and cocked it.

There was a thunderous pounding on the front door. "Police! Open up!" Philippe hesitated for a moment, just long enough for two policemen to break the door open and rush into the room, their guns drawn.

Philippe's eyes grew wide. Then he lowered the pistol and slumped to the floor. "I'm sorry. I'm sorry," he sobbed.

Was he apologizing to the man he tried to kill? Or to me? Or was it to his unavenged family? Whoever it was, Philippe's perceived failure had left him a broken man.

Suddenly he pointed the gun at his own head and closed his eyes.

"Oh, no you don't," said one of the policemen. He grabbed the gun, hauled Philippe to his feet, and handcuffed him.

The other cop helped me up. "Anyone else in the house, miss?"

"No."

Rimsky remained in his chair, his expression blank.

I turned to the officer. "How did you know?"

The young officer put his handgun into its holster. "We got a call from the Pineland Park Police warning us."

Garrett. Of course. I wondered where he and Sloan were.

The two officers escorted Philippe, still sobbing, to the door. I was saddened at the sight of this wretched man who had dedicated his entire life to revenge. His demeanor was that of one who had lost his purpose for living—hopeless, resigned, and utterly desolate.

CHAPTER 23

Trout Fork had never seen a party like the one Alma and Gil devised the following Sunday for Hank's homecoming. Even though it was the day before Labor Day, a very busy time for tourists and fishermen to be visiting Trout Fork, Alma was determined to close the café at two and invite the entire neighborhood to celebrate.

Gil's barbeque grill was set up behind the stores, and as Garrett and I left Alma's cabin that afternoon, we saw him out there cleaning it. Hank stood by his side. He was thinner and paler, but the huge smile coming from within his bushy red beard lit up the whole yard. He held a bottle of Evian water and saluted me with it.

"Hi, Hank," I called. "Good to see you home."

"Thanks to you, Ryn. Thank you."

Hank had returned to Trout Fork two days before. Garrett had expedited his release by talking personally to the judge. Once Philippe confessed to Sarge's murder, there was no reason for Hank to be kept in jail. So Garrett brought him home to the people who loved him. And what a reception he received. Alma wept and couldn't stop hugging him. Gil grinned and pumped his hand over and over, as though he couldn't believe his eyes. Madam

Gauzie fussed and fluttered around him like an insane moth near a light bulb, offering to cook for him, do his laundry, trim his hair and beard, anything she could think of. I think it was sheer desperation on Hank's part that caused him to finally relent and allow her to clean his store in preparation to open up the next morning.

Garrett and I had stood aside and watched the joyful celebration. Then he said, "I'd like to stay, but the chief wants to see me." He kissed my cheek. "I'll be back later."

I watched him drive off. I had yet to tell him I had taken the job with the paper. I wasn't sure why. Maybe it was that there was enough hubbub surrounding Philippe's capture with all that entailed, and we hadn't had a quiet moment since then.

I thought back to the day Garrett and Sloan finally arrived at Rimsky's house. The Littleton police had taken Philippe away. I had made tea, and Mr. Rimsky and I sat together in his shabby living room while I listened to him reminisce about his days in the Marines.

Now it was Sunday afternoon. Ashley and Zoe had served breakfast and lunch, then closed the café. I had jogged the trail with Jack early that morning, stopping to sit on my favorite rock to take in the scenery and enjoy the tranquility. The early morning sun dappled the stream as the water danced among the rocks, splashing its way downstream. Two fishermen in waders stood midstream casting their lines into the water. A magpie chattered amiably to a bluebird in a nearby tree. Jack dug in the pine needles at the end of his leash. I sat back and sighed. Nothing would bring Sarge back, but Philippe was in jail, along with Captain Williams and Bodmin. Hank was home, and I was about to embark on a new career. All was right with the world.

I had returned to the cabin, and after feeding Jack

and showering, I went in the back door of the café to find Alma still grinning ear to ear. Was it just Hank's homecoming that caused her happiness? When I asked her, she told me she and Robert had had a "heart-to-heart" talk that weekend and that Robert was "weakening."

"What does that mean?" I asked as I sniffed the sausages and bacon on the griddle.

She smiled in a way that reminded me of a schoolgirl with her first crush. "Well, you know the hang-up to our getting back together has always been location. He wouldn't leave his job with the Denver firm, and I refuse to sell and move up there. Last night, for the first time, he said he's thinking about opening his own law office in Pineland Park."

"Whoa! That's great. So when's the wedding?"

She laughed. "We have a long way to go before we set a date. But I really do believe it's going to work out."

"Ashley must be thrilled."

"I think she's afraid to get too excited until things are more settled, but she's glad she won't have to move to Denver and change schools."

I stole a tiny piece of bacon off the grill, popped it in my mouth, and blew on my fingers.

Alma rolled her eyes. "Get out of my kitchen before you burn yourself. I'll send your breakfast out to you. Garrett is out there waiting for you."

I pushed through the swinging door to the dining room and spotted Garrett at his usual table by the fireplace. He wore a snug shirt that showed off his arms and chest and a pair of cargo shorts that were equally becoming to his legs. He looked up and smiled as I sat at the table, but his smile turned to a frown as he looked behind me.

I turned to see Dansby Blanchard enter the café. He waved and strolled over to our table.

"Ryn, I'm glad I found you."

"Hi, Dan. Sit down."

He pulled a chair out, nodding to Garrett, whose smile was forced. "I have news for you. I've asked around and guess what? There's a job for an assistant manager at one of Vail's biggest resorts. They're starting to collect resumes and will begin interviewing next week. I know a girl who works in the HR department. She said she'd look out for your application and give it special attention. Isn't that great?"

I glanced quickly at Garrett. His smile had disappeared completely.

I put my hand on Dan's arm. "I appreciate you thinking of me, Dan. I really do. But the thing is…" Garrett looked at me hopefully. "The thing is I have a job. I've taken the position of managing editor of the Pineland Park newspaper, the *Star*. In fact, I start Tuesday."

Ashley was passing the table at that moment, and she stopped and stared at me, her mouth wide open. "No way!" she nearly shouted. "That's great! Did you tell Mom?"

"Not yet. This is the first time I've said it out loud. I like the way it sounds."

Ashley dashed toward the kitchen and burst through the swinging door. I heard her say, "Mom, guess what!"

Garrett's expression was one of relief. He grasped my hand. "When did you decide?"

"I think it was when I was sitting in Philippe's garden wondering whether I would live to see the sunset. All I could think of was…well, you. I knew I didn't want to leave you. While I was waiting for you and Sloan at the coffee shop, I called Cosgrove to tell him I would take the job."

Dansby got up from the table. "Well, congrats, Ryn. I hope you'll be very happy." He cast a glance at Garrett.

"Best of luck to both of you. I'd better get back to Vail. Oh, by the way, I'm getting married."

I looked up at his boyish grin. "What? When?"

"In October. Now that I know you'll be sticking around, I'll have Kira send you an invitation."

"That's wonderful, Dan. Congratulations."

He went to the ordering counter, got a coffee to go, and left the café, whistling.

Alma brought my breakfast to the table herself and gave me a huge hug. "I knew you wouldn't be able to leave us. I just knew it. You'll be staying with Ashley and me for good now?"

"I haven't worked that part out yet. I'll need to find a place to stay in Pineland Park eventually. I can't be driving back and forth in the winter, but I'd like to stay with you for a while, if it's okay."

"Okay? It's wonderful." She hugged me again and headed back to the kitchen.

"Seems it's all settled then," Garrett said, squeezing my hand. "I'm glad."

"Me, too. Who would have thought that coming back to Trout Fork to help find Sarge's killer would turn out this way?" I dug into the pancakes, thinking about Philippe and all that had transpired. "By the way, what did you find out from Philippe? Did he confess to the other two murders?"

"Oh, yeah. He was very forthcoming. Seemed almost glad it was over, relieved, you know? It was one of the most methodical crimes I've ever heard of. He got that job with the Veterans' Association decades ago, specifically so he could track down the four Marines from the helicopter. Then two years ago, he started bumping them off one by one, all on August seventh, the date his family members were executed by the Communists.

"He booked his vacation to Trout Fork this year,

watched Sarge for patterns of behavior, then followed him to the campsite the night of the seventh. If we hadn't caught him, Arnold Rimsky would have been the final victim, planned for next August. But you were right—he knew he was about to be caught, so he moved Rimsky's execution up a year. He told us he followed Sarge and Hank to the campsite that night and waited until they drank themselves into a stupor. Hank passed out, and Philippe sneaked up on Sarge while Sarge was writing something."

"The note to Gil about Greer."

Garrett nodded. "That's when he hit him on the head and broke his fingers. Hank must have been really out of it because he never moved."

"One thing I don't understand. What made him burn all of Sarge's clothes and stuff in the fire that night? Did he ever say?"

"I asked him about that. When he saw Sarge's clothes, the fatigues he always bought at the army surplus stores, something in him snapped. I guess the sight of those clothes brought back memories of that day on the helicopter and put him into a rage."

"He had a flashback."

"Something like that. Anyway, he said something came over him, and he rampaged around the campsite wrecking everything and tossing stuff into the fire."

I shook my head. "Harboring that much hate for that long is unthinkable."

Garrett shrugged. "In this job, I've learned not to underestimate people's ability to do the unthinkable."

"Speaking of your job, what did the police chief want the other day?"

His boyish grin flashed.

"What?" I said. "Did you get fired or something?"

"Far from it. You're not the only one with a new job. Meet the new captain of precinct number two."

I sat back, nearly speechless for a moment. "That is just wonderful, Garrett. You deserve it. It's about time they recognized your talent."

He laughed. "Either that or he was desperate to re-place Williams, and no one else wanted the job."

"Oh, don't you believe it. The chief is a smart man."

Once the café closed at two, the celebration started in earnest. Residents poured in from the cabins, loaded with food, games, and gifts for Hank, who sat at one of the picnic tables, set up in back of the stores. He seemed genuinely touched by the outpouring of affection from the Trout Forkers, his eyes growing misty at times.

Gil was busy at the grill, turning the steaks and ham-burgers with an expertise born of many a barbeque. I ap-proached him and told him about Garrett being promoted to police captain.

He nodded. "I hope he can clean up that precinct. Makes me sick to think about it."

It saddened me to hear that his unwavering pro-police stand had been shaken by the corruption in that police force. "I feel the same way, but I look at it this way. Hank is free and the guilty man is behind bars. The system sometimes works slowly and ponderously, but it usually does the right thing. No legal system is perfect, but I'll take ours over any others I know of." My words sounded like they'd make a good slant for the *Star*. I smiled to myself. I was already thinking like a newspaper editor.

Gil sighed. "I guess you're right." He cleared his throat and added in a husky voice, "My son called. He'll be released soon. I told him he could come here, and we would work something out." He gave me a small smile. "No matter what he's done, he's still my son."

I patted his arm. "I'm sure you're doing the right thing. You won't be sorry."

I wandered over to the table where Madam Gauzie sat with Hank, who was still holding court like a monarch accepting homage from his subjects. The table was piled with gift-wrapped boxes and cards. He had nearly emptied his store of beer and soda for the party. Coolers sat on the ground in various places, and the party-goers were helping themselves. Hank was still drinking Evian.

"That's a great idea, dear," Madam Gauzie was saying. "AA has helped a great many people."

I sat with them. "You're thinking about Alcoholics Anonymous?" I asked Hank.

"Yep. I had a lot of time to think in jail. It's time I stopped looking backward and starting planning for the future. I've been stalled for too long waiting for my wife to come back. We're divorced. That's the end of it. I've wasted too many years finding comfort in the bottle. Those days are over."

"Will you stay in Trout Fork? Keep the store?"

"I know I won't leave Trout Fork, but having a liquor store isn't the best choice for a recovering alcoholic." He paused. "You know, that's the first time I've admitted it, the first time I've used the word."

Madam Gauzie chimed in. "I think it's wonderful, Hank. I'm proud of you."

Hank's eyes got misty again. "Thanks, Madam G."

Garrett's news about his promotion got around quickly, and many people came to him with congratulations.

Some offered advice about things that needed more attention from the police. Others joked about having parking tickets fixed. He took it all in with good humor, and I could see he was becoming as attached to this little town as I was.

What was it about Trout Fork that drew people in, settled them down, and made them part of itself?

As though to confirm my thoughts, Zoe passed by chatting with one of the younger local fishermen. Her appearance had changed completely from weeks before when she was influenced by Derek and his wild and dangerous lifestyle. Her green eyes were bright, her skin clear and glowing. Alma had told me she was taking Zoe under her wing, teaching her as much about the restaurant business as she could. That would be wonderful for Zoe. It would also make Ashley's going away to college in a couple of years easier on Alma.

We partied until well after dark. Garrett and I made plans to take a short trip through the mountains the next day for one last day of recreation before we both started our new jobs the following day.

Ashley and I finally said good night to everyone and went back to the cabin. Alma and Robert had already retired, and the cabin was quiet. Sasha and Jack seemed to be the only ones wide awake, and they wanted us to play with them, which we did, tossing toys for them to chase and bat around with their paws.

Eventually, we were all worn out and lying on our beds. Ashley cuddled Sasha to her and gazed out the window pensively.

"What's up?" I asked.

"Just thinking about Philippe. You know, he seemed so kind, so helpful, such a great guy. Then he turns out to be a killer. It makes me think you can't trust anyone in this world. There are just so many liars, so much evil."

"Being raised in New York City, I got to a point where I felt the same way. But I realized you can't think like that. The bad guys get all the press and notoriety. We hear so much of it we start thinking everyone must be evil. But it's not true. Look around. Of all the people you've known in Trout Fork, there's only been two really bad guys—Philippe and Zach. Everyone else is good and kind. That's what makes Trout Fork the kind of place it is."

"I guess you're right." She yawned. "Night, Ryn."

"Good night, Ashley. Sleep well."

I turned out the light and opened the curtain to gaze on the moonlit scene. Tiny grass shoots were already appearing, scattered among the burned-out area behind the cabin, a reminder that life renews itself continually, even after the worst happens.

Jack sat beside me watching the moonlit scene, his amber eyes sparkling. Then he snuggled under the covers, stretched out along my side, and sighed.

THE END

Author's Note

While every attempt was made to accurately portray the evacuation of Saigon in 1975, certain events had to be changed slightly in order to keep the plot intact. The USS Kirk did not take on board the type of helicopter that evacuated personnel from the Saigon embassy grounds. Those American aircraft, the Boeing Vertol CH-46 and CH-47 (Chinook) helicopters, manned by US Marines, landed only on the larger ships in the South China Sea. It was the Vietnamese-piloted UH-1 (Huey) helicopters that landed on the Kirk. None of those came from the embassy compound.

Also, the incident with the Marines having to use their rifle butts on the fingers of the panicked crowds is historical fact, but there is no record of that having happened on the helicopters. It was the Marines at the embassy who had to resort to that tactic to keep the crowds from climbing over the walls and overwhelming the compound.

About the Author

DM O'Byrne's first job was as a waitress. Now she's a writer of mystery novels. In between, jobs included English teacher, racehorse exerciser, jockey, accountant, golf resort assistant manager, writer, and editor. Her places of residence ranged from the Jersey shore to a lengthy sojourn in California and finally to the Colorado Rockies. Each profession, each location was rife with life lessons, fascinating characters, potential plot lines, and wide-ranging experiences. Sooner or later, they will all end up on the written page. O'Byrne is the author of *Dangerous Turf* and the sequel, *Three to One Odds*, as well as *Death in Trout Fork*, the first book in the Ryn Lowell Colorado Mystery Series.